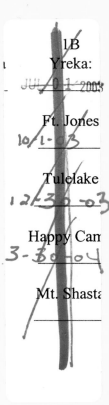

NO BUGLES, NO GLORY

**Center Point
Large Print**

**This Large Print Book carries the
Seal of Approval of N.A.V.H.**

ॐ श्री गणेशाय नमः

NO BUGLES, NO GLORY

FRED GROVE

CENTER POINT PUBLISHING
THORNDIKE, MAINE

This Center Point Large Print edition
is published in the year 2003 by arrangement with
Golden West Literary Agency.

The text of this Large Print edition is unabridged. In other
aspects, this book may vary from the original edition. Printed in
Thailand. Set in 16-point Times New Roman type by
Bill Coskrey and Gary Socquet.

ISBN 1-58547-275-1

Library of Congress Cataloging-in-Publication Data.

Grove, Fred.
    No bugles, no glory / Fred Grove.--Center Point large print ed.
        p. cm.
    ISBN 1-58547-275-1 (lib. bdg. : alk. paper)
    1. United States--History--Civil War, 1861-1865--Fiction. 2. Large type books. I. Title.

PS3557.R7 N6 2003
813'.54--dc21

                                                        2002031494

CHAPTER 1

Drizzle caught Benton Wall as he left the timber and rode out upon the slippery road. By the time he had traveled as far as the Cassville fork, drumming April rain was falling, and he slopped ahead through thickening layers of mist, feeling the cold misery of these weeping Missouri woodlands under his leaky poncho.

As he turned left, following weaving wagon ruts, the homesickness overtook him again; he almost forgot his dismal surroundings as he remembered cloud shadows passing on a rounded hill, tilled bottom fields laid open to the sun, gleaming, the spongy smells rising, and tufts of white drifting like loose cotton across a wide, blue sky. He saw and felt everything once more sharply, with a gripping ache, clean and vivid.

"Halt there!"

Benton reined in and raised his right hand, sighting a soppy Union picket in oversized coat and boots, rifle aslant, standing by the roadside beneath a dripping oak. The young face under the visor of the forage cap looked grim, and a voice, fluting up, ordered sternly, "Advance an' be recognized!"

Benton drawled, "Sergeant Wall—First Battalion, First Missouri Cavalry—going to headquarters," and walked his horse across the greasy footing.

The picket glared his suspicion and cocked his head. He had, Benton saw, farm boy and new recruit all over him, calf-eyed, fuzzy-cheeked, puffed up with duty; likewise, just plain scared.

"That's fer enough!" The snout of the muzzle-loader was making an unsteady arc.

"Hold your horses," Benton told him, halting. "I got a pass." He began digging inside his poncho, but the nervous waverings of the rifle barrel checked him, and he idled both hands on the pommel.

"Hands down! Stay put!" Half-turning, though mindful to cover Benton, the picket bawled into the dark forest behind him, his voice hiking higher, "Sergeant of the guard! Sergeant of the guard!" then snapped his head front.

Benton, eyeing the pointed rifle, grinned faintly and slouched forward, accepting the delay without comment.

Soon a heavy-set non-com, grumbling profanely, chomping tobacco, appeared on the double and split his glance between the two.

"Claims he's got a pass, Sarge," the picket sneered.

Expelling an accurate stream of amber, the sergeant sized up Benton and moved to Benton's stirrup. "Let's see it," he ordered wearily—the voice of an old soldier, rarely foxed. Benton handed him his pass.

"Talks like a Reb, Sarge," came the persisting distrust while the sergeant read. "An' I don't mean Missouri Reb. Got a funny drawl. Like them other two that passed a while ago."

The sergeant, ignoring the chatter, returned Benton's pass and waved him down the road. "Ain't seen you boys since Pea Ridge. Well, it's a mudhen's day." And wheeling on the picket, he observed with acrid disgust, "Next time you aim to shoot any Rebs, better ear back yer musket hammer, Strawfoot."

Taking the rueful picture of the boy's face with him,

6

Benton turned out to the messy road. Twice more he was challenged, several hundred yards on and again at the encampment's edge. Headquarters was a clapboard farmhouse, gray drab as the day itself, where the flag hung soddenly in front and men lounged on the muddy gallery and heads-down horses lined the picket fence. All around, until lost in the smoky haze of the fringing woods, stood rows of white dog tents and the larger "A" shelters and the conical Sibleys resembling Indian tipis.

Benton felt a getting ready here, for it was common camp-talk that General Van Dorn was massing again around Fayetteville, threatening to march on the Federal supply depots at Springfield and Rolla. Farriers' hammers made a constant din. From the northeast, down the road that split the green hills, Benton could see supply wagons, white tops bobbing, teams fighting the mud, struggling toward the churned meadow where the camp lay.

Voices rolled on the crowded gallery, German guttural mingling with the softer Missouri accents, and Benton, leaving his horse and stepping up, got the rankness of sweat and wet woolen uniforms like a solid flavor. He was passed inside, into what had been the farmhouse kitchen, now blue with cigar smoke and noisy with aides and clerks. A moon-faced civilian and two enlisted men waited on benches. Presently, in an off-room, he stood before a balding, bushy-browed man in rumpled brigadier's uniform, intent over a spread-out map.

Benton recognized General Sam Curtis, remembering him at Pea Ridge late that first day, in fading light, erect on a bay Morgan, calmly ordering the Fourth Iowa to face about, fix bayonets and charge.

Benton saluted and stood at attention until the general, raising dominant black eyes, said, "At ease, Sergeant. Orderly, have Mr. Hart and those two enlisted men step in."

In briskly ahead of the enlisted pair, the civilian was evidently in no happy frame of mind. He was soaked to the skin and no doubt piqued at delay. Without invitation, he placed his roly-poly, well-fed body in a chair by the general's table.

"Captain Hart," General Curtis said to him, "Sergeant Wall, here, completes your detail." He gestured around. "Sergeant . . . Corporal Doyle and Private Mears."

Hart merely nodded, and Benton met the gaze of a zealot's uncompromising eyes set in a humorless face made rounder and broader by a stand of bristly red whiskers.

Doyle just inclined his head, a muscular, bearded, tight-lipped man with a heavy cast to his features. But Mears, looking slight beside the blocky corporal, his slim face smooth and brown, grinned affably and stuck out his hand to Benton.

"Mr. Hart," the general continued, "is a captain on General Hunter's staff, Department of Kansas. However, he's found it wise to dress as a civilian while traveling through bushwhacker country."

Hart nodded sourly. "A situation we'd soon correct on the Kansas side if we had the men, General."

"Seems every commander needs more troops than he has, Mr. Hart. Or thinks he needs them." General Curtis was distinctly polite. "Grant included, down in Mississippi; I could have used General Hunter's strength at Pea Ridge—if he'd seen fit to cooperate. Fort Scott . . . one-hundred miles northwest of Springfield . . . was hardly in danger at the time." He shook his head, dismissing the subject. "Unfortunately, I cannot spare Hunter troops for Indian Territory campaigning while he's still equipping his Union Indians. General Halleck has advised me to act within my discretion, which I've done, by placing these three Texans on detached duty with you."

"Texans?" Hart pushed back of a sudden.

"North Texans to be exact, and a rather rare breed to find in the Union army."

"I assumed you'd pick Missourians."

Irritation ruffled the general's haggard features. He asked softly, "Pick? What is it, Mr. Hart? You people in Kansas still worried about Texas drovers bringing in tick fever? I suggest you keep in mind that this matter is not limited to your region. We're all affected. The war department is greatly concerned."

Hart subsided. "I understand, sir. It just seems a little strange that only Texans would volunteer."

"I requested Texans, Mr. Hart. North Texans, if possible, because they should know the country better. And if you're surprised at having only three men assigned you, remember that a larger force, if I could spare it, would create suspicion and endanger your mission."

By now, Benton had stamped Hart as a politico. Commands were loaded down with them, though the war itself was weeding out some of the worst incompetents. Benton, intent on the general for further inkling, saw it wasn't forthcoming yet. Beyond volunteering for duty in the southern part of Indian Territory, he had no idea where this led, and he guessed from their faces that Doyle and Mears were equally in the dark.

It seemed a long wait before the general cleared his throat. "You will leave at once, proceeding northwest to the vicinity of Jasper County. Captain Hart will be in charge and guide you to your destination. There, by whatever means you deem best, you will attach yourselves to one of the bushwhacker bands operating under Doctor Skaggs . . . You men from the Army of the Southwest will pose as escaped Rebel prisoners, which shouldn't be hard for you. You fought with Colonel Ewing, Third Texas Cavalry, at Pea Ridge. Captured by the Second Missouri Cavalry, you were taken to the Cassville stockade and have just made good your escape. One of my aides will help you work out details of your story. You'll be issued the proper Confederate uniforms to change to once you get past our lines . . . Captain Hart knows his part—a Missourian, a Rebel sympathizer, forced into the Union army; now a deserter. You've met on your way to join Skaggs' men."

Benton flinched inwardly, freezing his face to mask his bitter disappointment. Just four men! Three rump-sprung cavalrymen and a Jayhawk politician going on a God-knew-what mission into guerrilla country! There wasn't going to be a fast Union lunge, horsed up with hundreds of hardtailed troopers, ripping across the Territory as far south as Red River, as he'd thought and gambled on, with one Sergeant Wall, while conveniently out on scout, slipping over on the Texas side and hanging up some hides to dry before slipping back.

"Sir," Benton said, feeling his way, "you mean we're to report back location of the bushwhackers' headquarters?"

Curtis' headshake was sympathetic. "Wish that was it. What you men have to do is far more important and risky.

Skaggs is gathering several hundred men at a place called Parkinson's farm, in the hills southwest of Carthage. He has, we hear, some kind of vague lieutenant-colonel's commission. His bushwhackers, along with what he can recruit, are being enrolled as Confederate Partisan Rangers. When he's ready, the plan is for him to join forces with General Pike's Rebel Indian Brigade at Fort McCulloch, Indian Territory."

Benton's attention warmed. He'd heard of Fort McCulloch, the new Confederate post across the Red in Choctaw country on the Blue River.

". . . We know this from papers found on a party of Rebel officers wiped out on the Verdigris by Union Osages. Seems the Confederates were bound for Colorado Territory to recruit and stir up things." Curtis' voice picked up gravity. "You will see how all this fits when I tell you Pike has ordered his Seminole Indian Battalion to march on Forts Larned and Wise in southwestern Kansas. Comanches and Kiowas are expected to join the expedition; some Shawnees, Pottawatomies. If the Kansas outposts fall, Fort Laramie's next, with the West cut off from the Union . . . New Mexico, Colorado, Utah, California, Oregon—the entire works. Gentlemen, fewer than four hundred men are holding those frontier posts. Pike and Skaggs will have in the neighborhood of fifteen hundred. Several thousand, if Larned and Wise fall. Indians like a winner. Furthermore, the South would like to force us into dispatching troops out there from Grant's command, thus relieving the pressure in Mississippi. Something we cannot afford just now."

General Curtis paused and his fatigued eyes seemed to size and measure each man. Benton observed him narrowly, his thoughts running ahead.

"With Skaggs' so-called Rangers," Curtis went on, "Pike's Seminoles will move north soon after the Confederacy pays their annuity, in the next four to six weeks. Around a hundred-thousand in silver. Your orders are to stop that annuity between Fort Smith and Fort McCulloch. Make certain Pike never gets it to hand out. His Indians won't fight without it. If they get it, we understand they will move whether Skaggs gets through or not. However, we have nothing in the Territory large enough to stop him."

Benton had heard enough. Four men—provided they shook clear of bushwhackers and Seminoles—jumping a guarded silver train! Eyes on the mud-tracked floor, he realized that, save for possibly reaching the vicinity of Red River, this nowise shaped up as he had expected.

"If caught," Curtis elaborated, "you will be shot as spies. Our nearest force to you will be at Fort Gibson, where we have a few loyal Cherokees. Otherwise, you'll be entirely on your own." He pushed his solemn glance at the three uniformed men. "You can still back out. I'll take no half-hearted men. I can get others, Missourians, but I prefer you for reasons already stated. Speak up."

Mears shuffled one boot. Doyle scrubbed the back of a hand over his bearded chin and appeared annoyed. Hart seemed unconcerned either way. The silence congealed. Benton said silently: it's full of flaws, it's insane, fantastic. But I'm going.

"Then it's settled," Curtis said, a little sadly, Benton thought. "Good luck."

CHAPTER 2

They rode northwest in the clammy rain, glumly, hearing the steady sucking of hoofs in fetlock-deep mud, moving between endless shaggy hills in a morose world of cold, gray light. A stinging wind came up, flinging rain-shot against their wet faces.

It was late afternoon, and no change in the dreariness, when Hart ordered a rest and rode on, alone, to look over the road ahead. They had passed the last Yankee cavalry patrol several hours ago and, by this time, were on the edge of queasy country, more Confederate than Union in sympathy, or just as much, certainly.

Corporal Doyle bent over, broke off some twist tobacco, ground it in his left palm and eyed Benton as he got a stubby, foul-smelling pipe going. He had a dark face, wild and strong, the kind that appears to mirror something powerful and deep, yet contains it within fixed limits. His black eyes were large and couched back under ledges of heavy brows, his nose too large, his blunt hands and hairy wrists so wide and thick they seemed outsize even for his horse of a body. Below his forage cap the hair was blue-black as an Indian's, straight, in loose shocks. He could be edgy tempered, Benton had discovered, at times remarkably profane, and then, in contradiction, gentle voiced with horses, by turns silent and talkative. Now he spoke.

"So yore from north Texas, Sarge?"

Benton nodded.

"Aroun' where?"

"Bonham."

"Cotton, huh?"

"And mules. My family had a place not far from Red River."

Doyle's face underwent a sudden change. "Quality folks, I see," he said with a crisp, scoring malice. "Me—I got no use fo' gentlemen."

It was so unexpected that, for a moment, Benton could find no reply. He felt surprise and then his anger piled up, but it came to him this was no time for fighting among themselves. "I said *had,* blast it. Maybe it's all gone. You know that part of Texas?"

The corporal had a doubting look, as though Benton's comments about lost property lacked foundation. "Enough. Lived west of Bonham. My old pappy was a soul-saver. Preached an' farmed a little; mostly preached. Hell-Fire Doyle."

Benton remembered. He had seen the elder Doyle, a strange, gentle man, large, slow-moving, patriarchal, astride a brown mule, going about speaking of brotherhood and compassion for all. Kind of odd, folks said, but harmless. A little like that crazy John Brown from Kansas. Except Hell-Fire, the reverse of his name, preached against violence and was condoned in a district itself divided over slavery issues.

"I remember your father," Benton said. "But I didn't know him."

"You wouldn't," Doyle replied bitterly. "We didn't go down the same road with you gentlemen Walls."

Quite suddenly, Benton reined closer. "Whatever's in your craw, Doyle, spit it out!"

Before either could do more, Mears was breaking in loudly, "There's the Cap'n. Come on."

Benton, turning slowly, saw Hart in the middle of the muck, signaling.

"Some other time, Brother Wall," Doyle said, a grim promise in his tone. Benton, riding on, heard Mears' sardonic banter.

"Don't mind telling where I'm from. Just Texas, all over."

Benton looked back without speaking, Doyle's startling attack like bitter bile in his throat. A thought took sharp clarity: he'd have to fight Doyle soon, and he'd have to beat him or return to Cassville.

Onward, the rain eased up, and they passed a fat barn and two-storey house rising at the end of a rail-fenced lane. Mears was like a hound on scent as he turned to ponder a low shed, noisy with cackling.

"You boys ride on a piece, slow like," he said, his forager's eyes gleaming, and was gone before Hart could protest, kicking up mud as he loped up the lane. Benton could hear his clear, cheerful whistle as he turned in.

When Mears caught up with them later, he was grinning broadly, toting a squawking red hen. He'd been gone at least half an hour, so long that Hart, nettled, had halted for him.

"You stole that in broad daylight?" Doyle demanded, awed.

Mears seemed offended. "What makes you think I'd steal it?"

"Now did I say *steal,* Brother Mears?" Doyle was sneering. "Excuse me. Reckon you just tol' the lady you was a hungry soldier boy, didn't you?"

"I have my ways, Corporal," Mears confided, winking, mysterious.

Captain Hart wasn't impressed. "Mears, there will be no

more of that dashing off unless I order it. Understand?"

"Yes, sir!" Mears answered cheerfully. A minute later he leaned toward Benton. "Kinda disrespectful of vittles, wouldn't you say, Sarge?"

Still drizzling, the sky was darkening fast when they stopped in an oak thicket off the road and fashioned a lean-to with ponchos and rustled up firewood, the four of them communicating in miserable grunts. Doyle, grumbling, took flint and struck sparks from a D-shaped piece of steel into tinder and started a fire. With fat hen, baked over rail-fence coals, and coffee-dipped hardtack from haversacks, tempers fell away and it grew warm under the lean-to, almost comfortable.

Benton, turning his horse blanket to dry, learned the long ride hadn't altered his first estimate of the Jayhawker captain. Hart took himself seriously and spoke with a predictive frown, giving, now and then, a hint of the rabble-rouser and a fondness for Fourth-of-July bombast. He sat off to himself, though keeping near the fire, seeming to nurse his thoughts over a cheroot, showing scant stomach for soldiering and hardships. And yet here he was, on as foolhardy an undertaking as any man could tie himself to. On that reflection, Benton reconsidered, and decided he knew the man not at all.

As for the others, he recognized in them the dodges and expertness of old soldiers. Doyle, he put down as a pugnacious man, welcome in a close-quarter fight, and what Mears couldn't manage through brute force he could by stealth and cleverness and quickness. There seemed, Benton thought, a vestige of education and good manners about the smaller man which he sought to cover up with rough talk and deliberate bad taste. Benton judged him to be about his own and Doyle's age, in his middle twenties, except that he had an older look, worldly, dissipated, wise, as if weary of seeing and experiencing many things.

Presently Doyle started in, almost congenial, as he wiped greasy hands on his trousers. "Now how'd you do it? How'd you get that chicken?"

"Said I had my ways." Mears was being mysterious again, but like all born foragers he was proud of his ability.

"Ways with women," Benton suggested, idly.

"What woman'd take a second look at a little dried-up runt like him," Doyle argued.

Mears smiled, a slow and confident smile, his straw-colored hair showing neatly combed in the fire's glow. He sent a quick hand darting inside his tunic. "Oh, I wouldn't say that, Corporal," he murmured, pursing his lips, and suddenly dangled before them a pink garter, delicately ruffled. Doyle slapped his leg and brayed like a mule. "This gal, now, what's she—"

"Please," Mears stopped him, raising a restraining hand. In his changeable features it was hard to tell where mockery ceased and gravity began. "I never discuss my lady friends."

"Oh," grunted Doyle, his mood changing instantly. "Just another peacock gentleman, huh?" His sour look included Benton. Nobody spoke after that for a space and Benton saw all eyes shift upon him. Mears' timed laugh followed, scattering the tension. "Well, what we need is a drink!" Going to his saddlebags, the Texan rummaged and came up waggling a bottle that showed amber full. He pulled the cork with white, even teeth and handed the bottle to Hart; and when the whiskey had been once around, he brought up a harmonica and breathed into it. Patting his left foot, he tore into *Eating Goober Peas*. After one verse, he sang the chorus in a pleasing tenor voice:

Peas! Peas! Peas! Peas! Eat-in' goo-ber peas!
Good-ness how dee-licious,—eat-in' goo-ber peas!

Doyle, in disgust, put his hands to his ears, though he was grinning faintly, and when Mears went on playing, he sang with the music:

Just be-fore the battle, the Gen'ral hears a row
He says, "Th' Yanks are comin', I hear their ri-fles now!"
He turns aroun' in won-der an' what d'you think he sees?
Th' Geor-gia Mi-lit-ia, eat-in' goo-ber peas!

Tapping, bobbing a man of ample exhale and inhale, Private Mears blew through half a dozen lively verses, joining Doyle on the chorus each time, until, at the close, he dropped his hands, out of breath, and passed the bottle again.

"That's a Rebel song," Hart said, frowning.

"Reb and Yank," Mears said. "Must be a hundred verses."

Some of Hart's aloofness mellowed with another drink. "I want you men to tell me something. Why did you volunteer? I'm curious."

Mears hesitated and shrugged. "Just a fool notion. Thought there'd be a little frolic, maybe."

"How about you, Corporal?"

"I got wind they aimed to put me in a frog-swamp camp, guardin' Reb prisoners."

"Man, that's the truth," Mears supplied with a grin. "They always pick the ugliest ones for guards."

"Shut up," Doyle muttered. "Nobody asked you to horn in."

After a moment, Hart inquired, "Sergeant Wall?"

"Can't say exactly, Captain. Why does any man volunteer? Maybe he thinks where he's going will be better than where he is. One thing, I figure the big war's about over in Missouri, all but cut-and-shoot raids. I'm not much of a camp soldier."

All had evaded, Benton sensed. Mears covering up with indifference; Doyle's reasoning perhaps the most logical, though still farfetched, and Benton himself talking around the question.

Hart looked unconvinced. He helped himself to Mears' shrinking bottle before speaking further. "I am a lawyer by profession. Therefore, it's my training to look for facts and motives behind actions. Veterans, men like you, don't offer their services—risk their lives—without some strong reason. Flag . . . women . . . home. In your cases, I should say the chance to go home."

"Home!" Doyle snarled the word. "If I went home, I'd get hung!"

"There's a fact for you, Captain," Benton said. "Holds for all three of us. We don't hanker to have our necks stretched. Reminds me. We'd be smart to shuck these uniforms tomorrow. Put on our Rebel clothes before we start. A sight safer in itchy country."

"Unless," Doyle worried, "we git shot as spies, like the gen'ral said. Now, Cap'n, you tell us why you came along."

"Glad to." Hart's face took on a judicious expression. He

scratched his round belly and let them ponder momentarily what he might say. "A sense of duty, gentlemen," he told them, and Benton thought to himself: another bare-faced lie. "A feeling of destiny. As General Curtis told you, this is a mighty important mission. Our whole western country at stake—that's why. I'm a Free-State man. Strong Union man. Suffered for it, too. Been at this game a long time . . . fighting for the Union. Always. Before the war, I led raids into Missouri to free slaves." He ran his glance around, as if he must impress upon them the dangerous nature of his work. "I can tell you we took our hard chances."

"Did some hosses an' mules git freed, too?" Doyle asked dryly.

Hart, unabashed, said, "Only when necessity dictated, if we needed transportation for the slaves." He met their stares without a flicker.

"Understand you Jayhawks played another little game." Doyle's voice wafted the same dry note of inquiry.

"How's that, Corporal?"

"Sometimes, after you took slaves to Lawrence, you'd go back to Missouri an' look up the masters. Offer to return their property fo' about five-hundred dollars a head. Wasn't that how it worked?"

"By some unscrupulous men, so I'm told," Hart replied coolly. "Mine never did. I wouldn't allow it. Against my religion. I let the slaves go free, treated them as free men. Found work for them."

Doyle turned silent, brooding, an undisguised dislike edging into his eyes. Hart, Benton reflected, was either a self-righteous babbler or the coolest liar ever encountered. Benton gazed across at the Jayhawker, estimating many things.

"About the silver," he said. "If we get our hands on it. What disposition do we make of it? The general seemed to leave that up to us."

"Bring it back," Hart said unhesitatingly. "Thought that was understood."

"Quite a tote, Captain. Horseback. On the run, maybe. Need a pack train or wagons."

"We could cache it somewhere," Hart said.

Doyle advised, "Hell, throw it in the river."

"God forbid!" exclaimed Mears in a sorrowful voice. "Why not just bury it, like the Cap'n says?"

"So somebody could sneak back an' dig it up?" Doyle's mouth was firm. "First place, we'll have us a fight gittin' aholt of it. Won't be time to scratch up cover like a cat."

Talk dropped away. Benton became aware of a stillness. Rain was no longer pelting the ponchos overhead; he could hear their picketed horses stamping.

Hart rose with a yawn and took a skyward look. As he left the fire and went out to the horses, Doyle muttered after him.

"Blue bellied abolitionist! Black Republican!"

"Hey, hey." Mears made a low tsssking. "Why, that's secesh talk, Corporal. And heah you are wearin' Yankee blue."

"I'm still a Union man."

"You just said . . ."

"Shut up!" Doyle continued to glare in the direction Hart had taken. "It's him—bastards like him that started the goddamned war—th' loud-mouthers, th' do-gooders. Sonsabitches, they are! They'll never die in battle. We'll do that!"

"Not if I can help it," Mears said. Just then, Hart started back and Mears softened his voice, musing, a speculation in it that came out mixed with cynicism. "Wonder if Indian silver helps make a good Union man?"

They stirred to a gray, cheerless morning, threatening rain again, to the stiffness and grumbling of a wet bivouac. After coffee, hardtack and salt pork, they changed to linsey-woolsey uniforms, complete even to the correct number of sleeve stripes for Benton and Doyle. Mears, dubiously, inspected his loose-fitting blouse and trousers, made for a larger man, and the rounded crown of his gray hat. "Colonel Ewing's homespun Texas Caval-ree. Heah we come!"

"You forgot your Lone Star belt buckle," Benton indicated. "Texans wore 'em at Pea Ridge."

"What we do with our blues, Sarge?"

"I stuffed mine in that hollow tree over yonder. As for our sidearms, mounts, saddle gear, I guess we relieved them off a Yankee patrol." Benton glanced around. "Unless somebody has a better story."

Hart nodded in affirmative agreement. Mears carried his uniform to the tree, cached it, and Doyle, taciturn and surly, did likewise. When they had removed ponchos from the lean-to, it was time to travel.

Benton gathered up saddle, horse blanket and bedroll and turned. At that moment, going to his horse, he bumped into the equally laden Doyle. Or Doyle bumped him. He never knew. He lost his grasp on the bedroll; it slipped to the ground and a small book spilled out. There was a little run of time as he juggled the McClellan saddle and held on to the blanket, too busy to retrieve bedroll and book.

Doyle's gaze was like a file. "Reckon you want me to pick 'em up? That it?" He peered down and up. "Pomes, it says. A little book o' pomes. Gentleman's fancy readin' matter. Now ain't that nice?" He made a low, mocking bow and cooed, "Sorry, yore grace, just happens we're plumb outa niggers to wait on you today."

Benton gripped the saddle and blanket, still intending to pass. But something in Doyle's face, in his voice, told Benton unmistakably that he couldn't just pick up his belongings and move on. If he did, Doyle would think him afraid, and there'd be no working with the man in the uncertain days ahead. This could wait no longer.

Deliberately, with reluctance, without particular anger, Benton dropped the saddle on its side and the blanket on top and faced him. "Still stuck in your craw, is it?"

"I'll stoop to no man!"

"Nobody asked you to. You think because—"

Doyle interrupted savagely, "Don't tell me what I think!"

"Fair enough," Benton said, his voice quiet. "Why talk? We'd better settle it now."

Doyle's black eyes hurled a brittle pleasure. Sneering, he tore at his jacket, flinging it away, and peeled to his gray flannel shirt, never taking his eager stare off Benton.

"This is ridiculous," Hart said. "Stop it!"

Mears murmured, amused, "Oh, let 'em fight . . . the fools."

Hart protested no further and somehow the captain and Mears, standing by, watching indifferently, struck Benton as prophetic. Was this how it was going to be, he and Doyle doing the fighting and taking the chances?

"Captain," Benton said, "we can't fight among ourselves

and go on. It's got to end now, right here, or we're dead ducks down the line."

He shed his blouse and spread his feet and raised his fists, sizing up Doyle's formidable torso in swift regard. Not waiting, Benton moved in on the slippery grass, shifting back and forth.

Doyle barged forward like a Jersey bull, fists swinging as he lowered his head. Just when Benton started to duck aside, Doyle, unexpectedly, checked himself and shot a long left that landed flush on Benton's cheekbone. It sent his head humming, and the first thread of real anger went raveling through him, and he fell away, acknowledging a new respect for the man. Doyle could fight any style—as long as his temper did not run riot. Both men slipped as they maneuvered. Doyle followed up eagerly, and Benton sank a left to the corporal's hard belly and punished the square jaw, then slid off out of range. Doyle was stung. He tore in savagely throwing roundhouse rights and lefts, getting angrier by the instant.

"Y'fight like a damned gent, too—come on!"

Benton took severe, lacing blows around the body, another, that almost tore off his head, half spun him. Doyle's fists, he knew full well by now, could kill a man. Benton clamped his arms around Doyle and held on until his senses cleared. Stepping away, he wiped blood from his cheek as he continued to circle, drawing the man's rush, and when Doyle loomed close, Benton, dodging and pivoting in, smashed the dark face twice. He jolted Doyle back; Doyle cursed and charged in again, his nose muddy with blood. A swinging blow caught Benton in the chest; it knocked him back, it hurt him, and suddenly he felt Doyle's wild fists on his arms and shoulders.

Benton ducked clear, putting daylight between them. Doyle attacked recklessly, furious to reach close quarters. Benton crouched down and slugged the unguarded stomach, two punches, and next the heart. He heard a short, grunted gasp. By then, he was switching to the jaw.

Of a sudden, Doyle went down on his rump and skidded in the churned up ooze. He regarded Benton a dull moment, deeply astonished. He gathered himself and scrambled gamely upward, headlong, though a good deal slower this time.

Benton cracked him at the peak of his rise, along the jaw. Doyle fell again. He struck on his side, his head dragging low, his hands catching grass and mud. He propped himself up and Benton saw the battered ruin of the mouth, the damp shocks of black hair matted across his forehead.

"You"—Doyle gasped more than he spoke—"you fight right well fo' a gentleman. Next time . . . on drier footin'."

"On drier footing," Benton told him, "you'd kill a man if you hit him square," and began collecting his saddle gear.

As Benton rode with the others under the sullen sky, every part of him beginning to throb and ache now, it was as if Doyle's hard knuckles had jarred old scenes alive, unforgettable places and people, and made them stand upright again in the mind.

. . . He and Crockett traveling toward Bonham that peaceful-seeming early spring day hardly more than a year ago. Crockett unusually quiet.

Roiling, a ball of dust formed on the road ahead. An uneasy sensation started up in Benton when he sighted the rider, quirting, punishing his horse as no man would unless his life teetered in desperation.

"Looks like Martin Abel's old sorrel," Crockett said. "Runs all tuckered out. Martin's in trouble."

"He's been talking Union mighty strong," Benton recalled. "Too strong for his own good."

They reined to one side and waited, watching as the sorrel, a heavy-footed animal at best, closed the distance in broken stride. The rider—and Benton saw by now it was Abel—hesitated and then, in recognition, quirted harder and came on.

Rushing up, Abel yelled, "Switch horses with me! Quick!"

"What's wrong?" Benton suspected the worst. Abel's long, pointed face was pale under its dusty film, as if all the blood had run out. He twisted his body, glancing jerkily over his shoulder.

"Knowles—Larkin Knowles—his committee! Gonna hang me!"

Benton didn't move, not yet willing to believe that men had lost all reason over a senseless war just started, that neighbors were ready to prey upon neighbors because they disagreed.

"Benton, for God's sake gimme your horse!" Fear bulged Abel's eyeballs. "You—Crockett!"

Crockett squirmed and glanced at Benton, who also hesitated. Here in north Texas lived a number of small farmers raising mostly sheep, horses and cattle, men who had no interest in slaves. Martin Abel, an outspoken man, was one of them. Giving Abel a fresh horse would have but one meaning: the Wall Brothers were lining up on the Union side.

"Benton, look!" Crockett was pointing.

Benton threw a quick look along the road, curving off in the direction of town. A stir of dust was there, coming fast. He dismounted at once and held out the reins. "Take him, Martin. Your best chance is to get across the Red."

Martin Abel, in frantic haste, voiceless, was down like a stringy cat and aboard Benton's bay and hauling around and slamming off at a run. Benton stood a moment or so, indecisively, and took the sorrel's reins.

"We're in for it now," Crockett said gravely, though agreeing with what Benton had done. A little reckless glint mounted in his eyes. "Want to ride for it?"

"They've spotted us," Benton said. "Just make it worse." But suddenly he was reconsidering. "Crockett, you go. Cut across the fields. They needn't know it was you. Go on!"

"Leave you here to face Knowles?" Crockett's voice was sharp.

"Time somebody did."

"No," Crockett said. "We stay together."

"Then let me do the talking."

"All right. But we don't have to take anything."

Looking at his brother, Benton felt an unspoken concern. Crockett was three years Benton's junior, blond, trigger-tempered. Like the Lanes on their mother's side—the Southern side of the family—whereas Benton favored the darker, placid Wall strain. Between them, after their father's death, they had worked the plantation at a profit. And now their future was coming to a sudden head, for they would have to decide the extent of their loyalties. It could be, Benton was reminded bleakly, that they had made that decision already.

He watched the snarl of dust with his heart striking faster strokes against the wall of his chest. An interval passed, then the sound of hoofs was upon them. Some twelve or fifteen hard-riding men on blooded horseflesh.

Larkin Knowles rode in front. He reined in so abruptly his blood-red bay went into a bit-fighting dance. The others pulled up in the settling dust, every man reading the story of the used-up sorrel.

"What the hell'd you do?" Knowles' mouth was grim. A blazing anger whetted his eyes. "Swap horses with Martin Abel?" He carried a coiled rope in his left hand and the walnut stock of a shotgun hung at his knee in a leather boot.

Benton faced them, assessing their tempers, and knew a numbed surprise when he found Todd Vaughan, Jim Trask and Henry Jackman. His own friends. Men he visited with on Saturdays around the courthouse square. Men like himself—cotton and mule men—now changed, fused into a single body, a red-eyed mass without reason or mercy. He put down the others as Knowles' real rabble-rousing followers, the cussers and spitters, white trash ranting about rights and running over the next man's while keeping a sharp lookout for profit.

He saw this in one sweeping look, and he said distinctly, without apology, "Anything to stop a hanging."

A man slapped his saddle in disgust. "Play hell catchin' him now."

"Half you men ride on," Knowles instructed, his manner authoritative. "River's up. He'll think twice before he tries to cross."

The bulk of them cut away, galloping, all but Vaughan, Trask and Jackman and three of Knowles' cronies.

"Martin Abel's big dog in a secret Union society," Knowles said. "Been meetin' nights in the woods, just to stir up nigger trouble. Well, we took care of that." He pitched his knowing look around and stepped his horse in, an overdressed man in knee-length black boots and loud blue trousers, low-crowned beaver hat and a red and white checkered waistcoat which bulged out over a small shoulder holster. A dirt-common man of enormous vitality and shrewdness, growing wealthy because he dealt in shades most men shunned. "Abel's a snake-in-the-grass traitor. We've voted to hang him."

"Better stick to mules and horses," Benton told him coldly. "Let the authorities handle such matters. Let the law."

"Law?" Knowles, contemptuous, revealed square, brown teeth. "Ain't no law but us. County Vigilance Committee. We aim to hunt down the traitors. Every mother's son."

"I hope you know there's a great difference between Union men and fire-breathing abolitionists."

Knowles shook his head. "Same stinkin' litter."

"I don't agree."

"Then you're another one time's about run out on, Wall. War's done started good up to Fort Sumter. By God, if you ain't for us, you're against us!"

A reasoning voice broke in—Todd Vaughan's, a quiet man whose worried eyes said he hadn't full stomach for this—"Benton, your mother was a Southern lady. A real one. You owe it to her, her memory, to be with her people."

Feeling tore Benton. "That's the hell of it, Todd. This thing's split right down the middle. My father was born in Indiana; came here thirty-five years ago. He loved the

South, but he believed in the Union. I won't speak for Crockett. But I—well—I feel the same way my father did."

"Hell, let's go back in town for a drink." It was Jackman, a come-here Mississippian, calming the row. As he swung his horse, Knowles' instant voice lashed at him.

"You took an—oath No Mercy to Traitors. Now you turnin' soft first time some blue-belly speaks up?"

Jackman came slowly around, red-faced.

Knowles dug his long jaw at Benton. "Nawsir, it's time you tawed up. You an' your brother. Git on one side th' crik or th' other."

Crockett Wall said sharply, "Isn't that mighty strange talk coming from an Illinois man? A goddamned Yankee?" A wild, hot temper boiled in his gray eyes. "You are from Illinois, aren't you, sir?"

Knowles quieted. He did not answer, but his stare widened dangerously.

"I wouldn't expect you to admit it," Crockett kept after him relentlessly, his speech rising. "You'd hardly want it made public they ran you out for shady stock deals. Same way you got started in Bonham."

Knowles whipped up the rope, his face taut.

Benton was moving with him. He grabbed the bit of the trader's bay and forced the animal backward, causing Knowles to miss Crockett and, off balance, clutch the pommel of his saddle for support.

Knowles righted himself instantly. Something quick ran across his face. His palish eyes were pieces of flint under the cliffs of his brows.

Startled, Benton saw Knowles' right hand sliding inside his vest. Yelling in warning, striding from the head of the horse, Benton glimpsed the shine of Knowles' derringer. He flung up a warding hand—felt the jar along the bones of his arm as a roar sounded above him and seemed to hang everlastingly on the hot air. He spun to see about Crockett, aware that he'd knocked the weapon from Knowles' hand.

Crockett sat pale and tense, unhurt.

Benton stood back, a towering anger ripping up through his wave of relief. The gleam of the hook-handled little pistol at his feet snapped him downward. Scooping it up, he hurled it away with all his strength and confronted Knowles.

"Go on!" Benton ordered.

"We ain't through with you," came the matching tone.

"Don't ever set foot on our land—we'll run you off." Pointedly ignoring Knowles, Benton turned and included Vaughan, Trask and Jackman in his next words. "You're welcome—when you change company."

Knowles jerked reins to go. There was a forward movement among the riders, but not entirely. Jackman didn't stir. He said, "Count me out, Knowles. Too many private grudges in this to suit me."

Trask and Vaughan were also holding up. As if of one mind, they sided up to Jackman, the three of them forming a solid split.

Knowles glared at them, too taken aback to speak.

"Same heah," said Trask, and Vaughan nodded.

Knowles had no reply. In another moment he sank spurs and took his men down the river road at a hard run. The other three, looking sheepish, turned for town.

Benton watched them and afterward, thoughtfully, mounted Abel's sorry animal. "We'll stop by the Richmonds, borrow a horse."

"We can't go on this way," said Crockett.

"We can't—I agree."

"Think Knowles will pay us a visit?"

"Will when he gets enough men in front of him."

"How about Henry Jackman, Todd and Jim?"

"I'm not sure."

They rode for a time, and Crockett observed moodily, "We could sell out."

Benton scowled at the thought. "Not to Knowles. He'd like to have Cherry Point—cheap. Trouble is, a man leaving the country has to take what he's offered."

Crockett was tight-mouthed. He seemed to be only half-listening.

"Knowles is shrewd," Benton said. "Buys up whenever he can scare a Union family into moving north. He knows the Yankee fleet will blockade our ports. When that comes, he can haul cotton to Old Mexico and fill his pocketbook. Damnit, Crockett, I'd burn Cherry Point before I'd let him get his greasy hands on it!"

Crockett nodded. Cherry Point's future was a problem that had gnawed them since early March, when Texas voted for secession. It was home. If they sold, it would go for only part of its real value. If they refused to sell, they could expect barnburners and persecution, intimidation and ruin—probably what Martin Abel was running from at this moment.

Benton said, "We won't give it away. You don't want to sell. Neither do I."

Crockett turned, his face tightly drawn with the agony of decision. "We won't have to, Benton. I've made up my mind. I'm—I'm going to the Confederate army."

Benton stared back in stunned silence, and yet he didn't feel a total surprise, for he'd noticed the signs lately—Crockett's increasing moodiness, the drift of his thinking.

"Right away?" Benton asked.

"Next few days."

"I hope you're not going just to help us hold Cherry Point? Not compromising?"

"It isn't compromise, Benton," Crockett stated firmly, with care. "It's the way I feel. The side I want to fight on. You and father . . ." He broke off.

"I know," Benton said. "We always felt stronger the other way. But none of us ever came to blows about it, did we?"

Crockett returned him a warm smile. "I thought you'd understand."

"I think so," Benton said, without looking at him. "Just don't do it for me."

They left it there, finished and yet an unfinished thing between them, and a mile onward, walking their horses, they turned off the pike up a familiar lane that led to a two-storey clapboard house, cool and weathered gray under ancient oaks. A Negro groom trotted out on the graveled drive. Old DeWitt Richmond, gouty, proud, sat in a high-backed rocker on the long veranda. Now he rose stiffly, unsmiling, standing with the aid of a hickory cane.

"Afternoon, gentlemen."

His greeting, thought Benton, sounded cool. "Afternoon, sir," Benton said cheerfully.

Richmond's gaze, watery but alert, pale against liver-spotted skin, traveled over Benton's contemptible mount. "Never saw sorrier horseflesh, suh. Do just as well afoot."

Benton, aware of the old man's fiery sentiments, explained in no more words than necessary what had happened on the pike, passing over the final row with Knowles. "Now, sir," he said, "I'd like to borrow a horse."

Richmond thumped his cane. "You deserve to walk, suh, he'pin' Martin Abel!" For a moment he drove all his fierce feeling at the brothers; then, as if the sound of his harshness sobered him, he said in a somewhat calmer voice, "But I do deplo' the likes of Knowles. Men who'll get rich off blood an' destruction while we eat pove'ty pie."

There was a brushing movement at the door, in the cool shadows, and Benton's entire body warmed as Hannah Richmond came out to stand by her father. She had a graceful way of walking that drew a man's eyes.

"Father," she chided, "why don't you ask them in?"

At Hannah's invitation, Richmond called the groom to take their horses and fetch a fresh one. Crockett, always the gallant, stepped down first. Benton was much slower, in no mood to visit the Richmond household, hostile of late except for Hannah. He was thinking of her as he dismounted.

"Sir," Crockett addressed Richmond, "there was no other course for us, since we didn't want to see a man hanged."

"I realize how it was, at the moment. But remember this—you an' Benton cain't remain neutral much longer. Feelin' runs high. That should be plain by now."

"It is, sir."

"Crockett's no neutral," Benton prompted. "He's decided to go to the army."

"My boy, I'm pleased indeed!" DeWitt Richmond offered his hand to Crockett, who flushed and said, "A local company. The Invincibles."

"We shall drink a toast to you, young suh. Why, I remember when your parents married . . ."

Their voices faded as Richmond, hand on Crockett's elbow, guided him inside. Hannah paused on the porch and took Benton's arm. "What happened?"

"Larkin Knowles' committee was after a farmer named Abel. I gave him my horse and he got away."

She stared at him in surprise.

"They intended to hang Abel," he stressed. "If I——"

She stopped him with her eyes. "I mean what really happened, Benton? That wasn't all, was it?"

He watched her closely, astonished at her perception. Hannah Richmond was one of the first girls he remembered, and she was still the prettiest by far. It seemed to him that every part of her, precisely and completely formed, had been poured into the mould of her high-necked dress, not an inch of cloth to spare. Her full mouth, now, was barely parted, a mouth he'd kissed and found exciting, her light brown hair in tight curls that showed golden glints. He admired her deeply and still he felt somewhat puzzled by her, a failure of comprehension he laid to his ignorance of women or the mere mystery of women in general.

"Crockett brought up Knowles' past," he said. "Knowles went for his little pistol. I knocked it down. He meant to kill Crockett."

"But Abel's a trouble-maker," she said.

"His life was in my hands. I couldn't let them hang him."

She shrugged as though to dismiss the subject. "Now that Crockett's going, what do you intend to do?"

Glassware tinkled inside. DeWitt Richmond, his voice

reminiscing, stronger, vitalized by fond memories, was speaking of service in the Mexican War.

"I honestly wish I could go with Crockett."

"What is theah to stop you?"

He replied quietly, "I don't believe like Crockett, though I don't argue his right."

"You heard what father just said?" she countered on a note of impatience.

"And he's right. Every man's got to decide."

"Father's been mightily put out with you, Benton. How you've acted . . . carried on about the Union." She stirred the rounded tip of one pretty shoulder. "You know, you could lose Cherry Point. Father expects the state to impress Union property."

Something stabbed Benton. "Not with Crockett in the army. Now, if I have to leave the country, Cherry Point is still legally protected."

"Benton," she said, looking up under long lashes, and it wound through him that she had a particular way of speaking a man's name, making it sound big, important, intimate, giving it a pre-eminence, "if something happened, though? I mean in the war, to Crockett? What about Cherry Point, then?"

He stepped back. Resentment put an edge to his voice. "Nothing will happen to Crockett."

"I hope not," she said. "I just want you to look out for Benton Wall." She moved in, again gazing up at him. Her long fingers strayed to the lapel of his coat, a pleasing, special thing which had its instant effect upon him. He looked down and saw the unchanging interest in her eyes, and a sudden rashness came over him, and he found his arm around her waist. At that precise moment, she lifted her parted mouth, closed her eyes. He kissed her and felt the pressure of her body as she swayed against him.

He held her until she drew slightly away, murmuring, "Benton, you could raise cotton for the government . . . stay heah. You could take the oath . . . be sure of holding Cherry Point."

He let go of her gradually. He stood free, a tiny eddy of disappointment whirling through him. He said, "Take the oath of allegiance to the Confederacy—lie—stay home—be a speculator while Crockett goes off to war?"

She looked boldly into his face. "Why not? Other men are already doing it. You know it isn't just Cherry Point I'm thinking about."

He didn't answer; he felt bewildered, sensing an urgent need in her, the need of any woman to keep her chosen man safe, but wishing she had not picked this way to show it.

Then old DeWitt called to them impatiently. Benton turned to go without her, caught himself at the final moment. She took his arm and they entered a lovely, high-ceilinged room of rich colors and ornate furniture, of quiet and ease, the feel of thick carpets underfoot. He never came here that he did not think of Cherry Point's plain parlor, simple except for the many shelves of books of his Yankee father. Folks said the Richmonds lived high at Windwood, far beyond their means, that old DeWitt indulged his only child to the extreme of lavishness. Though the Richmond residence did not match the sweeping elegance of the square, pillared mansions seen by Benton on the Mississippi up from New Orleans, magnificent structures gleaming white in the hot sun, at least Windwood had its own aura of refinement here in the Red River Valley, less than a hundred miles from raw Comanche country.

They drank a toast to Crockett, another, and for a time the room was as Benton recalled it best when a boy, careful of his manners—vivid, cheerful.

Afterward, on the drive, old DeWitt hobbled out to see them off. "Benton," he said, not unkindly, "remember any fence is a damned hard seat. A man cain't straddle one fo'ever."

Twilight haze blurred the dusky fields when the brothers, returning from town, approached Cherry Point. Leaving the road, they entered a long double row of lofty pecans, planted years ago by the practical-minded elder Wall for both useful and eye-pleasing purposes. Inside the tunnel of trees, which hid the house from view, Benton halted. "Let's go around," he said, troubled. "Come in by the barn."

"Knowles wouldn't dare jump us here, would he? On our own land?" Crockett laughed, but it was a short laugh. "I'd as soon ride on."

"I'd feel easier if we didn't, since we're unarmed."

Crockett said no more and Benton turned off, angling across a field of young corn, circling in. Shortly, the whitewashed quarters of the darkies could be seen, just a few dimly lighted. Benton passed this side of the low buildings, and going on became aware of something missing from the familiar early evening pattern—the soft hum of voices and dusky children playing in the hard-packed yards. He rode on and looked toward the big house. It was dark, the lack of light there striking him as unusual at this hour, when Ned would have their supper cooked and waiting in the oven, the dining room aglow in candle light.

As they reached the open door of the high barn and dismounted, a figure darted out from the rear of the house. It was Ned, his white head like bobbing cotton as he ran up.

"Git—yo'all! Dey's white men aroun'!"

It happened before they could swing back to the horses.

A shout came behind them at the corner of the barn. "You Wall boys stay right where yuh're at!"

Benton could think only of his pistol in the house. He jerked his arm in that direction and the three of them started running.

"Goddamn yuh halt!"

No one let up.

A shotgun roared as their boots rapped the back porch, and Benton heard Crockett's cry and saw him pitching forward as a shout rose, "I got 'im!"

Benton caught Crockett, got under him and drew Crockett's arm around his shoulder. With Ned helping, he half-carried, half-dragged Crockett inside, into semidarkness. Ned slammed the door and bolted it fast. Outside, boots struck the hard yard. Another blast shattered a kitchen window.

"Around front!" The same voice each time. It registered unmistakably upon Benton. Knowles' dominating, commanding voice.

Boots went pounding around the house.

Benton moved mechanically, in a stunned state of mind. He got Crockett to the parlor and laid him on the horse-hair sofa, left Ned moaning over him and sprinted down the hall to his bedroom for his revolver. Running back, coming to a shattered rear window, he saw men scrambling for cover.

He swung to the parlor again and saw shapes scurrying among the trees.

Benton eared back the hammer, fired. There came back a shrill yelp of pain. Buckshot rattled like hail on the front porch. Men kept shouting.

Benton called to Ned by the couch. "Can you tell how bad Crockett's hit?"

Ned gave no response. Benton called again and Ned's continued silence caused Benton to spin around.

"Mistuh Crockett—" Ned moaned. "Lawdy Gawd—" He couldn't say the rest of it.

Benton felt the rapid pump of his heart. He whipped across to the couch, seeing Crockett's dim, upturned face in the murky light, and the instant he looked he knew his brother was dead.

He stared for an awful, endless time. He could neither believe nor accept what he knew to be true. It took the yelling outside, renewed, menacing, to shake him to his senses. He made a savage turn to the nearest window, engulfed by a murderous fury. He heard glass tinkle in front of him and realized he'd knocked out a pane and was pointing the revolver. When a man ran for a tree nearer the porch, Benton fired. The figure stumbled, seeming to float several steps before sprawling.

That stirred up the deep-toned shotgun blasts once more and the buckshot drumming the clapboard walls. And a new sound, the higher cracks of rifles.

Benton continued to fire, moving back and forth from the windows, and when his weapon snapped empty he stayed there, stubbornly, expecting them to rush him now, and hoping they would, aching to hurt them some more.

A hand shook him roughly.

"Mistuh Benton, you high-tail it! Dey gonna kill you next!"

Benton was listening. There was a stillness outside, a lull, a pause, until the familiar bawling voice came, "You men watch th' barn! Get ready!"

Ned said, fast, "Dere horses—dere jest no'th in de woods!"

Benton, still watching, spotted several men behind the trees, working toward the barn. They were on all sides of him now.

"We'll go together, Ned. Stay here they'll murder you, too."

Ned stared at Crockett's body and moaned, "Somebody gotta stay wid him." He was crying softly, swaying over the couch.

"We can't help Crockett any more." Benton choked on the words, hated them for their finality. He went to a rear window, saw the influx of figures around the barn and filing through the trees which flanked the house. He stepped back, his mind yanked tight. He hefted the empty revolver like a chunk of rock, realizing there wasn't time to run to the bedroom and search for the waxed-paper cartridges he seldom used.

"Ned," he said, "when I break this back window, we'll run out the front door. Grab their horses. Now . . . slide the bolt easy."

Ned shuffled to the door.

Benton heard the soft rub of the bolt nick the quiet, but he delayed just a little while longer. Like Ned, the thought of leaving Crockett's body was intolerable. He turned, looking backward again. Then he could wait no longer. He threw the revolver through the window, wheeling away with the tinkling crash and the following shrill cries of "Here he comes! Kill 'im!" He gave Crockett's pale face a lingering look and sprang out the door held open by Ned. Benton cut west with his boots crunching gravel.

His steps slowed as he discovered himself alone. He stopped and looked back. There was no sign of Ned, though he distinctly remembered that Ned had come out on the porch behind him.

He ran back several rods and stopped again, hacking for wind, in a struggle of self-damnation. Ned hadn't followed at all. He was sticking with Crockett's body and he might well die for it. And already it was too late to go back, for Benton could hear men running around the house toward the front drive. If he went, at the most he couldn't account for more than a man or two before they blasted him down. And just now, looming bigger, of greater importance than the mob violence he couldn't undo tonight, and the Crockett he couldn't bring back, was the eventual returning and the proper settling up in full. As he stood there, it all hardened in his mind.

He turned with a sense of emptiness, of naked loneliness, and started off, running quietly.

There were other events—crossing the swollen river, the surface of the cold water shining like slick grease as his horse fought the swift current—thereafter, hiding by day, traveling by moonlight—the guarded mountain passes into Arkansas—stealing food as he slipped around towns and camps of soldiers—behind him, for all doubting Unionists to consider, Martin Abel's body swaying stiffly above the sandy river road. . . .

CHAPTER 3

By mid-morning of the next day, the sullen sky turned clear. In wooded country beginning to flatten out to the west, they looked down upon a tiny settlement lumped hard by a bridged stream.

"Center Creek," Hart announced, satisfied, as a man would who had come a far distance and hit his destination on the head.

"Parkinson's farm," said Benton. "It's in the neighborhood?"

"Is. But I don't know where. Have to do some inquiring down there." Hart nudged his mount down the sloping road.

They jogged past the few scattered houses, sighting no one, and came to the general store, where a fleet-looking, well-coupled blue roan gelding stood tied.

Hart went inside first, followed by Benton. At their entrance, a rawboned man, wearing incongruous new sergeant's stripes on the sleeves of his homespun shirt, turned from the counter. He stared them up and down, fast and blunt, turned back and took his purchase from the storekeeper and shouldered by the four men. Quickly, Benton heard hoofs booming the bridge planks.

"Morning," Hart greeted, walking across.

"Mornin'," said the storekeeper, a paunchy, balding man whose careful eyes fixed them over silver-framed spectacles, whose snuff-dipper's mouth, puckered, brown at the corners, reserved still further judgment.

"On our way to Parkinson's farm," the captain said.

"Can you direct us?"

"If a man knows whar he's headed, a-body'd think he'd know th' way."

"If we knew exactly, we wouldn't be asking."

Meanwhile, Doyle had advanced to the cracker barrel, and was helping himself when the storekeeper said sharply, "Git outa that!" Doyle jerked, his hand spilling crackers back into the barrel. As he obeyed, Mears, down the counter, raised up and folded his arms across his chest, innocently enjoying the corporal's dismay.

Benton, seeing the situation was getting out of hand, said, "We're Confederates. You can see that."

"Uniforms ain't always what they seem. It's whut's under 'em that counts."

"Meaning what, now?"

The paunchy man looked uncertain.

"You're afraid we're Yankees. That it?"

"I ain't accusin', mind you."

"Of course, you're not," Benton said agreeably. "Don't blame you for being careful with strangers. In your shoes, I wouldn't give a man the time of day. But it happens we're Confederates. Now you just tell us how to find Parkinson's place and we'll be on our way."

"Jest don't let on who tol' you how t'git thar." He gave them directions, then repeated fearfully. "Don't you let on now. Skaggs, he'll burn me out."

"Oh, we met a man on the road," Benton assured him. "He told us."

In the saddle, Benton missed Doyle and looked up to see the corporal striding brazenly from the store, dangling two long rolls of smoked sausage in one hand while he balanced a hatful of crackers in the other. He slowed his step as the storekeeper, on the porch, stiffened up, glared, started to protest, appeared to reconsider under the circumstances and, instead, forced a hard-giving smile of reluctant assent.

Leering like a black pirate, Doyle marched out to his horse.

Across the bridge and down the road a piece, Doyle divided the sausages, a half for each man, and passed the crackers.

"You're getting more like Mears every day," Benton told him in mock gravity. "Shows what association will do."

"I don't agree," Mears contradicted. "Doyle has no finesse whatever when it comes to foragin'. He makes common thievery of an accomplished art. Just grabs and gets caught in the act, else stalks out for all the world to see."

Doyle's jaws were bulging. His answer came muffled. "What's the difference, long as a man gits what he's after. That finessey, you call it, ain't my style."

"Well, it pays," said Mears, and calmly took from under his blouse a wedge of yellow cheese.

Doyle blinked, stumped. "When—how'd—you snitch that?"

Mears gave a superior smile.

They ate as they rode and, for what seemed a long time, they jogged steadily, in watchful fashion, sighting neither man nor animal, yet sensing that they rode in the wake of movement, of watchers so near Benton could feel their invisible presence.

Twisting, the scuffed road bent into the dark mouth of a wooded ravine, and there Benton saw them. The woods seeped men and horses; they blocked the road and took up positions on both sides. Benton could feel hesitation gripping the four of them, then they were riding on as before.

When they stopped, a whangy hill-country voice came at them, "Jest whar yuh headed so danged fast?"

It was the quarrelsome-looking man who had ridden hurriedly away from the store. He seemed larger and even uglier behind the Sharps carbine he handled with indolent ease, and from the appearance of things was in charge. His men were a crusty, scrubby bunch as looks went, a study of odds and ends of uniforms and farmer's attire. A dirty butternut jacket here and there; one man in Yankee trousers. Most in homespun. Nonetheless, well armed, well mounted.

"Skaggs' camp," Benton said.

"Whut makes y'think Skaggs mought be 'bout hyar?"

"Runs this district, doesn't he?"

"Yuh claim to know, Soldier Boy. We-uns is astin' yuh." The long jaws worked a moment on an enormous bulge. There was a *phut-ting!* as he spat his distrust.

"Look," said Benton, "three of us broke out of the Cassville stockade. We aim to join up with Skaggs. Be obliged if you'll take us to headquarters."

"Him"—the suspicious eyes were pecking at Hart—"whut 'bout him. He ain't in uniform."

"Let him tell you," Benton said. "We met on the way."

"Glad to," Hart offered. "You men wouldn't expect a deserter from Sigel's dirty Dutch division to wear his blues in Confederate territory, would you?" Hart sounded convincing, and he was cool.

"Yuh could both be lyin' like a weasel. I'God, yuh could!"

"Why not let Skaggs decide that?" Benton said.

" 'Cause if I let the wrong men through, hit's my hide," came the frank reply. "I dunno. Them uniforms look moughty fresh t'me. Fresh duds allus makes me leery. I'll do my own decidin' hyar."

Phuttt! An amber stream splattered the forefeet of Benton's horse.

"Yuh're hankerin' t'see the colonel. Reckon yuh can jest tussel fer hit. Git down, Soldier Boy!"

Immediately, the bushwhackers began forming a semi-circle, grinning and calling. "Show 'im, Tadlock! Muss up that purty suit!" There was an expectant glitter on their faces.

Tadlock slid down and Benton followed, tossing reins to Doyle, who grunted between his teeth, "Sarge, let me take him."

Benton, flashing him a look, was surprised to see the usual surly hostility missing. He shook his head and draped his jacket over his saddle.

"Awright," Doyle said, as cross as ever, "get yore blasted head kicked in."

Benton turned. Tadlock was waiting, a born brawler's grimace overspreading his lean, black-whiskered face, his slab body bent, his long, powerful arms set to pound or grapple or gouge as he advanced.

And Benton knew: no straight-up fight this time. Not two men merely trading licks.

Tadlock leaped in, swift, gaunt, grabbing for Benton's body and bringing up his knee. Benton took it high on his thigh. Pain shattered up through him. He broke Tadlock's hold and smashed Tadlock's face. Tadlock, snarling, wiped

47

blood off his mouth and advanced again, suffering three blows to one, but he was inside Benton's guard.

Benton felt his shoulders grasped, felt a boot ramming behind the calf of his left leg, felt himself tripped and falling backward and saw Tadlock following up swiftly. Tadlock's broad thumbs were gouging for his eyes, missing, yet jabbing and bruising the flesh on Benton's cheekbones. Benton jerked his head; he rolled with a surge, kicking viciously at Tadlock's scrambling shape, and broke free to his feet, seeing how it had to be if he won.

Tadlock came tearing in, long reaching, the unwashed smell of him like a stale wave. Benton let him come, let him almost close, then drove his knee, low, to the base of Tadlock's exposed belly.

An astonished agony contorted Tadlock's face. He mouthed a torn, "uhh," doubled up, and Benton straightened him with an uppercut. Tadlock folded and fell in the horse tracks on the chopped road, hands clamped across his lower bowels, writhing, his face ashen, his legs locked.

"Wal, I'll be damned!" a man cried. "First time Tadlock's been whupped." And there was no regret in the voice.

"He ain't stud no more."

Benton couldn't drag in enough wind. Heaving, he considered Tadlock without sympathy, realizing how near he'd come to losing and their mission to failure. He felt dull and tired, his elation fading before a feeling of distaste, deeply bitter at Tadlock and his men for what they had forced upon him, the raw, animal brutality they had compelled him to use.

This is it, he thought, the way it will be.

"Waited 'most too late," Doyle reminded as Benton put

on his jacket. "Why I wanted him. More my style." Then in a tone that brushed approval, but not quite: "But yo're learnin'—fo' a gentleman."

Benton eyed this unfathomable man. They were going to lean on each other many times hereafter, he thought. And it was an odd change, but Benton found that he was beginning to like Doyle.

An escort in charge of a corporal took them up the ravine, which turned out to be the back door to a stand of rough hills. Half an hour later, Benton saw the ripples of an old field, wide in extent, fringed with tents and crude brush shelters, picketed horses and clumps of idle men. Across a small, clear stream, silver against the dark hue of the timber, stood a large "A" tent; behind it, obscured, square and low in the oak shade, two log houses and a scattering of long sheds.

Without delay, the escort crossed the creek and loped to the tent, where two bearded riflemen lounged on guard. The corporal got down, was admitted, and Benton heard voices strike up and go on for a minute. He wasn't prepared for the young-looking, middle-aged man who came out first, expecting, instead, the usual rough-and-ready bushwhacker commander dressed in a variety of clothing.

Not at all. This spare, erect man had a lieutenant-colonel's double stars on each side the collar of his gray, double-breasted frock coat and elaborate gold braids looping his sleeves, and sky blue trousers; the blue Confederate regulation, all right, though a color seldom seen on captured regimental officers in this second wearying year of the war.

Benton saluted smartly, aware that Doyle, Mears and Hart did the same.

Skaggs—and this was the Dr. Skaggs beyond any doubt—touched the brim of his hat, and in that moment Benton learned something, if the vain black plume flaring back from the soft gray hat, and the red shirt beneath the coat hadn't told him beforehand. Skaggs doted on the salutes.

Bits of stories about him tumbled in Benton's mind. A doctor, a poor one at that, whose interests lay outside his profession. Disappointed office-seeker. Duelist. Ladies' man. A martinet feared alike by his men and Missouri citizens. Also, a cunning guerrilla commander.

"I'm Colonel Skaggs."

Benton nodded.

"I'm told you just whipped Sergeant Tadlock." Skaggs had a deceptive softness when he spoke.

"Yes, sir," Benton drawled and waited, unsure, for Skaggs' reaction. Suppose Tadlock was a favorite of his?

"Tadlock had it coming," the colonel said, smiling. "Been too uppity since I promoted him. Now"—Skaggs scrutinized each man in detail—"you say you've broken out of the Union stockade at Cassville? You want to join my command?"

"Yes, sir."

"First of all," Skaggs reasoned, "why didn't you return to your regiment?"

"Tried to, sir. Colonel Ewing's Third Texas Cavalry. But Yankees are thick as fleas below Cassville since the Pea Ridge fight. We couldn't get through."

"Ewing's cavalry?"

"Three of us are north Texans, sir. From down below Indian Territory."

50

Skaggs displayed an increasing interest. "How well do you know the Territory."

Benton felt temptation, sudden and inviting, then realized if he spread on the lies and was found out too soon, he'd jeopardize the lives of all four. He said, "Some, Colonel. Been to Fort Washita and Gibson; on up the Texas Road," which was solid truth he could stand on; beyond that, having seen the wide, rutted slashes of the emigrant road, his knowledge was fairly limited.

Skaggs appeared to accept the account, though in this short time Benton had learned the colonel could exhibit apparent friendliness one instant and, in the next, turn alertly suspicious. There was a changeable, erratic quality in him, an infinite slyness, that threw Benton on guard.

"The other man," Skaggs said, indicating Hart. "What's your story?"

"Deserted Sigel's dirty Dutch," was the easy reply. "Met up with these Texas boys."

"And your uniform?"

"I reckon," said Hart in an unhesitating imitation of a Southerner's soft accent, "it's still 'longside the damn Yankee sutler whose clothes I'm wearin'."

That stirred some laughs from the escort and was, Benton sensed, the best answer Hart could have given.

But Skaggs hadn't yet let Hart off the hook. "The Dutch? What were you doing with them?"

"I'm a lawyer, Colonel. From up Jackson county. My hard luck to be in Saint Louis the day Sigel formed his division. Truth is, the damned Dutch plain volunteered me. 'Fore I knew it, I was in the goddamned Union army."

"You, Corporal!" Skaggs, his suddenness startling, pivoted on Doyle. "How did General Pike's Indians perform under fire at Pea Ridge?"

The question bothered Benton. If Doyle . . . He was relieved as the big Texan drawled with a straight face, "Got licked, sir."

A curious self-satisfaction succeeded the colonel's stern look. "Like the rest of you did?"

"We's awright, sir, 'til Genial McCulloch got killed. He—"

"Would you say Pike's Indians fought well?" Skaggs shut him off, bringing Doyle back to the subject.

"Wal, sir, they got their own fashion o' fightin'. I heard some took Yankee scalps. Can't say I saw it, though."

"In all," Skaggs led on, insisting, "would you say they fought without much organization or skill on the part of their commander?"

"Colonel, I was too busy to watch Indians. All I know it was a messed up fight."

All the while, Skaggs was nodding in agreement. Suddenly, he looked up and drilled his gaze on Mears. "What regiment captured you?"

Mears lied without a hitch. "The Second Missouri, sir."

"Cavalry?"

"Yes, sir. We got cut off. Rear-guard action."

Skaggs stared at them a long moment, no sign whatever on his lean, straight-nosed face. Finally, he said, "A good thing it was cavalry—not infantry, in which case I'd have no use for you," and about-faced to a stocky man in greasy butternut blouse.

"Captain Yandell, your roster's short. I'm assigning these men to your company."

"I can use 'em, Colonel."

Benton felt easier, thinking Skaggs had dismissed them. But the colonel turned again. He tugged at his beard, reflecting, "Ewing's cavalry, you say. Come to think of it, I have several men who served with Ewing at Pea Ridge."

"Likely, sir," said Benton, with a placidity he did not feel. "We got busted up. Scattered bad."

"No doubt. Your leadership was inferior," Skaggs stated and left them for his tent.

Captain Yandell barked an order and Benton wheeled with the escort, aware of a great relief. Now that they had passed inspection, he was surprised to find his skin slick with cold sweat under his shirt. Well, thank God they'd played it straight. No involved yarns that could trip up a man, no claiming kinship to General Lee or Jefferson Davis. And then he sobered. It had been almost too easy, for Skaggs was far from a fool.

They splashed across the creek toward more tents and brush shelters scattered under oaks. The corporal halted.

"They's one thing you Texas boys better keep in mind," he said ominously. "Colonel's plumb tetchy about it. Nobody crosses th' crick less'un he's got orders from his company commander. In such case, he goes direct to head-quarters tent. Never—never the cabins."

Mears opened his mouth to speak, but closed it as the corporal rolled his eyes and said, "Don't ast me why. Jest remember."

Benton agreed with a nod.

"You boys make 'selves t'home now." The corporal swept an ironic hand. "Fried chicken ever' day."

When the escort was out of hearing, Benton motioned

everyone together. "If these so-called Ewing regiment men show up, and something tells me they surely will, first thing they will ask about is our company. Myself, I can't call a single company commander we captured from Ewing's regiment."

Doyle said, "By Gawd I do. He was a young Reb cavalry cap'n at Pea Ridge in Ewing's regiment. Took him with our wounded. Name was Neal. A Cap'n Neal. He tol' me 'fore he died. Weatherford, Texas boy. . . . Promised I'd write his folks down theah."

"Naturally, you did," mocked Mears, arching his back and striking an exaggerated pose of remorse. "The Damn Yankee War Department regrets to—"

Benton saw it forming, the violence pouring into Doyle's face like a darkening storm. Benton said flatly, "Hold it, you two. Mears, halter that play-actor's mouth. Doyle's given us what we need—a real name. Captain Neal was our company commander, if anybody gets nosey. But don't volunteer any information you don't have to. Above all, stick together."

Mears held his tongue. Doyle's black eyes still glittered; in a surprisingly controlled voice, he addressed Mears alone. "Happens I did write the letter. Sent it over next day with a buryin' detail."

The little Texan was surprised into silence. Benton took advantage of it to head them for camp, wondering as he did so, about the strange paradox that was Doyle. Of all men, hating the South, its class distinctions, its gentlemen, with the banked-up, acid bitterness of something secret balled up inside him, Doyle, the least sentimental of men, seemed the least likely to do a gentle thing like writing that letter.

Leading them in, Benton saw a sort of irregular company street flanked by tents and brush-roofed huts, horses picketed to the rear. Men loafed and smoked and chewed tobacco in the oak shade, mended saddle girths and bridles, aired blankets and cleaned carbines and revolvers. The four riders attracted no more than passing attention, as if new arrivals were not unusual.

Benton chose a site near the rear, where the encampment angled around the foot of a timbered hill. If need be, a hurried man could take the path climbing the hill; meanwhile, it was a convenient place to observe travel between the company bivouac and the headquarters tent. In all, Benton estimated sixty or seventy men made up Yandell's company.

They unsaddled and picketed their mounts, afterward cut brush and saplings from the slope with Doyle's hand ax. Mears dogged his end of the chore, and Captain Hart applied himself with no more diligence. They were two of a kind, Benton decided, drawing closer together, though Mears was far the superior soldier. They were the first to quit work.

Benton stared after them, vaguely troubled.

"Not Mears' game," Doyle remarked. "Too much sweat. As fo' Brother Hart, it's agin his religion. Said so the first night, remember?" Doyle made a face. "My pappy said never trust a man what's pious in public. Steal you naked in January. An' I say never trust a Jayhawker anytime." Having spoken, Doyle searched for another sapling to cut.

And, over again, Benton felt the contradictions Doyle posed, acting one way and speaking another, like a man yanked two directions at the same time, revealing a Texan's contempt for all Jayhawkers while he spied for the North. From Doyle's occasional references to his father, Benton gathered that Hell-Fire was dead. If so, why had Doyle volunteered—if not to go home? Certainly not for the mere adventure of it, not for the very strong probability of losing his life. Benton had the impulse to ask him, pointblank, then reconsidered. Doyle's motives, like Benton's, were private. Until the proper time, Benton would respect them.

Benton said, "Hart seemed cool enough when Skaggs questioned him."

"But how would he stand up in a shootin' match?"

Doyle went to chopping, and presently Benton, during a resting spell, focused his attention on the intriguing path that wound up the slope. "Let's see where that goes, Doyle."

Doyle showed a quick interest. They started climbing.

Near the summit, a man emerged from behind a thicket. He swung the nose of his carbine in their direction. "Whoa, boys." His glance read Doyle's ax. "Plenty brush down below."

"Just looking," Benton said.

"You've looked. Now skedaddle."

Benton didn't argue. As they turned down hill, Doyle muttered, "Leastwise, we know the back gate's shut."

"Makes a man wonder," Benton said, "if desertions run extra high."

Together they began dragging and carrying the last of the cuttings. On the final trip in, Benton noticed a rider putting his blue roan across the creek, bound for camp. "Looks like our friend, Tadlock," he said. "Guess he's in Yandell's company."

When they had dropped their loads, Doyle ventured up camp. He returned after several minutes, nodding. "Tadlock, awright. But he won't bother us for a while. All he could do t'git off his horse."

While Doyle built up a fire, Benton fetched water, and as the bacon and coffee smells became stronger, a boy, fourteen or fifteen, all hands and feet, walked over. His hungry glance went hopefully from first one man then another. He was grinning cheerfully all the time, speculating on the food and yet undecided, it seemed, how to go about cadging a share.

"Join us," Benton invited, and received a rebuking look from Hart. "Get your cup and plate. Sit in."

"Much obliged." The newcomer, his grin spreading, was gone immediately.

"By God," Hart objected, "if you propose to give everything away—"

A keen dislike sprang up in Benton. "My rations. Not yours."

Quicker than Benton thought possible, the boy was back, rattling tin cup and plate and knife and fork. "Man, that smells like real coffee! No damned okra seeds an' parched corn!"

"Abe Lincoln coffee," said Benton. "Borrowed off a Yankee patrol. Come over here. You'll eat with me."

"Sweetened it up a mite, eh, takin' it off'n Yankees?"

Mears finished mixing dough on a square of oilcloth. He hacked off a strip, forced his ramrod through it and placed the works over the fire. "Where's the commissary, boy?"

"Name's Ernie—Ernie Fletcher." His voice was changing. He moved awkwardly. He grinned anew, his teeth large and spaced in a homely, friendly face, out of which stood a fleshy nose, pimpled skin and brown, easy-natured eyes. A thin tracery of a moustache struggled above a thick upper lip. "Last commissary I seen was a widder woman's house. Got me a little corn meal 'fore she run me off."

"So if you don't forage, you don't eat?"

"Kee-rect," said Ernie, alertly readying his plate when Benton swung toasted bacon his way on the tip of his ramrod. "Hell of it is," Ernie went on, "country's 'bout cleaned out. Reckon we'll have to move purty quick."

"Wonder where?" Benton asked, not pressing it.

"Injun Territory, guess. Big doin's." Ernie Fletcher spoke between rapid bites and gulps. He accepted his new comrades completely, and his willingness to please with answers quickened his expression. Furthermore, he was the center of attention here, his comments sought after, a rare experience for him in a camp composed chiefly of older men.

Benton passed him more ramrod bread. "Surprised you boys haven't knocked off some Yankee supply trains."

"None clost, I reckon, else we would. Just organizin' now, we are. Musterin' up." He spoke with a weighty importance in his up-and-down voice. "Some maneuverin' an' drillin'. Some pistol-gun practice." He stayed on after he'd eaten, volunteering endless information, of such general nature, however, that Benton decided the boy's knowledge was limited.

Benton said, "Bet the home folks would like to see you, Ernie. Sometime out on forage detail, you might just keep riding. You might just do that, Ernie."

Ernie turned wistful. He said, guardedly, "Oncet you git in with bushwhackers they's no goin' home. 'Less'un a man's dead or the war's over." In the same breath, as if he'd said too much, he jumped up, exclaiming, "Plumb forgot t'water them horses."

"Say," Benton called, stopping him, "who's our platoon commander, if we have one?"

"Why . . . Tadlock is," Ernie said uncomfortably and hurried off.

The four around the fire traded looks. "That," Mears said, grimacing, "makes everything rosy."

Around four o'clock riders swung down the company street, led by a man so broad that he filled and overlapped his saddle. Mears was sleeping; Hart was smoking a cheroot while he contemplated the headquarters area across the stream. Doyle, cleaning his carbine, switched around at the hoof clatter. Benton watched with a sense of impending trouble as the horsemen padded on.

They rode up and halted, and the front rider said, "You boys from Ewing's regiment?"

Benton nodded. "If you mean Ewing's Third Texas."

"I mean what I say. Rode with the colonel, myself."

"At Pea Ridge?"

"At Pea Ridge. Where else?"

"Just wondered," Benton drawled, neither friendly nor unfriendly, thinking the man sounded more Missourian than he did Texan.

"You won't have to when I'm through."

Benton understood now. They'd come to check on the new Confederates, to bluff and threaten and confuse, in hopes somebody would make a mistake. Not an easy one to fool, Skaggs wasn't convinced as to the references of his reinforcements; or perhaps this was a test for all doubtful new men. Anyway, these were Skaggs' bruisers, his handy men. Another Vigilance Committee.

There was a blur of motion past Benton. He saw Doyle marching out, hands free.

"Stay out of this, Doyle!"

Doyle paid no heed. A rod from the man, he slackened and rubbed his hands together in a relishing way. "I say yo're a liar—a double-pronged, puss-gutted liar! Never was down to Pea Ridge! An' yeller plumb to th' bone!"

They met in a stamping of boots and solid grunting, as two wild bulls colliding in a pasture. Doyle's opponent loomed half a head taller; thicker, too—he had no waist. His hat flew off during the preliminary bumping and exposed flat ears and a bullet head riding so low on beefy shoulders there seemed no neck in between. But he was slower than Doyle, who, after the first scuffling, stepped clear, feinted as he had Benton in the mud, and landed a straight left to the jaw. Benton expected Doyle to rush in afterward, wildly, to lose his head. But the Texan drew off coolly, taking the man's guard with the same ducking motion, and smashed the right side of the scarred face. The blow was timed just right; it made a crunching sound, it knocked the bush-whacker back on his heels.

Around them Benton glimpsed men running up, he heard them calling. He glanced back to see Doyle shake off two blows to the chest and pound the barreled belly. Broken wind husked out of the man's throat. He studied Doyle with a kind of insolence, yet desperation, and apparently determined to end the affair before he ran out of steam. He filled his great lungs and charged, suffering a rain of blows. Gore smeared his face. His rush carried him against Doyle, which was to his liking. He threw his blows lower, aiming for the under stomach, for the crotch.

Benton yelled to Doyle, "Stay away from him. Watch his knees."

Doyle shot both fists to the shapeless mouth and the shattered nose, a look of pure pleasure upon him, for this was the slam-bang style he understood best and preferred. He charged, he flanked, showing nimble footwork for a large man, and pounded one ear, then the ribs and over the heart. And when the bushwhacker, showing pain, raised his arms higher and waded in to attack, Doyle drove his shortest punches to the paunchy belly. The marked face blanched; the man gasped. He surrendered ground for the first time.

Doyle was after him savagely. So far, he'd fought a careful, stand-up fight, punching and maneuvering. Now he simply lowered his head and rammed the already battered belly. It was a surprising change of tactics, and his man uttered an injured cry and retreated on wobbling feet. Doyle sledged the ruined face.

A vague stare fixed the bushwhacker's eyes. He regarded Doyle dumbly, slack-jawed, helpless, and pitched to the ground.

Doyle stood free, his mouth crooked as he labored for breath, his defiant face shining out its wildness and his black, Indian-looking hair hanging wild, accenting that violence.

"Anybody else heah from Pea Ridge?" he called.

There was some shuffling and look-trading, but no takers.

Two men, hesitantly, dismounted and pried the downed man to his feet. But he couldn't stand, he was still in stupor. His bullet head rolled. He wobbled that unfocused stare a moment, and collapsed. It took a third man to help tote him off.

Benton stepped across to Doyle. "You'd done the same to me if you'd fought like that."

Doyle simply turned away, striding for the creek.

CHAPTER 4

Shabby daylight broke against the east in a murky streak. A breeze wandered out of the southwest, rattling the dry, brittle leaves of the drooping brush shelters, scattering the first smoke of the breakfast fires.

As full light flamed, fall-in orders came from the center of the company street. Other camps were stirring in the distance. Benton could hear the barked orders. He and his party, having farther to go, were the last to line up for roll-call.

Tadlock, afoot, out front with another platoon leader and Captain Yandell, cut-glanced them. He growled the roll, reported to Yandell, then began taking the names of new men, writing laboriously in what resembled a black tally book. When he came to Benton, he observed the sergeant's stripes a malicious moment after Benton gave his name.

"Soldier Boy, yuh're jest a buck-ass hyar. Remember that. Don't git uppity with orders." He hesitated as if he welcomed trouble.

Benton stared straight ahead, woodenly, not speaking.

His silence, when retort was expected, angered Tadlock.

He searched for a new point of harassment and his gaze marked the stripes again. "Take 'em off."

"You try it, Tadlock. You try it."

"We'll see," Tadlock swore and passed on.

After dismissal, as they walked back, Doyle said, "Ain't fo'got you licked him. Ain't goin' to."

Following breakfast, *Boots and Saddles* shook the hillsides, and men stood to horse. Yandell's command shattered the jingling and stamping:

"Prepare to mount!" Hands grasped reins and pommels, feet sought stirrups. "Mount!" and the company swung to saddle.

"Form fours—trot!"

Yandell rode to the open ground of the long-abandoned field, where, alone on a rise, Colonel Skaggs awaited his command. It formed rapidly below him in company fronts. Benton counted four additional companies besides Yandell's and figured about three-hundred men in all. After commanders faced to the knoll and reported, Skaggs touched spurs. He loped to the right flank, cut his mount about and swept along the face of the command in a rushing gallop, erect, head right, pale eyes inspecting, two Navy revolvers belted at his waist. At the end, he turned back to the center and whirled his horse to a spectacular stop. All done exactly, like a well-rehearsed act, a pretty piece of show-off riding.

His commanders rode forward then and saluted for orders of the day.

They drilled through most of the morning, letting up only to rest the horses. But these were scarcely the maneuvers of Union horse regulars, of Confederate regulars, either; little here to remind Benton of adherence to Scott's Tactics. There wasn't a saber in the entire command. Colonel Skaggs had his own conception of handling guerrilla cavalry.

"Yip-yip-yaw—aw-aww!"

Benton was startled for a moment. He'd forgotten the terrifying Rebel yell. In the next thirty minutes he was busy keeping up. Small units of horsemen, often in separate fours, would slam headlong in a short dash and veer off, crouched low, shrieking like Plains Indians. Never in wide compact company fronts, never a massed charge across open stretches. Go around. Flank. Cut in and out. Strike fast, pull away. Superb horses and Navy revolvers, carbines and shotguns.

One company in particular stood out. "That's Cap'n Fant," someone said. "Ain't he a hell-roarer!"

Doyle and Mears handled themselves as well as the rest, Benton saw. Hart, red-faced, his roly body suffering, grumbled and cursed. Sometimes he lagged, making a man wonder if he hadn't learned horsemanship in a Kansas infantry regiment.

Climaxing the drills, Skaggs dismounted the command as skirmishers and with horseholders taking reins, sent the others ahead in short, quick dashes. Next, as a lone bugler blew *Charge,* he advanced one company—demonstrating, attacking—then drew it back in a simulated retreat, while the four reserve companies, two on each flank, closed the jaws of an ambuscade. Through it all ran the element of trickery.

Ernie sidled over just before Yandell's foraging expedition

formed. He was still there, chattering in his exhaustless way, hungry for company, when Tadlock came along the street.

He turned in. "Stay with yuhr own mess," he ordered Ernie. "Wall, report to headquarters. Shake a laig." Tadlock went on, turning slowly so Benton couldn't miss the smirking satisfaction.

Ernie didn't obey immediately. He seemed to want them to know he had a will of his own. "Tadlock worked me over when I joined up: Can't take care m'self like you new Rebs," he said and left them.

Benton, watching Ernie go off, pondered the summons. Did Skaggs intend to pin him down closer about details of Ewing's command? Was it for the licking Doyle had administered?

Hart broke in on his thinking. "I'm going to tell you something," the Jayhawker said. "This magpie-chattering boy, this Ernie—run him off next time. I don't want him around camp."

"Need every friend we can muster, don't we?"

"Tadlock doesn't want Ernie over here. He'll make trouble for us if we rile Tadlock."

"Tadlock can go to hell," Benton said.

Doyle butted in on a knowing note. "Wasn't Ernie, be somethin' else. Th' sonofabitch. Him beatin' up a boy, too. One of us have to kill him yet."

Hart said tersely, "Watch your tongue, Doyle!" He raked the three of them with his eyes, singling out Benton. "I remind you—all of you—of one thing I believe you have overlooked. By due and proper authority I am in command here. We have a job to do, and we must not draw attention to ourselves by creating unnecessary antagonism."

Mears gave a seconding nod. Doyle glared, his jaws working.

And a feeling, quite suddenly, was kicking through Benton. He admitted Hart's position; that was General Curtis' order. It was the overimportance of the man that rankled.

"It's a petty thing, Captain, to run off a homesick boy. Frankly, I refuse to do it," Benton finished and walked past Hart to his horse.

Colonel Skaggs was alone in his tent, two sentries posted outside. He sat at a portable desk which Benton guessed had once belonged to some unfortunate Union officer. Completing the bare furnishings were several field chairs and a brass-rimmed picture frame, overly large, enclosing a formal-appearing piece of printed paper, filled in here and there with hand-written script, bearing a signature executed in flourishes and centered, in capitals, in broad, impressive type, the words: LIEUTENANT-COLONEL.

It hung on the tent pole just behind Skaggs, prominently, at eye level, so that a man facing the colonel gazed directly at it.

"At ease." Skaggs returned an indifferent salute and registered an approving expression as he hooked a thumb to indicate the frame. "I see that you are observant, Sergeant. For your information, you are looking at my commission from General Price. I expect the Confederacy to do better by me in the near future," Skaggs informed him. "No less than a brigadier's stars from the Secretary of War." His confidential air vanished. "Sergeant, you Texans have beaten two of my best men, handled them severely."

"Was that or get whipped, sir," Benton replied warily. "When—"

"Never mind the details. I am fully aware of them. I only hope your powers of observation and listening are as competent as your fists, knees and heads." The spade beard parted in what should have been a smile but wasn't. "What can you tell me concerning the disposition of Federal forces west of Cassville?"

"Well, sir"—So this was the reason for calling him in. In it, Benton sensed another trial. If he seemed too well informed, the colonel might suspect. If he told too little, was too vague, he could still invite suspicion—"I can give you my impression. What we saw getting away, when the Yankees had us blocked off from the south. What we gathered as prisoners."

"Let's have it."

"There's a big concentration all about Cassville. Supply trains coming in. Big parks of wagons. Appears like the Yankees got everything sealed off clean along the Arkansas border." Make it sound big.

"Into the Territory as well?"

"Can't say, Colonel. But I wouldn't figure that far."

"My intention," Skaggs said, confiding again, "is to avoid any large force that might hinder my advance to the southwest. Not until we're supplied, anyhow."

"In that case, sir, I'd say march West to the Fort Gibson— Fort Scott road." Point him toward the Territory without delay. Get him going. Swing him wide.

"The old military road?"

"In that vicinity, yes sir. Keep on it until you pick up the Texas Road."

"Why shouldn't the Yankees extend themselves into the Territory?"

"Maybe they're watching Van Dorn. He retreated south in the direction of Fayetteville, we understood. If he moves north again, he'll stick to Arkansas. More settlements. Indian Territory's picked clean as a chicken yard. Was before Pea Ridge. . . . Unless," Benton said the other way, "Van Dorn should decide to run a flanker, come up through the Territory as a surprise."

Skaggs brought up a skeptical look. "A remote possibility—most remote, I assure you—judging from the caliber of rock-bound thinking we have in the Trans-Mississippi District." Displeasure roughed his brows. "I had hoped to pick up supplies in northwest Arkansas. Platters hereabouts are licked clean. Well, Sergeant, you are dismissed."

Benton saluted and turned on his heel.

Heading back, Benton thought of the colonel and the sly strangeness flickering in him, the thwarted ambition and arrogant self-approval wasting him. He returned to an empty camp, too late to catch the foragers, and for something to do set to examining his saddle gear. As he busied himself, he reflected how poorly fitted by nature he was for this sort of double game, lucky as they'd been thus far. He recognized his unpreparedness and foresaw involvement in happenings he was helpless to prevent. He'd witness outright murder and pillaging, for such was the pattern of the bushwhackers. He'd be wretched, sick, many times before he reached the end.

It was falling twilight when Yandell's foragers returned, most of them lightly laden. Hart toted a sack of unshelled corn, Doyle a small hunk of salt pork. They trotted in first.

"We separated," Doyle said in empty-handed complaint. "Lean pickin's, except Brother Mears. Look what he scared up, the little son-of-a-buck."

Benton turned, hearing a squawking. Mears trailed several rods to the rear, drawing the envious glances of less fortunate foragers. A brown sack, heavily lumped, sagged from his saddle. From it issued a raucous disturbance.

"Somebody's old red rooster," Doyle said with admiration. "Got t'hand it to that boy, if he does rub me raw at times."

The rooster wasn't all the loot, Benton discovered as Mears unloaded. He had a basket of eggs, an enormous slab of bacon, several brown sausages, a pan of yellow cornbread, two loaves of light bread and a blackened skillet.

"Well, was she young or old?" Benton baited him, and Doyle threw in, "Smooth-flanked or wrinkled?"

"Oh, so-so," Mears answered airily and, as usual, left them guessing the details.

During supper, Benton said, "Where's Ernie tonight?"

Doyle pressed a look at Hart, who said after a moment, "I ordered him to stay away. Follow Tadlock's orders."

Benton set his cup down with care, thinking how they had to pull together or fail completely. He studied the cup at length and then he said, "No call to do that," and when Hart had no reply, he said further, "Ernie can eat with me."

Hart's roly shoulders upped and fell, which could mean anything.

Cagey, thought Benton, and considered him again. The overfed body, the red-whiskered jaws crammed full, the zealot's eyes as unbending as ever, the moon face. A feeling of repugnance filled Benton.

Hart finished his meal in silence, rose and unrolled his blanket. He was snoring when Mears drifted up the company street, where mess fires winked and men's slow voices carried pleasantly across the soft night.

Benton and Doyle watered the horses, picketed them for the night. Still thinking of Ernie, Benton motioned Doyle to accompany him. When they reached the shelters where Ernie quartered, Benton glanced over the reclining men but failed to see the boy.

He turned to retrace his steps, then held up as the spirited notes of "Goober Peas," with variations and frills, beat down the street.

"Looks like Brother Mears got hisself a little crowd," Doyle said, interested. "Let's see the show. Where Ernie is, prob'ly." As Benton hesitated, the friendly tone of Doyle's voice hardened. "If it's high class enough fo' you."

"When," Benton clipped, losing patience, "will you get that out of your head? I was taking another look for Ernie. Come on."

Doyle swung with him, not commenting.

Lanterns threw yellowed light on men standing and clapping and tapping to the lively mouth organ music, which shrilled off as Benton and Doyle arrived. Mears, holding forth in the center, was wiping the harmonica when Benton looked in from the back of the crowd.

Someone called to Mears and the little Texan, in his mysterious fashion, squatted down and rolled his eyes around.

"What was the first thing you said?" another asked.

Mears hesitated just enough before he replied. " 'Lady,' I says, with my hat off, 'could you loan a po' little Confed'rate boy a skillet to fry some meat in?' "

Doyle nudged Benton. "He's off!"

"When she hands me a skillet I says in my usual genteel manner, 'Thank you most kindly, ma'am. Now could you loan a po' little Confed'rate boy the meat to fry in it?' "

Under cover of laughter Mears took up his harmonica. Benton recognized "The Rebel Soldier" and presently he and Doyle were joining in the singing.

Two burly raiders skipped lightly out. They swept off sweat-greasy hats and favored each other with courtly bows. Then, hats donned, one chucked his comrade under his whiskered chin and, like ponderous circus bears, they stamped into an awkward but enthusiastic round dance. It ended violently when a trampling boot trod tender toes. A yelled pain, a curse, and the injured party's swinging fist struck his partner's jaw, knocking him into the laughing crowd.

Mears, exhibiting great gusto, led on through more verses and finished with a mournful flourish that produced a storm of applause. He bowed front, he bowed left and right and, spent, slumped down on a log, his impish face aglitter, exulting.

The crowd didn't want to let him rest. But, as though his actor's sense of timing told him this was the moment to stop, Mears murmured, "That's all tonight, boys" and slipped away.

He wasn't in camp when Benton and Doyle returned, nor when they went to bed. It was late when Benton heard Mears come in. He arranged his blanket, sat, pulled off his boots and yawned. But he didn't seem ready to retire.

"What's up?" Benton asked.

"News, Sarge."

"Turn in," Doyle growled.

"You'll wake up when you hear this," Mears said.

"Better be good."

"It is."

Doyle rolled over, observing Mears. "Another stretcher about skillets an' girl garters?"

"News, I said. Big news."

"Like hell, I bet."

"Truth. Listen, you-all. I crossed the creek, looked around. Colonel's got him a girl over theah."

CHAPTER 5

Once again in the early morning light Benton saw the unkempt raider companies lined up on the slope and Colonel Skaggs sitting his horse in review. After taking reports from his five commanders, Skaggs raised a rolled newspaper high above his head, held it there dramatically. Then, swiftly, he slapped it against his left palm.

"Listen, men," he called out in his inflammatory, carrying voice. "You have just been declared outlaws by the Feds. The Yankee paper in Carthage carries an account of it. What they propose to do to you." He stood higher in his stirrups. "By order of General Halleck—commander of the Department of Missouri—you have been deprived of all civil and military rights. After this day you will be shown no mercy. You will be shot down if you surrender."

Skaggs lowered himself in the saddle, letting the announcement sink in, and Benton could hear the angry muttering rise around him.

Skaggs' voice, like metal on metal, stilled the command. "Any person caught harboring you or giving you food will be arrested and tried by a Yankee military commission. You know what they're driving at here—your friends, your families, your wives and sweethearts, your old folks—even your kids."

Well, Skaggs had timed it just right and added a rabble-rousing touch of his own. The order wasn't new. Benton had heard it some weeks ago. Skaggs had obviously held off until he could make maximum use of it, to give him an excuse for any extreme he had in mind.

Skaggs' uplifted hand quieted the muttering again. "From now on we show no quarter to any goddamned Yankee soldier or sneaky Yankee sympathizer. We take no prisoners! This morning we're breaking camp for Indian Territory—"

Benton felt the rapid catch of excitement. They were actually going, at last.

"—Captain Yandell's company will form the advance. Then Captains Fant, Anderson, Bushrod and Olinger, in that order. Southwest of here we expect to find a Yankee supply train going in the same direction. I trust you know what action to take?"

Yelling and shouting rose from the men.

"I see that you men who've been with me before haven't forgotten. We pull out right after you've been issued extra uniforms."

"Extra uniforms?" Doyle muttered as Yandell took the company, in column of twos, across the creek toward the sheds. "Where's the first ones?"

Men moved busily around the sheds, in and out. Farther back, parked under the oaks, Benton saw covered wagons with hitched teams which hadn't been there yesterday.

"Dismount and form a line."

Benton and Doyle came down near the head of the column, close by a long shed. Mears and Hart trailed them.

Tadlock was the first in line. When Tadlock emerged, he was grinning as though he'd just heard a crude joke.

Benton stood still. His stare widened on the bundle of blue clothing Tadlock carried like some kind of grim trophy. Doyle remained stiffly quiet. Then it was Benton's turn. He ducked inside; two men sorted and paired from several high stacks. One pitched crumpled blue trousers and jacket at Benton, who turned outside and shook out the trousers, folded them thoughtfully and examined the jacket. A ripped place circled by a rusty red spot commanded his eye.

Revulsion and a needling fury crawled over him. These weren't new uniforms, stolen from a Yankee supply depot or wagon train. They were worn and soiled, blood-marked; they still stank of the dead Yankee boys off whom they'd been stripped, God knew where. He saw Doyle and he read, momentarily, the print of his own hidden outrage.

When all Yandell company men had been issued, Tadlock bawled, "Keep these Yank duds whar yuh can git at 'em fast."

They were preparing to break camp when Hart asked Benton, "How do you figure that no-quarter order?" The captain looked peaked around the mouth. All of them, even Doyle, looked grim.

"It doesn't change anything," Benton said. "Halleck's order came about, mainly, because Skaggs murdered Union patrols after they surrendered. Patrols and supply train escorts. My guess is that's where these blues came from. But Halleck's order grants Skaggs an excuse for whatever he does. Sky's the limit, though it always was."

As Yandell's company took the front position, Benton watched five spring wagons form in the center, all but one U.S. Studebakers, painted blue. The exception was an army ambulance, square-topped, side curtains strapped down, drawn by a pair of fast-stepping brown mules and driven by a burly young man. The girl reported by the nighthawking Mears wasn't in sight.

Once the wagons filed in, Colonel Skaggs struck a drumming gallop, swept forward to join Yandell, and the column stepped out, westward, crossing the creek and winding around behind the log houses and sheds to come upon a rocky road squeezed between tumbling, shaggy hills.

Beyond camp, Yandell called for scouts and flankers. Tadlock began pulling out his men. His gaze rejected Benton and fed on the contentious stripes, still resenting them. He spurned Doyle also, then sourly motioned for Hart and Mears. Next, he chose Ernie Fletcher. Some twenty men rode off.

Benton gazed after them, understanding why Tadlock wouldn't want him along but wondering why, when veteran bushwhackers were available, he'd picked Hart and Mears and Ernie.

"Hart got plumb chummy yesterday with Tadlock," Doyle confided as though reading Benton's thoughts. "Leastwise, he tried to."

"Politicking, I reckon."

"What'll it git him, heah?"

"Tadlock won't ride him, maybe." But now that Doyle

mentioned it, Benton questioned if that could be all.

Despite the up-and-down country, Skaggs traveled briskly throughout the morning, holding a steady trot. At intervals, scouts angled in from the roughness, reported, and rode out again. At noon, under a high, polished sky, Skaggs called a halt that carried over into the afternoon, a strange pause to Benton's thinking after the hard, constant marching since early morning.

Meanwhile, Skaggs and his staff conferred in the shade off the road, the colonel crouched, drawing on the ground with a stick, while his captains looked on.

It grew hotter, with the column, which had fallen out to rest, stretched below in irregular clots of men, horses and vehicles. From where he sat on the slope Benton could see the white, gleaming tops of the wagons.

He said curiously, "Noticed the girl yet?"

"Nope. Been watchin', too. She'll be in the ambulance, if Mears wasn't lyin'."

"Don't believe he was."

Doyle leaned over, his voice pitched low. "How can Skaggs expect to cover up he's got a woman along?"

"He can't, and I guess he doesn't have to."

"No doubt," said Doyle in mock seriousness, "she is his daughter. An' only chile."

"Oh, sure," Benton went along. "And something to steer clear of."

"Mears didn't."

"Keep it up he'll get lead poisoning."

"Mears, he puzzles me. Ain't interested in this heah war a-tall. Don't give a damn either way."

"He will if Skaggs pots him some night."

"Figure Mears will die happy. All he cares about is women, whiskey an' play-actin'. Maybe that's best, after all. Me, all I give a hoot about is—" Doyle's voice seemed to snag and stop. A guarded look stole over his face.

"About what, Doyle?"

The Texan was looking away, southwest, upon vast distances, his chiseled features grave. "Aw, nothin'," he said, late in answering, gruff and natural again.

"Forget it," Benton said, apologetically. "I spoke out of turn." He regretted that their conversation had ended when Doyle was on the verge of letting light on himself. Benton, in asking, had touched a sore spot, an old hurt.

It was after two o'clock when Tadlock, alone, rushed up to Skaggs and dismounted. Benton could see Tadlock's mouth working as he gestured west. Skaggs listened, interrupting now and again to ask questions and speak to his commanders. Soon the conference broke up and the captains saddled back to their companies.

Yandell passed an order. "Put on blue uniforms."

Doyle was shaken out of his moody reflections. He stood up. "Now what th' hell?"

"It won't be good," Benton predicted wryly and saw etched in Doyle's face the same unease he felt. Benton took longer than necessary changing to his rank-smelling blues. The clothing, which had belonged to a shorter, smaller man, gave him an unclean sensation. When ready, he looked to the rear. The companies were reforming on the road, to all appearances a Union column, complete with supply and baggage train. Shortly, the Fant and Bushrod companies cut out and clattered front, where Tadlock guided them off over the hill and out of sight. Skaggs started the command a little later.

When Benton came to the crest, the advance companies formed a double file of blue in the distance, shrinking rapidly over another rise. An hour on and Skaggs tarried again; leaving one company with the wagons, he took Yandell's remaining men and the fifth company to the peak of a wooded ridge, dismounted them in a frontal line.

There was nothing to see at first, no arresting movement, until Benton worked his gaze forward and then northwest. There, lower down, between a row of low hills, rolled some twenty wagons escorted by Union cavalry, trailing southwest on a march apparently intended to come in on the military or Texas Road going on down into the Territory to Fort Gibson.

Why was Skaggs holding up?

Even as Benton asked himself, a second line of Union horse appeared in the southwest, jogging slowly, on the same narrow road. Another quarter-mile and the two forces would meet.

Benton heard Yandell's acknowledging voice. "There they are, Colonel! Tadlock's bringin' 'em in just right. Like to edge in closer, in case?"

"And have the train spot us?" Skaggs overruled. "Tadlock knows how to work this. We'll let him be unless he finds trouble."

Little by little, the distance between the columns shortened; now less than two-hundred yards separated them. The wagon train stopped and two troopers rode out to meet the advancing horsemen. A brief parley followed, terminated when the escort pair waved the train ahead and swung back. Gradually, the two columns, ruffling low-hanging layers of dust, approached each other. There was no sign of alarm among the wagons.

Benton, pulled forward, tensely watching, realized how well-chosen the site was for ambush. The road, which skirted the low, rocky hills for easier footing before angling off into flattening reaches of prairie, was rough and rutted from the way the wagons jounced. And within the last few hundred yards it narrowed, cramped in places; there was no room to corral the wagons if somebody did give the alarm.

They were very close now. And just when it seemed the oncoming horsemen would have to draw aside for the wagons to pass, the column of twos split, left and right, unhurriedly, yet precisely, and began filing down each flank of the train. Still, nothing happened. Tadlock's men continued the plodding, uneventful pace.

It erupted suddenly, just as the foremost raiders came even with the tailend escort riders. There was a swinging inward and drawing of weapons—all in the same rapidly wheeling motion.

Benton saw the escort reeling and falling before he heard the first sounds ripping across the wind, flat, cracking, intensifying, and the discharges rolled together. Blots of dirty smoke puffed around the wagons. His protest welling, he saw the teamsters go next, either dropping down over the wagon wheels or crumpling on the seats.

Within seconds it ended, leaving milling blue horsemen and drifting powder smoke; men struggling to bring the frightened, plunging teams under control, and rounding up loose mounts.

Benton swore softly to himself, seeing the tautness of Doyle's face. He heard Skaggs order the companies forward, and was sick when, after a long gallop, close up, he saw the scene in detail.

He looked for the wounded, expecting their cries and groans, and suddenly realized no one had survived, not one. None of the blue shapes on the ground moved. It was a wipeout to the last man. One full company, plus civilian teamsters. Most of them had been shot in the forehead. The consistency like a trademark or grim label.

Troopers in the ambush party were already helping themselves to supplies in the brand new six-horse wagons, loaded above the sideboards, and the arrival of the supporting companies increased the confusion. There was a concerted rush for the wagons. A kicked whiskey barrel bounced off a letdown tailgate. Wielding an ax, a bushwhacker straddled it and started chopping a hole. Two huskies hefted a huge sack to the ground, knifed it open and began dipping up handfuls of sugar. Wrangling voices rose.

Skaggs broke it up promptly. "Captain Yandell—place those men under arrest! Mount up—mount up! Issue five days' rations all around. We'll haul the rest. Burn what wagons and supplies you can't use. . . . And dump that whiskey!"

There was a grumbling withdrawal from the wagons as the men obeyed, heads turned sullenly at the prizes they couldn't touch.

One rider sat apart, stiffly watching. It was Ernie Fletcher, looking green and drawn around the mouth, as if he'd been sick to his stomach. He seemed relieved when he noticed Benton, and he rode in next to him; for once, he had nothing to say.

Yandell made short work of the issuing and detailing drivers.

When the column was in motion again, Benton could look back and see plumes of burning supply wagons blacking the clear sky.

Toward evening, a broad creek barred the way. Wagons bogged down in the gummy bottom land and Yandell's company fell back to assist. Benton, seeing the ambulance mired hub deep before him, dismounted by the rear wheel. With Doyle and two other men each taking a wheel, he grabbed spokes and heaved, while the teamster cursed the straining brown mules. Bit by bit, the vehicle rocked forward, and settled back, still stuck.

Benton heard movement inside. He looked up to find a young girl considering him in a manner very like amusement as she held up the canvas curtain. There was a delay as the teamster jumped down to inspect the situation; the interval gave Benton time to note her small face and large, brown eyes. He had expected an older woman, certainly a matured one, hard-eyed, worldly, such as the camp-followers who rode the sutler's wagons in the wake of an army and plied their trade in the woods. But this girl had a casual prettiness.

His surprised impression of her deepened as she asked, "Do you want me to get out?" and leaned forth to see for herself.

"Better stay inside," he said, and it occurred to him that she was enjoying the inconvenience of getting stuck, welcoming the diversion. "We'll have you out in a minute."

More men, seeing her, came over to help, causing teamsters on the heavier-loaded wagons, forgotten for the moment, to shout curses at the laggards. She continued to observe their efforts, watching until, with a lurch, the ambulance lifted free. Whereupon, she dropped the curtain, and Benton turned on to the next wagon.

With the swollen creek between him and any possible pursuit, Skaggs ordered bivouac. Fires began blinking boldly through the twilight. Men gorged on lean side-bacon and fresh, crisp hardtack and drank strong Union coffee. Skaggs' tent loomed in the encampment's center, the whiter globs of the ambulance and wagons nearby, but the former, Benton noticed, was parked alone.

"Enjoy your scout?" Doyle inquired of Hart, his sarcasm studied.

The question nettled. "Could I help it if Tadlock picked me?"

"Could," Doyle persevered in the deliberate dislike, "if you quit lickin' his boots."

Hart paused over his supper. His bristly jaws chomped on a moment. "I suggest you curb your tongue."

"You might try makin' me, Jayhawker."

Benton stood up and stepped between them. "Ease off," he said and when both men settled back, he went to the other side of the fire, realizing that although he agreed with Doyle he couldn't permit the division among them to widen. He added quietly, without criticism, "That was a tough lay today."

Mears seemed keen to unload. He said, just loud enough to be heard, "They say confession is good for the soul. Not that I'd know about that. . . . Well, I was slow with my pistol, on purpose. The man next to me got his Yankee and mine, too." He paused. "Made me want to puke."

Mears wasn't funning this once. And Benton believed him. Mears had wriggled free, thanks to his usual cleverness. Squatting down, Benton was aware of a curious abeyance in himself, and in Mears and Doyle, as to how Hart had made out.

Hart, with care, ran a piece of hardtack around his tin plate, snapped it into his mouth and wiped greasy fingers on his tunic. He chewed noisily and swallowed, making sharp, whisking sounds between his teeth.

"It wasn't an easy fix to get out of," he said.

Mears' eyes went up, but he kept still.

"I wasn't fooled," Hart said, a bit smugly. "I saw what was up before Tadlock gave the order, after their two men rode back. I said to myself, 'I can't shoot a United States soldier. No, sir, by God, I can't. No matter what they do to me.' Had me a plan in mind when we rode up to the wagons. Just as everybody wheeled in, I reared my horse. Made him act up. It was all over by the time I reined him down."

Mears held his eyes down. Doyle poked at the dying fire.

Benton looked off, hearing boots. "Here comes Ernie."

Ernie Fletcher's expression had changed but little since the afternoon. He slouched down, holding a long-faced, pensive silence. In his dull eyes the cold-blooded horror around the supply wagons still persisted. A dream had died.

Benton let him be. All did except Hart, who flung Ernie an unfriendly stare. "Get back where you belong."

Benton angered. Damn the man! He said firmly, "Stay as long as you like, Ernie."

"Had supper?" Doyle took it up.

"Warn't hungry."

A man approached, tall and rawboned against the purple twilight. Tadlock. He came into the light, deliberation marking his long steps. He grinned when he saw Ernie, though it was nowise a humorous grin. He pushed back his hat over his narrow, protruding forehead and said, "Git a Yankee today, boy?"

Ernie might have drawn his thoughts through his mind and back again, he answered so slow paced. "Reckon ever'-body did. Couldn't miss. Like butcherin' penned hawgs."

Ernie's voice was bare of subservient boyishness. A crinkle ran across Tadlock's forehead; his thick eyebrows bunched until they formed a single line. "Anyhow, yuh got weaned today," he remarked. He turned to Benton with authority. "Wall—Doyle—company picket duty. Midnight t'dawn. Doyle, first watch." He walked off. In a few moments Benton heard the irksome voice drift back from the next mess fire.

Ernie said in a gloating whisper, "Tadlock thinks I killed me a Yankee. Well, let him think it."

Mears was curious. "How's that, young squirt?"

Ernie's guarded gaze strayed in the direction Tadlock had gone. "I didn't kill no Yankee. Wounded my man in the arm. Wanted them to make him prisoner. Except it didn't work out." Revulsion pitched up in Ernie's face; he looked ill again. "When he fell off his horse, somebody shot him again. In the head—between the eyes, with him askin' for mercy. Murdered him! A wounded man. Like he was jest a hawg."

"You're talking too much," Benton warned.

"Don't give a damn," Ernie replied, sticking out his jaw, "I don't look up to Tadlock no more, now I know what he is. This whole shebang. They ain't real Confed'rate soldiers; they're jest killers!"

Benton said, "Something else you can keep to yourself. Even around us. Tadlock didn't like your manner tonight. Hereafter, he'll be watching you."

"Let him." Ernie's enormous Adam's apple rode up and down like a loose hickory nut on the elongated column of his throat. His inconstant voice continued, now husky, now high. "I—I'm gonna pull out tonight."

Benton stared at him, and it came full force how much Ernie had matured in one violent afternoon, in a short span of hours. "That's desertion," Benton said, clawing for a way to shut Ernie up.

Ernie's grimness didn't fade a whit. "My mind is set."

Benton said, "Then unset it," knowing that it was Hart and Mears who had placed the sudden caution upon him that he couldn't communicate to Ernie.

"But you're my friends!" Ernie cried.

Benton tried to shrug him off, to pretend Ernie wasn't serious. "You've more sense than to try that, I hope."

"I am, jest the same."

"Why do you suppose Tadlock's making the rounds tonight?" Ernie only stared, stubbornly, and Benton said, emphatically, "Maybe more men, new men like yourself, couldn't take what happened today. Maybe they got the same notion. Fed up. Tadlock knows that; he's no fool. He'll watch extra sharp tonight for deserters. He'll warn the pickets."

"He didn't warn you."

"Not in front of you, no."

"Tonight's yore poorest chance," Doyle objected.

A new recklessness animated Ernie's homeliness. He estimated Benton, and Doyle, switching back and forth. "Tadlock, he gave me my only chance when he put you-all on picket duty."

"Try such a damn fool stunt on me," Benton discouraged, intentionally severe, "I'll bring you back by the ear, sure."

"Aw shucks, you wouldn't, I know." Ernie rose, showing a toothy, confident grin.

"Don't try me."

"Say 'bout three o'clock." Ernie had the plotting expression of a conspirator.

"Three o'clock, hell!" Benton said.

"Kee-rect," Ernie said, composed, bold. "I'll see you." He left them, going quickly.

He'll try it, Benton thought. He will.

"Boy means business," Mears confirmed.

Doyle's smelly pipe set off a series of frying sounds. "You aim to stop him, Sarge?"

"Don't know."

"Hell, let the young fool go," Hart said.

"Let him go," Benton echoed, rising, seeing the indifference in Hart's eyes which he had noticed before. "So Tadlock can run him down?"

He tore his gaze from Hart, afraid of himself for a moment. He could not comprehend the man at all. He unrolled his blanket, stretched out and turned his back to the fire, coming to grips with his thoughts as he damned Ernie's trustful utterances. There was only a trace of truth in Benton's warning that Tadlock would take additional precautions tonight—only a trace. Skaggs' command, for the most part, consisted of deserters, absentees, stragglers, horse thieves, murderers and robbers, posing as Confederate partisans. The woods were full of them, mounted bands leeching off the country, dodging service in the regular Confederate and Union forces. They could just as well pretend to be Unionists, though the Union would not recognize them, and the South, officially, did not. But they stuck together—they had to, bound by an iron discipline.

After Benton heard the others go off to bed, he turned restlessly, still wide awake. He reasoned that he wanted Ernie to leave, to be free; but not when Hart knew. Yet why, why did he question the Jayhawker captain? The man was in this as dangerously as himself or Doyle or Mears. He'd be shot just as quickly if found out. Hart rode Ernie to gain favor with Tadlock. That was apparent. Yet the boy had given Hart no cause.

Benton dozed. . . . A sound broke in. He opened his eyes to see a sentry shaking Doyle. When the Texan got up and started out to stand the midnight watch, Benton rose quietly and followed him to the horse picket line.

The big man turned at his step and Benton said, "Maybe we should get Ernie up."

"He said three o'clock."

"Too late. Be daybreak by five. He'll need more time. What do you think?"

Doyle was still sleep-fogged. "Figger Tadlock will take after him, huh?"

"I know he will."

"Awright. Better move fast."

Benton went back through the sooty light to where Ernie lay in a scattered group of snoring forms around a dead fire. He shook the boy and felt Ernie stir and come instantly awake. When they came among the Yandell company horses, Benton stopped and said gently, "Doyle and I figured you'd better high-tail it now, not later."

Ernie's voice faltered. "My horse . . ."

"He's right over there, if you're still set on going. We're not pushing you."

Ernie looked around, and although Benton could not see his face in the dark, he could sense his uncertainty.

"I'm goin'," Ernie said then.

Doyle, a broad shape in the darkness, drifted up. "Lead out a ways 'fore you mount up," he said in a hoarse whisper. "Head northeast."

Ernie's movements were nervous, and there was the realization in Benton how unprepared the boy was to be riding out there alone if Tadlock followed and jumped him. Benton said, "Good luck, Ernie."

Ernie whispered, "I'm much obliged to you both," and walked into the night, leading his horse.

Rigid, listening for sounds behind, Benton watched the high shape of Ernie's horse blend and dissolve into the night. For a little while there was the faint padding and grass-swishing of the walking horse, and then the prairie was hushed. Doyle stood as still as a statue. Behind them the camp slept.

Benton heeled about, enveloped in a tremendous tide of relief. "I'll stand watch. You get some sleep."

"Figger ever' gentleman should stand his own," Doyle answered, but short of his usual gruffness. "I'll be routin' you out soon enough."

It seemed but a minute until he was shaken awake and he sat up to face Doyle.

"Horses just went out," Doyle said in a half groan. "It's him, Tadlock."

Flinging off his blanket, Benton sought Hart and Mears and saw their sleeping forms.

"Tadlock . . ." he said, a sick realization pumping through his head.

"Him an' two more." Doyle turned incredulous, angry. "Now how in hell did he find out?"

Benton sagged down. And he'd been so positive of Ernie's chances! He said in a let-down voice, "How much start does Ernie have?"

"Hell, not much!"

Now, by God! he thought and felt himself rising, striding to Hart and grasping the lumpish shoulder.

Hart mumbled, raised up. "What . . . what is it?"

"You leave here tonight?" Benton's face was so close to Hart's he got the cheap cheroot smoke, the greasy food smell on the red whiskers. "You see Tadlock?"

"Me—Tadlock?" Hart's voice, thick with sleep, now hiked to an indignant splutter. "What are you trying to say?"

If Hart showed any guilt, the darkness covered it.

Benton's voice leveled. "Did you leave here tonight?"

"Why should I? Furthermore, I resent the question, whatever you're being so mysterious about. Now, sir, take your hand off me."

Benton let go, rough about it, not convinced either way, feeling Hart's fatty flesh slide away under his hand. He spied Mears sitting up and he said, "You been here all night?"

Mears pushed up straighter, his yawn prodigious. "Yeah. Right on my featherbed."

"Was Hart here all the time I was gone?"

"Hart didn't leave," Mears replied calmly. "What's the fuss?"

"Tadlock just tore out after Ernie—that's what. Somebody told Tadlock."

Realizing he was getting nowhere, Benton went back and sat down.

Later, he took his turn on watch, alternately pausing and listening. Off out there in the murky dark, three men hunted a frightened, homesick boy. As grayish daylight stripped away the night, he began to feel a small hope for Ernie.

CHAPTER 6

There was no sign of Tadlock when Skaggs made southwest after breakfast, a cloud of Yandell scouts prowling ahead. Neither was there camp rumor concerning the absences. These were tight-lipped men, taciturn, offering no opinions for strangers' ears. Yandell, himself, had roll-called Tadlock's platoon without reference to the absentees, causing Benton to wonder if Tadlock had carte blanche powers when desertions occurred.

Under a hot, blue sky the command halted for water. Benton rode into the shallow creek, let his horse drink and afterward turned up stream, above the muddied water, to fill his canteen.

He saw them as he headed back to the column with Doyle. Three men coming in on slow-footed horses; one— it was Tadlock—leading a fagged animal which carried a body tied across the saddle.

Benton stared with a sinking realization, and heard Doyle

commence venting himself in the incongruous swearing mixture he sometimes fell into. "Sonsabitches! Murderers! Heathens! Wal, the wicked will be turned into hell!"

"You're too loud, Doyle."

Doyle's black, furious gaze bored into Benton. "You figger it was Hart, don't you?"

"Hart or Mears."

"That's certain. Who else knew?"

"We'll find out," Benton said, "and when we do . . ."

He trailed off. Tadlock was riding by. His eyes took in the Texans for a moment. Other men stopped, staring silently as Tadlock, leading the laden horse, passed on to report to Skaggs.

In a few minutes, teamsters and riders returned to formation. Benton took his place and waited dumbly for the order to move. It did not come, and he looked forward questioningly.

Skaggs was holding another conference, a lengthy one. Nothing happened until company commanders swept past on the gallop. Yandell and Tadlock came jogging down the line. Yandell halted midway along his company's double file, faced in and barked his men to attention.

"One of you deserted last night," he started off, sharp and forbidding, loud enough for all to hear. "Private Fletcher, it was. Tried to get back to the Yankee lines." Yandell gazed with emphasis at Tadlock. "You know what the penalty is. You saw Fletcher's body brought in."

Rearward now, as Yandell paused, snatches of talk could be heard as other officers addressed their men in the same stern vein.

"After this," Yandell droned on, "we take roll-call three

times a day to check up on stragglers—if there are any. Double pickets will be posted at night. We want no word gettin' out where we're headed or as to our purpose."

Benton matched glances with Doyle.

Yandell was finished. He reined away, Tadlock trailing, and soon the company forded the little stream. At first, Benton thought the men ahead of him were swinging around a rough place. Several rods on he flinched, stiffened.

Ernie Fletcher's body, a bullet between the eyes, was propped against an oak by the trail for every passing man to see. A shallow-dug grave waited.

Benton, turning for one last look, saw two men with shovels filling Ernie's grave as the tailend of the rear guard cleared the creek. Staring, aching, he thought: when we ride back this way, Doyle and I, we'll put up a marker so his name won't be lost in these empty hills. And it came on him strongly that he was leaving Hart and Mears out of his future calculation, counting them out, when their mission had no more than begun.

All morning Skaggs maintained a fixed gait, not pausing, and by afternoon, making faster time through open prairie land, they struck a well-traveled trace—the Fort Gibson-Fort Scott military road, a broad scar stretching north and south, which also became the Texas Road. Skaggs turned south with all the assurance of a Federal supply train bound for Fort Gibson in Indian Territory, his men still clothed in blue uniforms.

Benton noticed that Doyle kept scanning the country. He said, "Look familiar?"

Doyle's face was wry. "Helped trail a bunch of mossy-horns this way in 'Fifty-Nine. Crossed the Red, came up the

Texas Road. Headed for Saint Joe. Wal, we never got theah. Armed settlers turned us back farther north. Tick fever scare. Lost our britches good. What stock th' damned Jayhawks didn't kill got scattered to hell an' yonder. Long ride home. I went back where I belonged, follerin' a mule's tail."

So Doyle had faced Jayhawker lead. That explained his unwavering enmity for anything Kansan. Benton stored the information away, including Doyle's trip through Indian Territory, as something to remember and perhaps call upon, and reflected how lean was his knowledge of Doyle, even though eating and sleeping next to the man and fighting him.

Colonel Skaggs skirted the Union garrison at Baxter Springs and hurried on. Before sundown, the column descended a cut between limestone bluffs and forded to the east side of Spring River, some miles below its junction with Shoal Creek at the tiny Quaker mission of Lowell, Kansas. They were, Benton knew now, getting within Indian Territory.

Alone, he walked through the sloping oak and hickory woods to the shining, pebble-bottomed river, farther up from where the command had watered. Fair light still held when he started for camp after a swim and a shave and washing his shirt, which he had waved about to dry and put on damp.

Following the bank, he rounded a tiny wooded point which jutted out into the river. He turned inland and stopped in his tracks, astonished to see a young woman less than two rods away. She sat on a flat rock overhanging the clear water, her back to him, her arms braced behind her as she turned her long hair to catch the lowering sun rays. Motionless, he watched another moment while she shook her head and brushed at her dark hair, as the sinking light picked up reddish flecks.

A sense of intruding, of gawking, crystallized in him. He turned to leave, and at that instant she moved as though hearing him.

"Sorry," he said, facing back. "I was headed for camp."

She observed him without alarm, with casual interest, a casualness which became searching. "Didn't you help push my wagon out of the mud?"

"There were several of us."

"I remember you because you don't have a beard."

He touched his chin and smiled. "That's a close observation. Well, I'll go now."

"The water's so cool and clear," she said, her voice holding him a moment longer. "My hair's a sight."

"On the contrary, it's quite pretty," he said, surprised at himself, and came to a speedy conclusion. Up close, she looked even younger than she had in the wagon. No more than a girl. Sixteen, seventeen. Small and rather slim and neither lovely nor plain, somewhere in between, and he discovered in her again the fresh, random prettiness he'd glimpsed the first meeting. Bare-legged, no stockings, wearing low-heeled slippers and a high-necked, blue cotton dress, faded after many washings, now too short to cover all of her graceful legs.

For the life of him he couldn't fit her with Skaggs. The connection posed an ugly question he didn't like, for it clouded his picture of her.

His compliments pleased her. "I do declare, you're the

first person that's said a kindly word to me but 'Climb in, hold on, git down.' You don't seem like the other men, somehow."

He smiled. "I thought most Southerners were considerate of women."

"They ain't all Southerners, not by a bootful. They ain't much of anything. Riff-raff. Unfriendly."

"Maybe they're afraid of the colonel."

"Well, that's the truth. Are you?"

"Let's say I prefer not to anger him."

Again, the little searching glint enlivened her eyes. She had a thoughtful, listening attitude. "*Prefer,* you say. You don't talk like 'em, neither. You surely don't. You've been to school."

"In Indiana. But I'm a Southerner," he said, though he had no intention of talking about himself.

"You never spoke you name." Her voice was pleasant, he thought. Very pleasant.

"Isn't important," he said, taking a going step.

"But it is," she insisted, so emphatically that he waited up. "Stay and talk to me a minute. You treat me nice. I'm not afraid of you because—because you're a gentleman!" she exclaimed. "You—"

His pained look checked her. "Not every gentleman is trustworthy," he said. "Remember that."

"But ain't you?"

"A gentleman? I'm not certain I know what a true gentleman is, or whether I'd like to be one. Anyway, being called one has caused me a little trouble lately." As he talked, the humor of it sank in. First Doyle and now the girl.

"Your name?" she went on. He gave in reluctantly, more

to get away, and she repeated after him, "Benton—Benton Wall. I'm Lettie Jo Capshaw. Now let's visit. Don't know when I've had me a good speak-out." She made a place for him on the rock.

He said, "You've been doing pretty well as it is," hesitated, and moved forward and sat down, feeling at once the laziness of the seat she had chosen, where the sun strayed through an opening in the woods and bathed the rock, making it warm to the touch.

She sat back, her eyes trailing across him. He saw a question, a faintly troubled look. "Reckon the men talk about me, don't they?" she asked. She looked older as she said that, more grown up.

"I joined up a few days ago," he said, "and I haven't heard any talk. But I imagine they've wondered what a girl like you, young and pretty, is doing here. Guess I have, too."

"Oh, it ain't what you think!" she flared, fully facing him, vivid color streaking her cheeks.

"It's none of my business," he said firmly.

"But it ain't so, Mister Wall! It ain't!"

He'd hurt her when he didn't mean to. "Wait a minute."

As suddenly as she had cried out at him, she recovered her control. "I know how it seems," she conceded quietly. "Not proper. In the colonel's ambulance. Off to myself all the time. They think I'm—his kept woman, don't they, Mister Wall?" She sounded miserable.

Benton seized the opportunity to divert her from a question he couldn't answer and which he had no wish to try. "You can drop the mister title."

"Why, you are touchy about it," she said, surprised, amused and equally questioning. "I thought every man liked to be a real gentleman." She looked straight at him. "You didn't answer me, Mister—"

"Benton," he provided swiftly, "and I have answered you as best as I can. You can't expect men who haven't seen a woman in months not to speculate and wonder about you. Don't you think it's a little unusual for a girl to accompany a bushwhacker command?"

"Not if she has to," she replied, looking off toward the river, glassy under the late sun. "Jayhawkers killed my folks. Burned us out." She went silent, and, seeing the sudden trembling of her mouth, he turned his head away until he, too, gazed at the river.

He said, "I'm sorry. What next?"

It was a moment before she resumed. "Oh, we didn't have much; not a big place. But my father raised good horses. We farmed up in Vernon county, near the Kansas line. Just the same we had our rights, even if we did favor the South. We didn't hurt those with Yankee beliefs." She had been speaking with a slow and studied recalling, wistfully, and now she ceased. "Here I am," she said, embarrassed, "talkin' to you like an old beau."

"Go on," he encouraged "Were you there when it happened?"

"Off to a neighbor's. Sometimes I wished I'd been, though."

"Don't ever wish that. It's a fortunate thing you weren't."

She turned curious, as if sensing a hidden meaning behind what he had said. "You don't give in much to your feelings, do you?"

"I try not to. We can't bring back the dead."

"I guess it's a good way to be, if you can," Lettie Jo said, settling her slim legs under her, tugging ineffectually at her skirt. "I couldn't farm alone. Everything was gone. The Jayhawkers ran off all the stock. No neighbors I'd burden myself on, and I couldn't reach my kinfolks in Texas."

He sat up. "In Texas?"

"Uh-huh. Sherman. That's why I'm here, Ben—Benton," she got out.

"That's better," he smiled.

"Doctor Skaggs—I mean the colonel—used to come by our house on his rounds when he campaigned for United States senator. He never won, but he always ran. When the war broke out, he used to hide his men in our barn. After the Jayhawkers came—"

He interrupted with a wave of his hand. "You keep saying Jayhawkers. How do you know?"

"The colonel said so."

"Was he there?"

"No—how could he? But he knew; everybody did. Jayhawkers'd been raidin' and burnin' through there."

He reflected on that, then said, "Go on with your story."

"Well, after that, I guess the colonel felt he was bound to help me, though I never asked him, hard as things got. He offered to carry me to Sherman and I said I'd go, him bein' an old family friend, you see. That is, to my Pa."

"Your mother didn't know him?"

"She did and she didn't. Ma wasn't interested in politics. Pa was."

Benton did not speak. He could see, at least he was beginning to see, he thought, the suggestion of several things. He didn't trust Skaggs, who had no mercy, no feeling for others; not when he allowed Tadlock's bullying cruelty and the murder of mere boys. Among a band of deserters and murderers and thieves, he ruled because he was harder than any of them. As for the colonel's tender regard for a homeless girl, a pretty one, a desperate one—well, that was incredible and wholly out of character. Furthermore, the command wasn't headed for Texas. Benton regarded her with sympathy, with pity, and was angry at what he knew. But now wasn't the moment to tell her, if he ever did. He could be of no appreciable help to her. Moreover, she wasn't his concern. This one time, he reflected—thinking of Martin Abel and young Ernie—he'd stand clear.

"So it ain't what folks might think," she said, her earnestness telling him she hoped he believed her.

"Doesn't matter as long as you get to Texas," he said, rising. "Time you went in. Much longer and the colonel will be out looking for you. Follow the bank down to camp. I'll go through the woods. Goodbye." His voice was brusque. One step and he turned, it coming on him that he had been foolish in talking so freely. "Do me a favor. Don't tell anyone you saw me. The colonel wouldn't like it."

Lettie Joe was standing, absently shaking out her glistening hair. "I'll think about it," she said, teasing.

He waited for her to go. Yet she gave no indication of leaving. She was studying him again, her gaze curious, reflective.

"What is it?" he said.

Her reply was spaced out, with a trace of wistfulness. "I was just thinkin' of all the fine ladies I'll bet you've squired about. The nice parties and pretty dresses—the soft fiddle music and dancin'. You a-holdin' hands."

"Lettie Jo, you have considerable imagination."

"Well, you're a gentleman," she pursued determinedly. "You are. Made up my mind about that. Guess it's your talk. That, and how you keep your hands to yourself." She had spoken on impulse; now she was blushing furiously. "You treat me like a lady, and I'm no lady. I never went to school as much as I wanted to."

"Lettie Jo," he said, touched, "it's what a person is that counts. Not what he wears or pretends."

"A man—" she said at once, "that's easy for a man to say, when he don't have to worry about growing old as a maiden lady. A girl's got to look nice. Have pretty things."

"I agree, but sometimes, even when she doesn't have them, she can look nice. Like yourself, for instance." He was, he realized, lingering again, and talking too damned much.

She laughed and was pleased and said, "Why, you flatter just like our devilin' Missouri boys—none of it true," and sobered, showing him an increasing interest. "Your school . . . was it a big place? Did you have many schoolmasters?"

"A small college," he said. "My father went there."

"Was there one for young ladies, too?"

"On the other side of town. Miss Emma Pevee's Female Seminary." He found himself touching his hand over his heart and bowing gravely. "Madam, our Conservatory of Fine Arts has an enviable reputation, and justly so. . . . The purpose of art is to develop in the student the power to respond to beauty of line, form and color. . . . Our Expression Department is unexcelled. Our moral culture the highest. We have done our best, and the past is not our goal."

She continued to smile at him, intrigued, entertained.

"You mean there wasn't time for dances?"

"Oh, there were some. Of a sort. Waltzes and quadrilles. Receptions and musicales. Occasional parlor dates. But Miss Pevee was like an old hoot owl, I'm afraid. One eye always open." He lifted a scolding finger, mocking. "Only genteel young ladies attend our noble institution, sir. And only young gentlemen may call."

She was beaming. "You did, I'll bet. Every chance you got."

"Frankly," he said, "I was scared to death of her. She was an old heller." He looked at the skidding sun. "Young lady, I think you'd better hitch along."

"Will I see you again?"

He hadn't expected such a question. He was stumped into silence, seeing what another meeting might bring, the complications and risks to his purpose, and yet he was dwelling on it with anticipatory pleasure in spite of his better judgment. "You want to get me shot?" he asked, not meaning to speak so harshly. "You go now."

She appeared to deliberate, and after a long moment she said, "All day I ride and look at the country. Nobody to talk to. Might you . . . have a book I could read?"

"A book?"

"Yes—something the young ladies at Miss Pevee's used to read."

Laughter rose in this throat, a laughter he throttled upon seeing her intense seriousness. "You're already a young lady, in my opinion."

"There you go. You're just nice. I'm not a lady and you know it; but I aim to be. I do. I wish," she burst out, "I wish I could be like one of Miss Pevee's young ladies!"

"Not many of Miss Pevee's young ladies had half your charm, Lettie Jo. You haven't a thing to worry about, believe me. Some young Confederate will see you don't stay a maiden lady. Mark my words. Just be yourself."

"Myself!" she exclaimed. "That's the trouble. I talk like a—well, like a farm girl because that's what I am. It ain't that I'm ashamed. It's—" The sudden light of inspiration widened her eyes. "Would you . . . teach me? Like a school-master? Would you? You knew Miss Pevee's young ladies. The subjects they studied."

He was taken back again, and also moved to an astonishing temptation that urged him to please her. She was dead serious. Becoming a lady, and whatever outlandish picture that might be, meant a great deal to her. He understood and he did not wish to disappoint her completely.

He said, "I'm no schoolmaster. Wouldn't be time for that if I were. But there's a little book in my bedroll. A book of Tennyson's poems. I'll fetch it for you when I can. Goodbye."

She turned with a half-finished expression and began picking her way over the rocks while he watched. She reached a clump of brush on the other side of the small inlet and there she half-faced him and waved before going ahead. When she was out of sight, he tracked back as he had come and entered the timber, walking thoughtfully.

He got a jar when, back in camp, Doyle told him immediately, "Tadlock's lookin' fo' you. Report to the colonel, pronto."

Going toward Skaggs' tent, Benton wondered if Lettie Jo had returned yet. He had allowed her plenty of time by walking roundabout through the woods, taking his time. He saw her ambulance parked off a short way from the other wagons, but she wasn't outside. Dusky twilight was overtaking the land, dimming the sky, smudging the shapes of horses and men. Early supper fires formed small yellow cones of light; wood smoke quickened his hunger.

A lantern glowed through the murky walls of Skaggs' tent; figures stirred in there, casting distorted shadows. Voices ceased as Benton was passed inside. Skaggs was concentrating over a spread-out map. Tadlock, standing, slouched, turned with a scowl.

"Whar yuh been?"

"Ever take a bath?" Benton snapped, and saluted Skaggs, who gave no notice to the byplay.

"You told me you'd traveled the old Texas Road," Skaggs said.

"That's correct, sir."

"You know where the crossings are and what to expect?"

Benton nodded. "Cabin Creek's next. But Doyle knows them just as well."

"Doyle?"

"One of the Texans with me. He drove cattle over the road."

"Ah, the big man, the fighter," Skaggs recalled. "Very well. Effective in the morning, I'm detailing you two Texans to go with Tadlock as scouts."

Protest kindled in Tadlock's yellow eyes. He tucked in his mouth at the corners, rusty with tobacco stain. It seemed to Benton that he intended to debate the order.

"You disagree?" Skaggs asked softly, in his deceptive fashion.

"Nawsir," said Tadlock, changing, the picture of respect,

appearing to down his grudging acceptance without malice. "Like you say, Colonel, we need men as knows the country. Jest hope they do, is all. Like they claim."

Skaggs dismissed them then.

Benton went on, aware of the muted horse sounds, the hungry voices, the bacon and coffee smells and the winking fires; and over there, among the white-topped wagons, he picked out the sallow flush of a lamp burning in Lettie Jo's ambulance.

CHAPTER 7

It was some twenty-five miles to the Cabin Creek crossing, Benton estimated, riding with Tadlock's scouts in advance of the grumbling column, routed out of warm blankets at 4 a.m. to cook breakfast and cross Grand River by Jordan's ford. As the light lengthened and objects took defined shape, he could see an attractive country unfolding—open stretches of high-grassed prairie rippling westward, timbered hills rising behind him to the east where the Grand flowed. Prairie chickens, disturbed by the thudding horsemen, fluttered off and settled down again, near enough for Benton to hit them with his handgun. Likewise, it was a lonesome country, showing no recent marks of human passage along the trail.

"Not a soul since we left Kansas," Doyle commented. "Where's all the Injuns?"

"They say most Cherokees live east of the Grand. More protection; they like hills."

"We'll need some ourselves in these smelly blues if Rebs jump us."

Presently Tadlock, in evident ill humor, spread his fan of scouts left and right and ahead, keeping the two Texans on the trail. Mears was somewhere on the flanks, one of the far-away bobbing figures, rising and falling with the pitch of the greening land. Hart rode with Tadlock; now, together, they cantered by.

"Some pair," Doyle said and spat his contempt. "Real school chums."

Benton gazed hard after Tadlock, the rawboned shape of him in the saddle. Every time Benton saw him, he was reminded again of Ernie Fletcher; and then the deep-seated angry bitterness would swell and burst anew to all parts of him, demanding that he act.

"Just fo'git it a while," Doyle warned. "If it's what I figger you hanker to do. Believe we got another job first, ain't we?"

Benton was surprised, not accustomed to hearing caution from Doyle.

"Kill him too soon you'll spoil everything," the big man reasoned. "Brother Tadlock will keep a little longer."

"Not much he won't."

"Better, 'til we reach Fort McCulloch."

"Doyle," said Benton, tilting his head to one side, "you're keen to get there, aren't you?"

"I aim to git it over with."

"Same here. But, meanwhile, I don't give a damn what happens to Tadlock and this riff-raff."

"Yo're hornet mad. All you can see is that sonofabitch free; poor Ernie murdered, no mark on his grave. Hell of a note, awright. Tadlock like a killer loose, laughin' in peoples' faces. An' I feel the same. Only how we gonna know about the silver if we don't ride into McCulloch with this mangy bunch?"

Up ahead, Tadlock and Hart had stopped in the road, waiting, and Doyle's voice shut off. When the Texans came up, Tadlock said, "From now on take the point." He was relishing something. "Colonel says yuh are scouts, so scouts yuh'll be—out in front. Hop to it."

Against the glassy afternoon glare, Cabin Creek's timber traced a dark, shaggy line. Other scouts came swinging in from both flanks, making for the crossing.

Just then, a horseman left the woods where the road entered.

"See that?" Benton questioned. "Our scouts aren't in there yet."

"He's wearin' blue."

"But nobody's ahead of us."

Benton, still in doubt, trotted faster. The horseman waved and continued to approach. He seemed to be watching beyond Benton, where Tadlock rode to the rear. Benton, turning, sighted the head of the column drawing into view and, in a moment, the swaying tops of wagons.

He looked front and got the explanation as the distance narrowed, got it with a start. The rider was an Indian on a poor horse, a Union Indian with a second lieutenant's shoulder straps and a rifle across his worn-out saddle. He saluted stiffly, correctly, grinning friendliness. His uniform looked new enough to have just been issued out of a quartermaster's wagon.

"What you got here, Lieutenant?" Benton asked, returning the salute, thinking it ought to have been the other way around.

"Union patrol," came the relaxed reply. "Cherokees."

Benton looked past him, seeing dismounted men and horses in the timber along the road. Not many.

"Better get 'em out of here," he said. "Quick."

Astonishment framed the young mahogany face. "My orders are to accompany your supply train to Fort Gibson."

It crackled in Benton's mind: the train Skaggs had plundered. His keyed-up senses took note of the scouts. In a minute they'd reach the road. Sweat was on him as he glanced behind and saw Tadlock running his horse, Hart trailing slowly.

"Lieutenant," Benton said gravely, "this is no Union supply train. If you want your men alive, go back! For God's sake take 'em across the creek."

"I don't understand."

Benton heard horses running hard. "Do as I say!"

"You wear Union uniforms."

"We're bushwhackers. Now ride hell out of here!"

But there wasn't time. Facing the creek, he saw the scouts closing in on the road, going into the timber.

"Here comes Tadlock," Doyle said, warning him.

With loathing for himself, Benton laid his carbine on the Indian, and as Tadlock clattered up, Benton ordered in a harsh voice, "I'm taking you prisoner!" Reaching, he seized the lieutenant's rifle.

Tadlock delayed long enough to shout, "Fetch him along to the timber!" and galloped down the road.

At last, Benton saw comprehension in the Cherokee's high-boned face. "You didn't lie," the lieutenant said, and shook his head, as if not understanding why Benton had warned him. "You are not Union." Fear had its hold on him for a miserable moment; then he showed the white man no expression whatever, and turned his horse when Benton motioned.

Coming under the mottled shade of the woods, Benton found the Union patrol bunched like cattle on the road, hands over heads; some fifteen troopers, their ponies as poor as the lieutenant's.

Tadlock had been questioning one of them. He turned away and spoke a low order, an action which sent a chill up Benton's back. It was plain as a bushwhacker stepped up to an Indian and gestured off into the woods with his carbine. The boy wavered between defiance and submission, until jabbed in the pit of his stomach. He turned with an expression of resignation and walked off the road, followed by the bushwhacker.

Hart trotted up from the rear. He held back, taking no part, not needed. Benton didn't see Mears.

It had fallen quite still in the dark timber. Benton was aware of small sounds: a horse moving nervously, a curb chain's chinking. He heard a hawking cough, its rasping, unnatural loudness. As yet, none of the remaining scouts had moved. He sensed a degree of unwillingness, broken when Tadlock, impatiently, signaled for the entire Union patrol to be marked into the timber.

Benton did not know he was going to speak, but all at once the words were out. "Tadlock—these men are prisoners—not spies!"

Tadlock jerked. "We don't take prisoners."

"They surrendered, didn't they?"

"Y'heard the colonel's order."

"That was in Missouri."

"Still stands."

"Let him decide this."

"She's already decided." Tadlock swung on his men. "Git a move on thar! I'God, move!"

At his bull-prod voice, the scouts began singling out Indians and herding them off the south side of the road. Benton sat watching. Tadlock, seeing the Indian officer still mounted, ordered Benton, "Him, too!"

Benton lagged, aware of the lieutenant mutely between him and Doyle.

A shot sounded. Tadlock roared, "Want me to git some-body whut will?"

In slow motion, though his mind mill-raced, Benton took the reins of the Indian's mount and led across the ruts, taking with him the picture of Doyle's troubled face at his action. Deeper forward, as the trees crowded more thickly, Benton saw with sickened eyes the scouts lining up the silent, solemn-faced Indians. Off a little way lay one blue figure, sprawled, arms out-flung, face down, as if he had tried to run. Powder smoke stank.

Benton skirted the scene, riding on. A man called, "Hell, ain't this far enough?"

"If I have to commit murder I'll do it in private," Benton replied and swung past, wide, to avoid the line of fire. He pressed on, seeking thicker, hiding timber, and when he found a place to his liking, he stopped and faced the lieu-tenant. Behind them, at that moment, a flurry of shots spat-tered, faintly muffled. The Indian flinched, but his mouth was set. He said nothing, he asked for nothing. More shots followed, closer together. A tiny span of time passed—and by now Benton knew it was finished. He took up his carbine.

Giving a trailing look to the rear, he pointed the carbine overhead and pulled the trigger. As the Indian waited woodenly, and the crash of the shot beat around them, Benton was telling him, "Get down. Keep going. Tell your commander at Fort Gibson three-hundred bushwhackers are coming down the Texas Road to Fort McCulloch." He added in apology, "We'll have to take your horse to make this look right."

It took a moment for the Indian to understand. Gradually, then swiftly, a light came into his dark eyes. He slid to the ground, his breathing rapid. Without a word, he turned and, running, disappeared into the gloomy timber.

He rode back, past the bad place in the shadowed woods where the Indian recruits lay in an irregular row. Like butchered hogs, Benton thought; like Ernie said. Well, the lieutenant was young and he was strong; he was an Indian and that was enough. Trouble, when it hit Skaggs, would come at the Verdigris or Arkansas river crossings. Let it come. He prayed it would.

CHAPTER 8

Benton reeled in his horse, an excitement pulsing in him as he stared southwest, squinting against the hard afternoon glare. In the distance lay the Verdigris river, its tracery of timber meandering in crookedly from the northwest to the crossing at the old Three Forks trading settlement.

Benton's mind was reaching far ahead, impatiently. Little more than a hundred miles stretched between him and Fort McCulloch. Beyond, south, Red River and home—and his reckoning with Crockett's murderers. But first he had a job to do.

He was alone today, riding under orders to scout the right flank of the Verdigris crossing for Union Indians. Doyle and Mears and Hart, meanwhile, were in a detail below the Verdigris ford, feeling out the approaches to Fort Gibson. A small party of Yandell's blue-uniformed scouts followed the trail toward the falls of the Verdigris, or Three Forks as it was better known. He could see them plainly, horses walking. A cocky outfit, it struck him, contemptuous of Indian fighting qualities and too careless for their own safety, lulled by the uninterrupted quiet since the Cabin Creek killings.

Benton, looking back up trail, was unable to locate the column. But he knew Skaggs was coming on without letup, intent on crossing both rivers and reaching Creek country, south of the Arkansas, before dark. Unless, Benton calculated, the young Cherokee lieutenant had made through to Gibson. It was a big question, certainly, what with Cabin Creek a punishing two-day ride to the north; unless the Indian had crossed to the Grand's east side and hustled himself a horse from the poor Cherokee settlements.

Riding on, Benton angled to his right for the river, to all appearances intending to prowl upstream as ordered. Once in the timber, however, he held up and killed a minute, his mind pinched on the ford and what might be there. He turned downstream, careful to stay out of sight within the screening woods, pausing, at intervals, to check on the bushwhackers going to the falls.

Soon he halted and tied up, now as near the ford as he dared, if trouble was there. Yet he was beginning to doubt that because of the continued silence as he left his horse and waded through underbrush and around tree trunks. He advanced more slowly, aware that he was making a small racket; he edged forward still slower and stopped. He could see the flowing river and hear the humming of the low falls; below them, he remembered, was the crossing over the flat rocks.

He blinked. Was it his jumpy senses or had something moved on the other side of the ford? While he peered, the chop of horses cut across the noisy falls. Foliage obscured his view, but that would be the scouts coming to the crossing, making their lazy reconnaissance.

All at once the horse clatter died, rubbed out. There came a high, half-drawn yell, another, muffled and not repeated. He heard nothing more. The compulsion to see sent him toward the river bank, toward a more open place.

Then, as he stood up, a Union trooper and an Indian materialized on the western bank, just above the cut-away slant where the crossing climbed from the unseen rocks. Benton hunched down hastily, parting the bush before him, feeling a tingle of elation.

He saw the Indian gesture for someone to cross over. A second Union man joined the first; other Indians appeared on the forested bank, until Benton judged twenty or more stood there. They stared, talking guardedly among themselves. After some minutes, Union horsemen humped into sight, leading four empty-saddled, wet-legged mounts up the ascent.

Not Indian ponies, Benton saw, but well-framed horses, heavy and stout-legged—bushwhacker stock, which told him what had happened.

He watched the crowded scene change in a matter of moments. Riders hurried out of sight; men faded into the trees and disappeared. Now the woods were as silently harmless as before.

It's set, he thought, and he started back, the picture enlarging in his mind. Waiting alongside the road, the Union Indians had cut down the careless advance scouts without firing a shot. This left the column unprotected in front, moving on a ford Skaggs assumed unguarded. Benton could warn Skaggs or let him go in. He thought on it as he legged faster for his horse. He had no regrets for the scouts; they'd been in on the Cabin Creek affair. Neither did he mind about the column. Wasn't he supposed to stop them, any way he could?

Yet, in the next few steps, he discovered it wasn't that simple. He'd completely forgotten Lettie Jo, he'd forgotten other reasons for being in Indian Territory. All he'd seen at first was the Union Indians balancing the scales, in which his own personal feelings surged strongly. Ernie Fletcher, for one.

His thinking was stranded at that point as he untied and swung to saddle. Then he saw it again clearly, like a picture pasted across his sight.

The four of them, if they were to stop the Confederate annuity from reaching Pike's Seminoles, had to come into Fort McCulloch as Rangers, under cover of Skaggs' hazy credentials. Only at McCulloch did they chance learning anything useful. It was bitter clear. Skaggs, damn him, had to get through; part of his command, anyhow. Meantime, there were the Indians set up at the ford. Benton felt a personal responsibility for them, for he'd put them there. He was in a scratchy place, caught between.

Riding northwest through the bottom-land timber, he saw the road still empty. He spurred up to put more distance between him and the ford; about a mile on he paused to wait for the column, his mind going back and forth over the circumstances. In half an hour he saw horsemen stringing along the road in double column, two companies in the fore, next the wagons, followed by two more companies.

Benton watched them while his thinking settled. He left the timber in a stretching run, riding for the clump of men at the column's head, and, rushing up, found Tadlock and Yandell on either side of Skaggs.

"Colonel," Benton said, calling out, "there's troop movement across the river!"

Skaggs showed alarm. He threw up his hand in the halt signal. "At the ford?"

Benton shook his head, pointed northwest. "Back in the woods. Looked like a patrol. About a mile up from the ford."

"Ford's took care of," Tadlock wedged in skeptically. "My scouts. Any trouble I'd know by now."

"Where in damnation are your scouts?" Skaggs snapped. "They haven't reported in hours."

"Reckon they crossed over, Colonel. Like yuh ordered."

Skaggs' temper flared. "I can remember my own orders without being reminded. I want to know why those men haven't reported."

Tadlock puffed up, stubbornness in his stare. "Means hit's clear up ahead, I'd say."

"With a Union patrol on our flank!" Tadlock's attitude, Benton saw, wasn't so much unconcern as it was to make light of Benton's value as a scout. Skaggs was edgy. He demanded of Benton, "Is there another crossing in the vicinity?"

Benton's headshake was negative. "This is it, unless you want to go way around."

Skaggs' manner spurned any such delay. "Which way was the patrol headed?"

"For the crossing."

"You didn't scout down that far?"

"No, sir. Tadlock told me to ride out the flank. Came in soon as I spotted the patrol."

Skaggs ran his fingers through his beard, brooding. "I don't like this. A small force—even a patrol, if it suspects anything—could damage us at the crossing. Delay us. Besides alarming the Fort Gibson garrison." He dropped his hand. "Captain Yandell," he said in his resonant voice, back arched, as if addressing a brigade commander, "tell Captain Fant to take his company across. Clean out that patrol. He's been itching for a fight."

"Hold up the train here?"

"Obviously."

Yandell blinked a moment and wheeled away. Skaggs, a crossness fleeting over his face, said distinctly, "Tadlock, I expect that crossing to be clear. To make certain, I'm detailing you along to scout for Fant."

Tadlock took the order with the offended air of a subordinate whose normally accepted opinion had been unjustly questioned, in surly silence. At the same time, Benton sensed as he had before, there were firm, old ties between the two, as evidenced when Tadlock expressed different views, and Skaggs, though ruling him down, never carried reprimands beyond a certain point.

But Benton, catching Tadlock's rebellion, decided this went deeper than any previous disagreement. Skaggs, actually, was beginning to doubt Tadlock's worth in strange country. In fact, the situation was shaping more favorably than Benton had hoped for while he waited in the timber, realizing, at last, he could prevent nothing this late, that here was an opportunity for the Union Cherokees to whittle on the column, pare it down, reduce its later effectiveness, while not exposing the wagon train to attack; that Skaggs would get through. He was too well armed and organized not to, and the Fort Gibson garrison was small.

"Sergeant Wall, you will accompany Tadlock," Skaggs said suddenly, shifting in his saddle.

Surprise and dismay kicked violently through Benton while, freezing his features, he gave Skaggs his brief nod, noticing, as he did, Tadlock's measly grin.

Hearing a company being ordered forward, he pulled out and halted, a pounding in his heart. He knew nothing of Captain Fant except he was considered a hell-bender who charged right up over the tent ropes. There would be no probing, little reconnaissance. Fant would lead them right into it, headon, Benton thought bleakly. This same Fant who'd figured in the wipe-out of the Union supply train.

Fant rode up. Never stopping, he motioned curtly to the two scouts, and Benton closed in with Tadlock. In his shapeless blues, there was little to distinguish the captain from a hundred other bushwhackers, bearded, untidy, mounted on fast Missouri horseflesh, the single gold bars of a Union first lieutenant perched mockingly on his shoulder straps. An ordinary looking man, the captain seemed, except for an extreme gauntness and his waxen complexion and the peculiar brightness, the staring quality of his blood-shot eyes.

"I don't aim for that blue-belly patrol to git away," Fant informed them. He rode on, trotting, now galloping, not slacking until the river trees rose darkly on all sides. At the lip of the worn slant gouging down to the water rushing over the flat rocks below the short falls of the higher reefs, Fant let up and studied the other bank.

To Benton's eyes there was no suspicion of danger. The wild woods over there some twenty-five to thirty yards, densely packed, overhung with vines, looked still and indo-lent. Across the open water, drowsy heat waves shimmered fitfully, glazing the shadowed face of the tranquil, tangled timber. Sound was the river brawling on to empty into the Arkansas several miles below.

"How deep?" Fant demanded, raising his voice above the roar of the falls.

"Ast him," Tadlock replied sourly, tipping his head at Benton. "He's our big guide. Been all over Injun Territory. Knows hit like a book."

Benton paid him no notice. "Up to a horse's knees," he told Fant, wondering if there was any means by which he could turn Fant up river.

"Been across it, have you?"

"It's swift, Captain," Benton discouraged. "Slippery. Easy to go over the falls." Yet, in citing the hazards, he grasped the futility of trying to swerve Fant when the man hankered to fight.

"My scouts crossed over," Tadlock shrugged. "Reckon we-uns can."

"If that Fed patrol's waiting for us, wised up, we're in trouble," Benton said.

Tadlock scoffed. "Why'd they wise up? Ain't we-uns blue-bellies?"

Talk seemed to annoy the restless Fant. He was hunched forward, one hand resting on the pommel, his round shoulders humped. He turned in the saddle. "You—" meaning Benton, "get out there. Lead us across."

Benton's pulse leaped. The fear of going kept him still, yet raced protestingly all through him. He had never known more acute dread, increased by the lack of motion. Benton was slow in obeying. He felt his mount's forequarters drop, felt the animal give and brace quickly against the pressure of the current sliding off the rocks to his right. His breath was shallow, shortened. Coming across like this, slowly, feeling his way, he realized he presented a perfect target. In his ears, beating fast, was the close roaring of the falls and the thrashing of the fording horses after him. He looked over his shoulder. Fant rode with his gaze pinned on the woods. Tadlock straggled at Fant's left.

Benton was rigid, tensed for the first shots. But they did not come. Halfway and the bank was yet cloaked in the fooling silence, peaceful, unruffled. But they're there, he thought—they're waiting. His horse quickened under him, striding faster as shallow water was reached; the churning and chugging behind lessened.

A chilly sweat bathed Benton. It had to happen now—and when the quiet persisted, he tried to believe the Union Indians had vanished, content to ambush only the scouts; tried, while his reason told him they had not.

Fant struck up faster. Benton, pretending to let his horse

feel the way, let him come even.

What seemed like an endless period dragged by, broken when Benton discovered the incline just ahead and the deep ruts going up. To have come this far, untouched, without a shot, was difficult for him to believe. And here, as a gift of time, unexpected, the high bank sheltered them. He glanced at Fant on his left and saw his fretting determination to hurry on. Tadlock rode lazily behind Fant.

Fant put his horse to the slope and Benton followed a pace to the rear, a frozen bunching filling the pit of his stomach. Still slightly behind, he could hear the company closing up rapidly, the horses kicking up spray. Now he was topping the slant. His eyes stretched wide, flicking at the trees and under brush and vines, and catching no stir.

He thought, They're gone.

The thought hung as his stare locked on blurred movement. Dark, gleaming faces behind felled logs and massive trees, among the hanging grapevines.

He gave a shout and leaped his horse away from the road, throwing himself low over the bobbing neck. For an empty, curious moment nothing happened—nothing at all. When the crashing did strike, there was no single, opening crack of sound; it was all together, a volley, the entire woods erupting violently.

Somewhere he heard a horse tearing off down the road. His own screamed and broke down. He lost a stirrup, he kicked the other free. He hit along the lip of the brushgrown bank, shaken hard, the breath pounded from him. He lay in a heap, unable to move immediately, until instinct drove him, rolling, over and over, his boots lashing stiff brush, then emptiness. He was falling, with the undertone of the falls and the plunging racket of the guns and the sudden yelling making a tumult in a spinning world. He grabbed with both hands. Brush scraped an arm; he grasped and missed. He grabbed again, in final desperation, and the fingers of his left hand snagged on rough branches. He seized hold, feeling the socket of his left shoulder give as the rest of him dropped. To his surprise the brush held. Next he was digging in with his boot toes, hugging, embracing. He twisted his head to see the whole confused scene, smoky, unreal, like a spectator.

The crossing was in an uproar, riderless horses switching around, bolting, sliding, hind quarters down, wild-eyed, some crashing over the slick rocks downstream; a few lunging up the west bank, stirrups flying. Others milled and floundered, while down on the water-swept ford riders lay like dark lumps of driftwood, stirred slowly by the pressing current. He saw one horse plunge straight over the rocks, dragging a foot-hung rider.

But toward the rear a loose order was taking hold. These were hard-twisted men, veterans, quick to recover from surprise, their level barrels blazing back as they turned and fired and made for the east bank and paused to fire again. Shouting, dark-faced riflemen, crying in elation, ran out and kneeled to lay an eager volley on Fant's retreating company. They drew a quick, spitting fire. Several went down. A shouted order called the others back.

Benton felt a looseness in the brush he gripped, a giving; abruptly he was punching his toes into the crumbling earth for support, feeling his boots digging in, breaking loose; then they caught and sustained him. He groped, his outstretched hands hooking on rock. Inch by inch, he began edging upward, aware of a slacked-off firing. He was within feet of a snarled thicket. Head throbbing, grunting, straining, he pulled harder, bracing one knee underneath, and managed to budge head and shoulders over. On hands and knees, he scrabbled forward and under and lay still, panting.

He lay on the right flank of the ford, where he'd turned in the first moments. His dead horse was a rod away. There was no gunfire in front of him, and he guessed most of the Union people were posted nearer the road in order to cover the ford, or were concentrating south of the road. If he crawled upstream, he'd be in the clear, calculating that Skaggs would be rattling up on the run, if he hadn't already reinforced Fant's company. The heavier firing over there sounded like it.

He started crawling, feeling sweat crack his skin. When he stopped and half-rose, head canted, he could almost count the Union shots, dying out, spaced. A conviction strengthened: the Indians were pulling out for the fort, which meant a small force, drawing off before Skaggs forced the crossing and came at them hard.

He retraced his steps, and by the time he was in close, both sides of the ford were quiet. Apparently the Indians had gone, leaving the road open. Captain Fant lay there, stone dead. Benton watched from cover while several riders filed gingerly across, climbed the cut and fanned out south. There was a pause. Presently, on the double, a platoon put out from the opposite side and jingled up the bank, spreading to scour the woods.

Tiredly, then, Benton showed himself, walking to his downed horse. When a man on horseback approached from down the road, moving against the flow of riders, Benton, busy skinning off his saddle, hardly noticed. The man kept coming. His persisting advance made Benton look up.

It was Tadlock, very much alive. His jaw hinged down and he stared mutely at Benton, his astonishment holding until he was turned aside by more jostling riders. Benton returned to stripping his gear. Catching a loose mount, he changed saddles, slung on gear, and attached himself to the passing double file.

He took stock as he rode along, very tired, neither elated nor regretful about Fant and his men. War was a dirty game because men, made in the image of God, died. Long before today it had knocked any nonsense about glory out of him—if he'd ever possessed much of it, certainly nothing to equal Crockett's youthful idealism.

He heard axes thunking as he neared the shaded Arkansas river bottom; going on, through the tall cottonwoods, he could see men felling trees and horses pulling logs. Though broad here, the Arkansas was fordable by sandbars halfway across, and it was to this farthest point, where a large raft was taking shape, that the logs were being snaked. Across the river horsemen hallooed back to the raft-makers.

Sundown hadn't come when Skaggs swam the last of his rear guard over and camped on a ridge above the bottoms, posting his right on a ravine and his left by a marshy run.

Benton, riding on, looking for the bivouac of Yandell's scout company, noticed Doyle making a fire. Before he could ride there, a fast-walking orderly hailed him.

"Colonel says report."

"Report?" Hunger rolled in Benton, hunger and

annoyance.

"Tadlock's chief of scouts. Not me."

"Tadlock's done reported." The orderly seemed about to blurt something. But, instead, he said, "I'd get fast, if I'se you. Colonel's right over yonder, sore as a boiled owl." He jabbed a finger for punctuation.

Turning toward the center of the encampment, Benton knew the last thing he needed was a cussing-out from Skaggs; the least he could expect was a severe dressing down, and perhaps suspicion, since Tadlock had told his version first. Benton felt an actual dread as he rode up and saluted.

Colonel Skaggs sat on a log, brooding more than usual, deeply preoccupied, oblivious of the orderlies pitching his tent.

Benton waited. Skaggs did not seem aware that he had ridden up. Finally, at length, Skaggs glanced up and returned the salute. "You may dismount," he said formally. His blue trousers and the skirts of his long frock coat were still wet from swimming his horse across the river. Temper burnished his gaze as Benton came down.

Skaggs spoke, at once to the point. "We took a bad mauling at the Verdigris," he said, stern and accusing, giving Benton no opportunity to answer. "Lost eighteen men, including Captain Fant, one of my best commanders. Seven wounded. Might as well say half a company. Now I've heard Tadlock's report, such as it is. So it's time for yours."

Did Skaggs suspect him? Through a cold apprehension, he made his account brief and stuck to the facts. Finished, he saw no change whatever in Skaggs' forbidding expression.

"Tadlock informs me they were Union Indians," the colonel said.

"Looked like Indians. Dark faces. Wasn't much to see."

"Our uniforms should have fooled any patrol. Certainly gotten us in close enough to take care of ourselves. Tomorrow we go back to our grays." Skaggs arched up and stood a moment, spraddle-legged, eyes on the ground, ruminating. "We found Tadlock's scouts in the woods, downstream. Knifed. I cannot account for it."

An insight bit into Benton's thinking: Skaggs wasn't concerned over losing men; he was angrily perplexed, incensed, because a prize deception had failed.

"Any notions, Sergeant?"

Benton took a while replying. "I wonder, sir, if some Indians got away at Cabin Creek?"

"But my orders! Every man—" Skaggs clamped his lips together, flushing, and eased off. "That could be, though Tadlock swore none did."

"Just the same, they were waiting for us today. They knew."

Skaggs was grim. "I don't intend for that to occur again. Not at the three remaining crossings, between our position and Fort McCulloch."

Benton's mind tore at the words and retreated. Was Skaggs, in his sly way, deliberately testing his knowledge of the Texas Road and the adjacent country?

"My recollection is five crossings, sir," Benton said straightaway.

"Five?"

"The North and South Canadian, Colonel. Muddy Boggy, Clear Boggy and the Blue River."

"Perhaps my map is incomplete."

"You're over the hump, Colonel. The Arkansas was your last mean crossing. Last big chance the enemy had to stop you."

"You sound positive."

"I don't look for many more Union Indians, if any, south of the Arkansas."

"And the nature of the country?"

"Hills. Prairie and timber. We can make good time following the Texas Road."

"We pick it up soon?"

"Southwest a few miles puts us back on it."

"Our next crossing"—Skaggs pursed his mouth—"is the . . ."

"North Canadian. About forty miles."

Skaggs' gaze never left Benton's face. His attention grew to a vigilance, constant, disturbing. He said on a note of impatience, "I keep waiting for you to show some curiosity, Sergeant."

"I don't understand, sir."

"Curiosity as to why I keep plying you with endless questions. Why I pretend a colossal ignorance of my own field maps."

"Guess it's to see whether I know the country like I say."

"One reason, yes." Skaggs stepped in, revealing a slanting smile. "The other is this. Effective immediately, you are my new chief of scouts."

Benton hitched a little straighter. This thing he thought he'd wanted—it was his, yet the implications threatened him. What if he refused to carry out murder? If he did, he was finished and with him the mission and maybe three men besides. He longed to hedge, to back out. But he had committed himself too readily. Been too eager to mouth information about the country.

Benton found his voice. "Quite a surprise, Colonel."

"You puzzle me, Sergeant. I expected you to thank me for your promotion."

"I wasn't expecting it. I'm new to the command, and there's Tadlock."

"Tadlock failed me," Skaggs said crisply. "Allowed himself to be sucked in, badly fooled. However, he will remain on scout duty with you."

That, Benton thought bitterly, will be just dandy.

"I can see you'd rather I transferred Tadlock to another Company," Skaggs said for him. "It isn't necessary. Tadlock has been reduced in rank. You understand? You will see that Tadlock follows orders. And you will guide us to Fort McCulloch without further mishap. Understand?"

Benton, meeting the chill of the compelling eyes, jogged his head up and down, and with each movement it was as if he agreed against his will.

"I'll get you through, Colonel."

He saluted and was ready to mount when Skaggs spoke again, turning him.

"Another reminder, Sergeant. My ward, Miss Capshaw, is riding in the ambulance, as you no doubt have noticed. I have issued a general order that no man, other than myself or her driver, engage her in conversation or approach her in any manner. Remember that and enforce the order if necessary."

Benton gave him a nod.

"Furthermore, this afternoon my advance captured an

Indian farmer. A gay fellow. Amusing. Wearing turban and blue hunting shirt. Looks like an Arab. But he's a Creek tribesman, I'm told. Rather he was. Tried to escape. We were forced to shoot him. There's a Creek village southwest of here. First thing in the morning you will scout out all approaches, preparatory to an attack before we resume our journey along your fabled Texas Road."

"Aren't some of the Creeks fighting with the Confederacy?" The moment the question popped out, Benton realized his mistake.

Skaggs had a flinty look. "General Pike won't like the idea of my stirring up his Indian allies, but in case the Creeks had a hand in the Verdigris fight, I propose to teach them respect for regular troops. I repeat, you will scout out the village and report to me soon after daybreak. That clear?"

Benton, mouth compressed, nodded, grasping, So we're Confederate regulars now! He mounted, and discovered he wasn't ready to go. "Colonel," he said, wondering how Skaggs would take it, "there's one more thing. I'll scout and I'll fight, but I'm no executioner like Tadlock."

He was surprised to see Skaggs grin, one corner of his mouth squinched up in that peculiar, humorless expression. "You mean there's a difference between killing a man who can't fight back and one in the heat of battle?"

"Is for me, Colonel. I won't kill a boy, dump him beside the road as an exhibition piece."

"More than exhibition, Sergeant. A necessary example of discipline where deserters are concerned. Well, you're frank and direct; I like that in a man, if he makes sense. I like your manner as a cavalryman. You show training, though not enough. You will kindly remember that my orders are to be obeyed—to the letter."

Skaggs' tent was up and ready, and he turned on his heel.

As Benton rode through the scattered camp, comprehension grew. He'd do as ordered or die. Skaggs required the services of a guide to Fort McCulloch. Once there, a man's usefulness could end suddenly. And why had Skaggs kept Tadlock in the scout company, if not to spy on him? Had Tadlock really been demoted?

Engrossed in thought, he did not see the ambulance until he was almost upon it, Lettie Jo beside it cooking over a fire, bending now to stir something in a small black kettle.

He reined to avoid her and saw the sudden motion of his horse attract her attention, and as she turned he noted how prettily the heat laid a soft glow across her cheeks. Recognition animated her. She straightened up with a quick smile, her manner all welcome. An instant after, her face dulled as he touched his hat in salute and passed on without speaking.

He found the three Union men wolfing down hardtack and bacon between swigs of coffee. Nodding around, he staked out his horse and fell to getting his supper.

Doyle took in Benton's mount with his practiced eye. "Swapped horses, didn't you?"

"Lost mine at the crossing. Union Indians. Guess you heard what happened?"

Doyle nodded, his interest quietly wise. "How in hell'd you git out?" After Benton told him, Doyle just shook his head.

Mears said sardonically, "Wouldn't it be ironical, one of us catching a Union bullet? Maybe all of us?" He presented that possibility still further with a careless sweep of his eyes around, and seemed disappointed when no one took up his bantering.

"It's not over," Benton said. "Tomorrow we hit a Creek village. And don't look so surprised, any of you. It's an order."

"Tadlock tell you?" Hart asked.

"Skaggs." Heads jerked. Benton had come here in dejection, in uncertainty; but now he saw an immediate usefulness to which he could put his dubious promotion. "I'm new chief of scouts. Tadlock's out."

Doyle was the first to react. He slapped his leg and brayed his exulting laugh while he directed a nasty look of triumph at Hart.

Benton said gravely, "We can't continue as we have been since leaving Missouri—quibbling, jawing at each other. It's work together or get rubbed out. From now on we scout together at all times. I'll see to that. I want—Skaggs to get used to seeing us that way."

He ceased, primed for Hart's antagonism. When the cool eyes in the round, whiskered face met his calmly, without differing, Benton felt a shallow surprise.

"That's sound thinking," Hart said. "We are bound by a common cause. Therefore, we must combine our efforts."

Doyle was grimacing, unimpressed. "Now somebody wave the flag an' we'll all march by." He cracked his enormous knuckles, studying Hart through skeptical eyes. "Thought Tadlock was yore great friend?"

"Ostensibly," Hart said with dignity. "At least I've succeeded in keeping him off us, don't you think? I also believe I've allayed any suspicions he might have."

Doyle, doubting, cut back, "Why didn't you let us in on

yore little plan?"

"Your acting was much more convincing this way. Tadlock thinks we're at each other's throats, growling, complaining, because I've seemed to side with him over Ernie Fletcher."

Benton couldn't digest that, quite. "Didn't you?" he inquired softly.

"Never." Hart's denial was absolute.

"Wal," Doyle sneered, "Tadlock's busted. How y'figger to oil his feathers now?"

"Maybe sympathize with him in his demotion. What do you think? I ask all of you," Hart underscored, but he looked at Benton as he spoke.

"Why bother?" Benton said. To avoid further talk, he seated himself on the other side of the fire and hungrily attacked his supper, contemplating Hart's startling metamorphosis.

CHAPTER 9

Benton's energy was building back. He lay flat, head resting on his bedroll, content to have even the hard earth quietly under his bruises. He watched Doyle rise and face south, staring moodily, big hands on hips, a remoteness in his eyes. He stood there a full minute or more, seeming lost to all but his concentration beyond the climb and dip of the broken land, across the wooded hills and clean streams and sea-like prairies. His attention broke; he strode off restlessly.

Soon after, Hart rose and winked, murmuring, "Believe I'll look up friend Tadlock," and disappeared in the dusk.

Mears yawned and tapped his mouth organ in the heel of his left hand, and blew into it, playing softly, with meditation.

"Let's hear something," Benton said.

"Not in the mood," Mears said, a rare refusal. "Man's supposed to play this thing, not think on it."

"Thinking," Benton said. "Like Doyle, thinking of home, maybe? How near Texas is, yet you can't go back?"

Mears cocked his head and shrugged, a cynical curl to his flexible mouth. "Be touching if I told you I longed for home. But I don't. Not even a little bit. Oh, it was quite an empire my father had on the Sabine river. Great passel of land and niggers. I was supposed to inherit it all some day. Travis Paxton Mears the Third. Son of the Honorable Judge Mears."

"Sounds worthwhile."

"Except I didn't give a damn for law or farming. Nor honor or duty, my father said. We never got along. He wanted a big strapping son. I was always small and scrawny."

"Any brothers or sisters?"

"Unfortunately for my father, no." The mobile face twisted. "I'm the last, and a black sheep, of a noble line which got its wealth by any hook available, so long as someone else did the sweating."

Mears seemed more natural as he spoke. The stamp of better days and better times told in his manner. He wasn't lying, Benton sensed; he asked, "You left home before the war?"

"Several years. My father kept sending me to various law schools, and I kept going in for theatricals and music and a good time. I put a good deal of his cotton money into circulation. Eventually, he tired of the expense and ordered me home. I returned, only to leave not long afterward." He paused to reflect on that and explained brightly, "In more exact terms, I was told to get the hell out, go north and stay north. Which I did. Sergeant, theah are a few things I perform rather well, if I may say so. I can act a part and I can play half a dozen musical instruments in the popular vein. I can purloin a man's purse or a fine horse from under a liveryman's nose and"—Mears had a sudden expression of pain—"I've a way with women. Sometimes I think it's a curse! In fact, a woman—a married woman—was partly responsible for my finding myself in uniform. If I'd been out west, in Colorado, the gold camps, I'd have stayed out."

"There was nothing to stop you from going west to avoid fighting, just as hundreds of Northerners are doing."

Mears' shrug expressed nothing.

"Your father," Benton said. "Ever hear from him again?"

"Never from him. Only indirectly about him. He raised a regiment, armed it at his own expense, took it to Virginia and got killed the first year of the war. Leaves no one at home. My mother passed on a long time ago. So I've no idea who has the place now."

"Has it?" Benton demanded. "It's still yours, unless your father gave it away."

"No one to give it to I know."

"So it's yours. After the war, go claim it."

"I detest that life. The damned high pride and the nigger trouble. Running a plantation isn't the easy, idyllic existence most Yankees picture it. You take care your niggers whether you can afford it or not, and why shouldn't you?

But my father was right. I have no inclination for duty. To me honor is a mask behind which gentlemen weave their machinations, either in New Orleans or Boston. I'm sick of the war. About all I've done is trade hot Southern pride for Yankee bullheadedness. They're both wrong, and each will destroy the other. We're eating our young, Sarge."

Benton raised up, a thoughtfulness coming upon him; his thinking circled, wandered, caught. Just barely, he could make out the white top of Lettie Jo's ambulance. He considered its proximity to Skaggs' tent, perhaps fifty yards separating them, and simultaneously he picked up the jingling and clopping of evening watering details trailing along the ridge toward the path descending to the river.

Pushing up, he explored his bedroll and found the little book and stuffed it inside his shirt, noting as he finished that Mears' mouth organ had ceased. On his feet, he stepped over and untied the picket rope from the iron pin and led the haltered animal away.

He passed other low campfires and picketed animals grazing the thin ridge-top grass, and reclining men, used up from struggling across the Arkansas. Pleasantly, the mixed odors of a weary bivouac came to him as he walked in a line with the ambulance: wood smoke and stale horse sweat, boiled coffee, frying bacon and tobacco smoke. His approach would take him by the tail of the wagon, close to timber, out of sight, and the chance to pass the book without notice, or, if Lettie Jo wasn't in sight, to pitch it inside.

Coming up, however, he saw the rear curtains closed. Voices murmured on the other side. Not pausing, he continued on and found Lettie Jo and her driver seated around the coals of the cooking fire, and was left with a vague disappointment. She swept a look his direction before he passed, walking to the rough path dropping down the ridge. He took it in lengthening strides as the grade dipped abruptly; once at the bottom, the sky's grayness was all but shut out, leaving him blinking in mealy gloom. The timber here was blackly massive, ancient, overspreading, its dead branches littering the soft floor underneath, with the damp breath of the river filling his lungs and the spongy bottom land and whirring insects dulling the passage of his horse. Mosquitoes and gnats hummed against his face; he batted at them absently.

A string of led horses filed by him, going uphill. At the river's sandy edge, where tallow light over the open river broke the murk, he came upon another watering party. Shortly, these men took their horses back through the timber, voices and hoofs and crackling brush persisting in sound long after Benton lost sight of movement.

Alone, he led down to the muttering, singing water; when the horse raised its streaming muzzle and turned, he climbed with it and sat down in the still-warm sand, holding the rope. He watched the big sky shift from evening to early dark, a vastness pricked with stars; he felt a cool wind sweep off the river. A grave thought sank. The book is all, he told himself. As far as I'll go. I can't be responsible for her; even if Skaggs isn't taking her to Texas as he promised. It would be cruel to tell her when he couldn't ease her problem. On the other side, was it right for her not to know?

Neither course gave him satisfaction.

He did not know when his senses first jumped alert to the new sound, it was so light and quick, a gradualness softly mulching in the sand. Suddenly distinct, like footsteps.

He sprang up, his eyes prying the dingy light toward the back-drop timber, his right hand on the butt of his revolver. He went stiff and suddenly dropped his hand when he recognized Lettie Jo. A light shawl lay across her shoulders, her voice was teasing. "You-all ready for the reception to start, Mister Schoolmaster?"

He was glad to see her and he wasn't. "There'll be a different kind of reception if your driver followed you."

"I slipped out the back of the wagon. He didn't see me."

"Step over here," he said, leading his horse off the path. He noted that she stood no taller than his shoulder, and he got the faint cleanness of soap and sachet scent. She disturbed him and the dark furthered a sense of remoteness, of just the two of them drawn together for protection. He caught himself thinking of her as a woman instead of a girl. An acute awareness of her swept over him. She looked older under the dusky, obscure light, perhaps so because of her hair, glistening even here, combed straight and arranged in folds on the back of her head; or perhaps because of the loneliness he read in her. Yes, that terrible and cruel loneliness had sent her trailing him.

"I saw you go by each time," she said. "I don't know—I just followed."

"A risky thing," he said. "Walking these river bottoms at night. And I don't know whether you've heard or not, but the colonel has issued orders that no man speak to you except him or your driver."

She looked up. "I didn't. He'd mean it, too. I'll go back now," she said, starting to move away.

"Not yet. I was going to put this in your wagon." He drew the book from inside his shirt and handed it to her.

She accepted with a startled cry of delight, handling the book carefully, caressingly, murmuring her thanks. "I'll read it fast as I can and return it."

"Yours to keep."

"Mine?"

He jerked and cocked his head. "Listen . . ." Horses walking and stumbling down the ridge, men's voices, came clearly. "We'll have to leave here," he said and yanked the halter rope and took her arm, guiding them farther into the timber. When he stopped, the noises sounded to his left at a safe distance. To silence any whickering, he laid his hand over his mount's soft nostrils.

Somewhere along the line of horses, hoofs started up abruptly. Brush snapped. After a great deal of jangling and cursing, the racket died and a call rose roughly in annoyance, "Damnit can't you handle that jughead!"

"Got creased today—he's jumpy," a voice grumbled.

"Well, hold him in!"

The detail tramped ahead, a heaviness, a weariness, in the slow-going movements. In a while, Benton could hear the horses at the water's edge. Afterward, for a time, he heard very little except the undertone of tired voices while the raiders waited. Once he got the drift of strong pipe smoke.

Lettie Jo had scarcely moved. She formed a small, indistinct shape beside him, standing close.

He bent his head. "You can go out to the trail now. It'll be all right." He sensed her hesitation and then she was going. Simultaneously the horses began scrambling up the river bank. She had frozen at the sudden commotion, and he pulled her back and faced the river, expecting the detail to proceed toward the ridge without delay.

Close upon that assumption Benton heard hoofs break out, the rapid movement a shying, skittish animal might make. Somebody yelled, "There he goes!" Boots padded along the bank.

Benton wasn't concerned until brush crashed in their direction. His horse danced nervously, and he shortened his grip on the halter, holding the tossing head down.

The brush crackling ceased and a hoarse cry followed, "I got 'im!"

But Benton's horse was still acting up; it veered sideways and slammed into a tree, throwing Benton against Lettie Jo, causing him to throw an arm around her to prevent knocking her down, and even then he went to his knees. They made a brittle scuffling that sounded extremely loud to Benton, who dragged harder on the halter and fought the horse under control.

"What th' hell was that?" Surprise and some fear mingled in the distant voice.

"Wild hogs, I reckon. Come on."

"Don't sound like hogs to me. Sounded sneaky. Like Injuns."

"Injuns, hyar?" There was a short, grunted laugh. "I'm goin' to camp."

There was no additional argument. Boots trailed off, then the quicker motion of a fidgety horse; next, more slowly, apparently the steps of the second man, noises that soon fused with the moving detail.

Benton went loose with relief and dropped the arm he had around Lettie Jo. But for the fortunate grab of a spooky horse's halter rope, they'd have been discovered together in the woods—the conclusion obvious. His plans wasted uselessly, wrecked because an impulsive girl had ventured after him. Cold sweat slicked his skin. Yet, when he turned to look at the pale oval of her face, he couldn't find anger. Hadn't he brought the book? Hadn't he looked for her?

"You'd better wait up a bit," he said, instead, though sharper than he meant.

He thought a coolness had entered her voice when she said, "I'm obliged for the book. Good night."

"Now hold on." Two steps took him in close, standing over her.

She said defiantly, "You don't think I can look out for myself, do you? Well—I can and I'm going."

"Give them time to reach camp," he said, more careful of his tone this time. Something was butting around in his head, something that bothered him and from which he shrank. It was a dangerous thing, but he had a tremendously protective feeling for her. "Let's go back a way off the trail. We need to talk."

"Talk—about what?"

He evaded with silence, for it still wasn't clear to him whether he ought to tell her about Skaggs. He walked on and paused on the river's edge, in the long shadows back from the open bank. "You're mighty young," he said, more to himself than to her.

The renewed light gave him a partial picture of her face, enough that he realized he'd said exactly the wrong thing. Her bitterness came out at him. "I'm not a girl any more. I grew up a long time ago."

"I didn't mean you hadn't."

She said, still bitter, "Maybe you never came home and found the neighbors standin' around—your folks dead

Your home burned. Just the stone chimney left." He stiffened, his sympathy welling. "Maybe you never lost someone close to you like that. Killed—murdered by Jayhawkers!"

"I think I know how you feel, Lettie Jo. How old are you?"

"Seventeen."

Possibly it was the unaccustomed feel of his hand resting on her shoulder, without his being aware when placing it there. For, without warning, she bowed her head and began sobbing quietly with a convulsiveness that ripped the heart out of him. He took her to him then, feeling the tremors working up through her while he tried to comfort her with clumsy pats. He stroked her hair; it was soft and smooth to his touch.

She lifted her head after some moments, eyes brimming, brushing with an uncertain forefinger; and he remembered his bandanna and dabbed the wet cheeks under the large eyes. She sniffled and he wiped her nose.

She said, ashamed, in a small and wretched voice, "A minute ago I was the one who'd take care of herself. I was grown up, I thought."

"I've seen men cry, Lettie Jo. Strong men. Brave as you ever saw. It's after things are over that you cry. Makes you feel better."

She shook her head unhappily. "I thought young ladies didn't show their feelin's."

"If you're referring to Miss Pevee's gently bred females, they'd scream at sight of a field mouse; and I doubt that any of them ever experienced what you have. Nor would they be as brave." An awareness of time jogged him. A latening stillness dominated the damp river bottom. No longer did he catch the occasional muffled stirrings on the ridge. He said, "I'll tell you now; may not get another chance." His tone left her quiet, waiting. "It's the colonel. What he promised you. About taking you to Texas."

"I told you he knew my pa," she said, faltering somewhat.

"Did he tell you he was going to Fort McCulloch, south end of the Territory?"

"Yes, he did."

"Did he tell you why?"

"No—but why should he?"

"He had reasons not to, Lettie Jo. Big reasons."

"I don't know what you mean."

"He didn't tell you he expects to command a brigade forming there, did he?" Benton said sternly. "His bush-whackers and General Pike's Indians. No, because he's going to Kansas—not Texas."

She winced as if from a blow. He heard her uneven intake of breath. "It's hard to believe," she said. "When he said he'd carry me to Sherman."

"This is his chance to play Napoleon to something bigger than a handful of bushwhacker companies," Benton con-tinued. "He's thinking of defenseless Union forts on the Kansas frontier. How he can take them and make a big name for himself in the South. Conqueror of the West—General Skaggs! Lettie Jo, he's still running for senator in a way. Still shooting for the moon."

She was shocked into silence. When she spoke, she seemed to voice a hope she did not quite believe. "Why—why can't he have an escort take me to Sherman?"

"Do you really believe he will?" he asked and cut short,

seeing they'd come up against the ugly hub of the matter.

"Why won't he?"

He set his eyes on her, wanting her to reach her own conclusion.

"You mean," she said, an unsteadiness in her voice when he didn't speak, "he aims to keep me with him?"

"Maybe you've got the idea." He kicked at the earth, he dropped his shoulders and swung his head in an up-and-down movement. "Now you know and there's no way I can get you out of it. None whatever. None I see."

She had been gazing up at him; now she dipped her chin.

"I don't like to tell you this," he said.

She grasped his arm. "I still can't believe it!" she cried, but with less conviction than before. A thought seemed to seize her. "The brigade, you call it. The Union forts. How do you know about such things?"

"I heard some talk."

"The doctor didn't tell you," she declared indisputably. "I know. He keeps things to himself. Oh, he'd tell his captains, but not a stranger. A new trooper like you."

"The doctor," Benton said dryly, "is not beyond bragging to a new man."

"But he wouldn't tell you about a campaign."

"Let's say I overheard it. You'll have to trust me, Lettie Jo."

She studied him searchingly and stood back a little way. "Benton," she said, groping, "sometimes I don't know. Sometimes you don't act like a Southerner a-tall. You never say Yankee—you say Union. Like it's something big and great; to be looked up to. Land sakes, you talk like you don't want the doctor to take those Yankee forts in Kansas!

Well, I do!" She showed him a defiance. "If there's any-body I want hurt, it's Jayhawkers!"

Inside him the flag of caution was raised. Lettie Jo was a Southern girl, a loyal one with sharp insights. And he'd let his tongue flap. "What would you do," he asked, "if I were a Yankee and you found out?"

"I'd tell the doctor!"

"Then what?"

"He'd have you shot."

"You keep forgetting I attended a northern school. That a good many Southern boys did. For your information, if it will make you feel better, I was captured at Pea Ridge. I escaped but couldn't make it back to my command, a Texas regiment. Took the only way out I had—attached myself to the nearest Confederate force."

"Oh, it ain't the school," she said, troubled. "Because you went there." She put a sudden, restraining hand to her mouth, an action that shattered the seriousness of their con-versation.

He had to grin at her self-correction. "In case you have any more doubts about me, your good doctor made me his chief of scouts tonight."

"You!"

He nodded once. "But if you still want me shot as a Yankee, just let on to him I told you about the forts in Kansas." He allowed her no time for conjecture. He was pulling on the halter rope as he finished. She stepped out with him, voiceless. Back on the path again, he walked without pause to the base of the ridge and motioned upward. "Go ahead. I'll wait a few minutes."

She did not leave at once, but appeared to consider a

thought. She half-faced him, half-turned away. She lifted her head and all at once she regarded him squarely. "Whoever you are, Benton, you're kind."

"Anything but that. I'm no help to you."

"I don't need your help."

The words rankled. "You still don't believe me?"

"I'm not worried."

"You ought to be."

"About him, the doctor? Nothing he says bothers me."

"You're sure of that?"

"Yes—"

She sounded convincing, almost. Yet he couldn't be responsible for her or become further committed than he was. Also, it was past time she returned. She delayed still, and he swung his shoulder to hurry her, and wasn't expecting her step toward him, her face uplifted, her hands on his arms. She stood on tiptoe, an insistence flowing through her touch. She kissed him on the mouth, an instinctive, hurried kiss, yet warm, and dropped her hands and turned up the path, gone before his astonishment broke.

His brain was suddenly foggy with tangled loyalties; his drive to revenge Crockett, the weight of importance that hinged on getting the Indian silver, his doubts about Hart and now this fresh complication which he could no longer deny even to himself. Wearily he leaned against a tree. First things first, he thought dully, and he took the path and led his horse past the darkened ambulance.

CHAPTER 10

Benton Wall had only a part of his mind on the Texas Road

drawing on before him, southwest, gouging the soft swells of the wild-flower prairie, curving around greening limestone hills tufted with post oak and blackjacks and blooming redbuds. The rest of him mused on the four of them riding together again, about as they had in Missouri at the outset, when Mears had returned with the fat red hen and afterward displayed the ruffled garter, to Doyle's vast amusement.

Yes, everything was fine, he repeated in thought—so fine he distrusted it. Since crossing the Arkansas, the column, back in dirty butternut jackets and homespun, had traveled in the leisurely fashion of Texas-bound emigrants. Skaggs seemed to welcome the lack of action. Tadlock, on the surface at least, had accepted his demotion. Today he rode on a flank, as far away as Benton could place him. Even the brief, one-sided skirmish at the Creek settlement had served one helpful purpose. North Fork Town, another Creek village between the North and South Canadian rivers was deserted when Skaggs charged through, warned, Benton was positive, by the neighboring Creeks above. Well, he figured, while his eyes ranged the country, we're getting close. Make McCulloch by late afternoon or early evening.

Hart spurred alongside, the embodiment of genial cooperation. "Look for any more Indian settlements between here and the fort?" He was continually asking questions as to the lay of the land, the streams, the Indians, familiarizing himself.

"No villages," Benton said. "Just scattered farms."

"Seems to me," Hart reflected, scratching his red chin whiskers, "we should try to remember the character of the country. Keep the landmarks in mind. Especially any likely spot to ambush the silver train."

"Just four men spreads it mighty thin. We'll have to think of something better than a daylight attack."

Hart agreed with a nod, in full accord. "I liked that gap we passed back there."

"Might do—if we knew in time," Benton said. "Mears, there's a job for you at Fort McCulloch—for all of us, in fact—finding out when the silver's due."

"Yeah," Doyle smirked. "Play the boys some tunes. Show 'em yore garter."

"An old story," Mears said, alertly on cue. "Got me a new one now." Turning, he searched his bedroll and brought out a fringed buckskin skirt, holding it high with both hands, between thumbs and forefingers.

Doyle grinned crookedly, but with interest. "Wal, how was it, Brother Mears?"

"My friend," replied Mears, making a show of calling on an exalted dignity, "a gentleman, a true one, never speaks of his conquests of the heart."

Benton interrupted them. "Column's closing up. Doyle, ride ahead with Mears."

As the pair made off, Hart resumed his geniality. "Sergeant, your work at the Creek village impressed me."

The obvious flattery placed Benton on guard. "I warned the first Creek farmer I found. He told the villagers. They got out."

"Weren't you a little worried over what Skaggs would do, when he discovered the Creeks gone?"

"Some were late getting out. Didn't make it. Guess there was enough blood to satisfy him."

Hart and Benton rode in silence for a while, and it

occurred to Benton that the captain had lost part of his roli-
ness. Everyday riding had conditioned him, melted some
tallow off him. He rode rather well by now; he appeared
capable and calm, determined to see their mission done. He
had a vigor not evident before.

"What," Hart asked, "if the Confederate money's ahead
of us? Already at McCulloch?"

"General Curtis didn't think so."

"If it is," Hart said, an aggressive fix to his chin, "I'd be
willing to take a chance."

"Don't worry—there'll be chances aplenty," said Benton,
finding in Hart's unfamiliar forcefulness, lacking until now,
another curious aspect. Nonetheless, he thought, reconsidering, it was exactly what they were going to need in vast
quantity.

Hart reined in slightly and, with a companionable turn of
his head, said, "Sergeant, I want you to understand one
thing. It's very important to me and, I think, to the successful discharge of our duty. Although I outrank you, and
General Curtis placed me in command, I've been willing all
the way for you to take over. I am still. More efficient. You
know the country and you've impressed Skaggs, which is
vitally important. One little matter bothers me, however."

"What?" said Benton, prepared for a complaint.

"You told Mears and Doyle what to do when we reach
McCulloch. I feel I ought to have similar duties."

"Keep your eyes open," Benton said and hesitated
impaled on his own vagueness, in which he realized a truth,
never could he bring himself to trust Hart completely; there
would always be a reservation or two. But, and he knew this
for truth also, he would work with the man as far as he

could, to the bitter, rag-tag end if he had to.

"That isn't much of an assignment, Sergeant."

"We'll know more when we get there. Just watch. Keep ready."

Benton halted. "Time you joined Doyle and Mears, Captain. I'm due to report back to Skaggs. Clear Boggy's not far ahead." He swung his horse before Hart could speak again.

At three o'clock with the Blue River just over the next swell of land, a single horseman appeared on the trail and stopped. Riding up, Benton saw under the stiff, gray wool hat the glittering face of an Indian, who raised his right hand from the shotgun across his saddle and signed that he would lead the column across the river to the fort. Benton sent Mears to the rear with the message and stepped down from his horse for a moment.

"Not much reception," Doyle said, aside, while they waited for the command. "Just one Injun. Wonder if Pike's sore, heard about the Creek village?"

"Probably every tribe in the Territory knows by now."

Not long after, Colonel Skaggs marched the head of his trailing riders between a double line of cedar trees past the two-storey Jonathan Nail house, which Benton remembered as a stage stop on the Butterfield Overland mail route before the war. The greenery of orchards, gardens and grape arbors flowed around the house and beyond.

Leaving the timbered bank on the west side, Benton gazed off in surprise. Instead of a small stockade as he expected, crouching apprehensively in the flats, Fort McCulloch was more like a fortified encampment in the classical style of a bygone era, an elaborate system of trenches and defensive works of recent excavation, something a student of world military history and a follower of Napier's "Peninsular War" might lay out. Upon a brow of low bluff, twin dirt breast-works in the shape of a Greek Cross protected the north and northwest approaches, a third Cross the southeast, all bristling with cannon.

Over the headquarters tent on a rise in the center a stiff wind whipped the Stars and Bars. Below, clustering on the plain, Benton saw cabins, walled-in tents, mess shacks and covered corn cribs and log and sod warehouses. Dog tents, huts and dugouts occupied the surrounding knolls and swells. A fort, he thought, in disbelief, with cannon, better than two-hundred miles from the Cherokee country Pike was supposed to defend. He guessed it indicated why the Confederacy, at times, seemed to be riding four directions at once in the Territory.

Jogging out on the flat below headquarters now filed a company of Indian cavalry, a giant white man in front. Skaggs' Indian guide halted and became like a post.

Skaggs, obviously put out by the delay, said, "Why are you stopping here? Lead us on to the general."

"You wait," was the blunt reply. "Gen'ul Pike, him 'bout ready talk."

Glancing around, Benton saw an extra reason for stopping. As if on signal, Indian cavalry—two companies on each flank—was converging upon the bushwhackers from the north and south. Skaggs saw them also; his head jerked. He looked right and left, so visibly aroused that Benton expected a defensive order. Just then, the approaching Indians paused some fifty yards away, staring silently, unblinking, and Skaggs faced front again, waiting out his indignation.

Pike came ahead, a luxuriously bearded man of striking personal appearance with a brigadier's three gold stars and a gold wreath on both sides of his coat collar. His massive body made the horse under him seem no larger than a pony. He reined in and touched a broad hand to his hat brim.

"I am General Pike, department commander of Indian Territory," he said, heavily. "I presume you're Skaggs."

Color pinked Skaggs' cheeks. "Lieutenant-Colonel Skaggs. With three-hundred Partisan Rangers from Missouri."

"Of course," Pike replied coldly. "The Lower Creeks told us you were headed this way. I believe they reported eight men killed, one a mere boy, and several harmless women wounded."

"A military necessity, General. Indians ambushed us on the Verdigris."

"Union Indians, Colonel. The Lower Creeks are allies of the Confederacy, treated as a nation."

Skaggs was silent a moment, agitated. "Can't we continue our discussion at your headquarters?" His lifted reins said he expected Pike to turn about and proceed.

Pike sat his horse stolidly, his hands idle. "We can discuss any matter here, in the open, before my Seminole friends." He gestured, indicating both flanks, then right, at a thickset Indian of wide mouth and heavy lips and intelligent black eyes. "My aide, Lieutenant-Colonel Jumper."

As his name was spoken, Jumper spurred even with Pike. His attitude was one of suspicious readiness.

"Colonel Jumper," Pike said, "commands the First Seminole Mounted Volunteers. As you can see, we have no uniforms except homespun and the gray hats. I consider myself fortunate to supply them at all. Despite the shortages and lack of training, they conducted themselves well at Pea Ridge."

"Pea Ridge," Skaggs said, arching his lip a little, "was not a victory for the Confederacy or its Indian allies."

Twin glints appeared in Pike's stare. "Contrary to treaty agreements, our Indians were ordered out of the Territory to fight. I told them to conduct themselves in their own fashion, using the bow and tomahawk if they wished."

"And the scalping knife?"

"Exaggerated. General Van Dorn had to blame someone."

"I see you share my opinion of Van Dorn."

"In one respect, perhaps. Circumstances have forced me to act on my own resources. Here I command the roads to Fort Gibson and Fort Smith, west to Forts Washita, Arbuckle and Cobb, as well as to Sherman and Bonham. The Red River valley is necessarily my base of operations, for I must draw all my corn, flour and bacon and ammunition, if I get any, from Texas, just thirty miles away."

"A long way from the enemy," Skaggs murmured. "I found the northern half of the Territory virtually defenseless."

Their talk dragged on. It was obvious to Benton that both commanders were sparring. Pike seemed suspicious of the Missourian's intentions and, until he determined them, would commit himself in no way. On the other hand, Skaggs, seeing Pike's unfriendly bearing, recognized a powerful threat to his great expectation to command the Kansas invaders. Plainly, Colonel Jumper had Pike's eye for that role. And so both, it appeared, were willing, temporarily, to draw off and deliberate before meeting again.

"My men are tired," Skaggs said presently, his voice altering to civility. "If you will assign us our bivouac area. . . ."

Pike was equal to the occasion. "Certainly, Colonel. Along the river. Colonel Jumper will show you. There's plenty of corn for your horses."

"Thank you, General."

"Now what the hell!" Doyle growled as they dismounted to make camp in the river timber. Benton could feel the unruly impatience in Doyle. The big Texan threw back his head, showing no inclination to unsaddle. "How long we gonna stay here?" he demanded around.

"Skaggs is playing it foxy," Benton said. "He aches to lead the Kansas invasion. I'd say Pike has other notions. Doesn't trust guerrillas. Skaggs above all, after what he did to the Creeks. Pike is foxy, too."

"Damned if they ain't!" Doyle bent in a ridiculing bow and perked his mouth, his manner bestowing, mocking. "Yo're obliged to some horse corn if you want, Colonel, sir. You shore are. Like hell! You back-shootin' sonofabitch! . . . Wal, Gen'ral, reckon I will have a little. Thank you kindly—you old coot!" He straightened and grimaced. "Who's gittin' foxed?"

"We will be," Hart fussed, "if we don't find out about the silver annuity for the Indians."

"It's not here," Benton said. "Otherwise, Jumper's Seminoles wouldn't be around."

The differing of opinion threw a tautness across Hart's

face. "What's to keep Jumper from collecting his money and waiting here for Skaggs? This is a planned campaign."

"Except Pike didn't figure Skaggs would jump the Lower Creeks. Pike's leery of us; maybe he was at the start. After what's happened, I believe he'd send the Seminoles on—if the money was paid."

Mears started warming up on his harmonica, blowing experimentally, a piece of this tune and that. Doyle wheeled. "Can't you let up on that damned mouth music?"

Mears sent him an indifferent look and continued playing. Doyle went to unsaddling, his movements hasty, temperish. So they were bickering again, Benton realized, himself included, turned irritable by weariness and the prospects of delay and the growing extent of the unpredictable action facing them.

Doyle turned back, his heavy gaze on all. "I say let's git it over with."

"Don't look at me," Hart said. "I'm with you. It's Wall, here, who seems to like the shade."

Heat burned up through Benton. Nothing had changed, he knew. But he stifled the impulse to take it up.

Murmuring over his mouth organ, Mears said, "Just can't wait to take on them fierce Seminoles, can we?" and returned to his aimless music, unconcerned again.

"We can't finish it here," Benton said. "Waiting for it to come to us. Quick as we get a good smell, we're going back up the road. Mears, after dark, take a stand by the wagons. Play for the boys. Keep your ears open."

Mears' hands came down with the harmonica. There was an air of preoccupation among the three as Benton unsaddled and turned toward the creek, leading his horse.

Looking back before he entered the timber, he saw two wagons filled high with ears of yellow corn being driven to the bushwhackers' camp. Beyond, prominently above the short plain, rose General Pike's flag and his white log-walled headquarters tent. Benton put his gaze north and south, taking in the main sweep of the encampment, reading strength in its orderly arrangement and size. Judging from the mounted Indians he'd seen, Pike's command outnumbered the bushwhackers three to one but did not appear superior in arms.

He looked once more at the Stars and Bars, looked thoughtfully, at length, and walked on, his mind on Lettie Jo, unable to forget her. Yet there was nothing, he decided suddenly, angry at himself, to hold him here much longer. At almost any moment he could ride off and cross Red River and start hunting for Larkin Knowles and his cronies. Nothing, if he locked his mind to all else.

On his return, he singled out the ambulance, and although he went no nearer, he could see Lettie Jo's driver much in evidence. He was always around, it seemed, always watching.

After mess, Benton saw Colonel Skaggs and Captain Yandell trotting off into gathering dusk for Pike's headquarters.

General Pike, briskly courteous and cool, offered them rawhide-covered chairs, saying, "You are quick, Colonel."

"Delays are inexcusable, General." Skaggs, straight-backed, sat on the edge of his chair.

"I trust you are comfortable in your bivouac, such as we can provide?"

"Quite comfortable, General."

"Tomorrow extra corn will be hauled over to you."

Skaggs did not respond, for he saw a continuation of the day's deadlocked parrying with this former Yankee school-teacher turned Arkansawyer, who was more student of law and history and the classics, Skaggs had heard, then a man of action. Skaggs envied Pike's knowledge, his poise, his position of command as a brigadier, and, more deeply, he hated the older man's thinly masked contempt for guerrilla troops. Still, he recognized formidable opposition when he saw it. Now, he pinched his beard, while his left foot tapped a nervous tattoo on the tamped floor.

Pike said, coolly, "Is there something else, Colonel? Some flour or bacon?"

"Let's drop the niceties, General. You know why I'm here."

Pike arched his eyebrows. "I thought you came to join my command."

"I came," Skaggs said, erect, direct of voice, "to claim *my command* of the western frontier invasion. An order to that effect was to come through to you from General Van Dorn on commendation from General Price in Missouri."

Pike's mouth settled. He looked weary.

At Pike's slack nod, a heady elation rushed over Skaggs. "I suppose," he pursued, "there was mention of my higher commission from the Secretary of War?"

Pike blinked rapidly. "Commission? It's customary for promotions to come after a successful campaign—not before."

"It can wait," Skaggs said after a pause, benevolently. "My men will be ready to move within a few days." He

154

stood, legs spraddled, his chin thrust out. He started to leave and was abruptly halted by the General's voice.

"I took Van Dorn's dispatch as a recommendation instead of an order, subject to my discretion," Pike was saying, flat and crisp.

"At any rate we're set."

"If you agree to serve under Colonel Jumper as second in command."

Skaggs was too astounded to reply instantly. He gaped and a soaring anger shook him. "Under Jumper!"

"You could do worse."

"A goddamned Indian!"

"I must correct you, Colonel. A Confederate Indian, and I believe in honoring our obligations to our Indian allies." Skaggs balled his fists. "Still a goddamned ignorant Indian, I ask you—do you intend to ignore Van Dorn's order?"

"I have no choice if we're to get this expedition under way. My Indians won't serve under you. Not after you attacked the Lower Creeks, their long-time friends and allies."

"I told you—" Skaggs' voice fluted up, and he stopped himself on Pike's checkmating stare.

"They don't trust you, Colonel. I've treated with Indians. All kinds. I know how they think."

There was a laden pause as they measured each other. Skaggs was aware of his own ragged breathing as he spoke on the same uneven beat. "Trying to make me pull out, General? Afraid—are you—my men will grab more glory than your simple Indians?"

A sudden flush stained Pike's high forehead. "I have explained my position," he stated, an acid bite in his calmness.

Skaggs uttered a snorting "Hah!" and was striding to the door, Yandell a step behind, when Pike said, "Colonel Jumper won't leave immediately, if you would like to reconsider."

Skaggs came to a standstill and turned his head, slowing in thought. "What's holding him up?" he asked, and the question kept expanding.

Pike seemed a count late in answering. "Supplies," he said, a guardedness leaking into his firm voice. "We expect them in a few days."

"From Fort Smith or Texas?" Skaggs spoke with a studied casualness.

"Both. Sometimes Van Dorn lets a little trickle through from Arkansas. What he doesn't appropriate and what those army worms, the speculators, don't steal from the Confederacy."

Skaggs' mind was clutching upon a conclusion, something he had overlooked in his anger. Supplies? Just that afternoon Pike had said he drew supplies from Texas. Did the self-righteous old fool, mouthing honor and obligations, think no one but himself and his greasy Seminoles was informed of the annuity? Skaggs felt like smiling, but he managed to present a respectful expression. "Give me a day or two to consider, General," he said, a heedful tone in his voice that had been missing before.

"Certainly."

"I'm also in the dark about your campaign. I'd like to know, if you care to discuss it tomorrow."

"Glad to."

"Then good night, General."

General Pike heard them mount and ride off downgrade.

He let his heavy body sag while he listened to the fading hoofs and the wind flapping the canvas ceiling of his bare quarters. A weariness weighed upon him, a repetitive weariness and discouragement. He thought: so Skaggs knows about the annuity. He knew, though he pretended not to. Nothing is secret in our army, among our flap-mouth officers.

CHAPTER 11

A stillness hugged the swarthy land when Benton saw Skaggs and Yandell return to camp. Instead of continuing to headquarters, the colonel pulled up and Yandell rode across and motioned for Benton. Doyle and Hart stared as he rose to follow Yandell. Mears had wandered away half an hour ago toward the wagons.

Skaggs swung down, turned his eyes on the nearest men and paced away from them, Yandell and Benton trailing. Skaggs stopped suddenly and faced about, an abruptness in which Benton could see a combination of black anger and sorely wounded pride. Skaggs was haggard, the lines around his mouth pinched and vengeful.

"Sergeant," he began, in his stringent voice, "you're leaving as soon as it's full dark. Take a week's rations and retrace our route up the road. Stop this side of Clear Boggy, where you can observe all passing parties. A small detail will do. More would be noticed. There's a ford on the Blue down below. About a mile. Cross there. Pike's Seminoles are all around his damned bridge."

Excitement took possession of Benton. He said, "All right, sir," thinking of his clumsy efforts to discover the very thing Skaggs now appeared to be telling him. "I can take the Texans and the Missouri man that joined up with us. We've been scouting together. We know the country."

"No," Skaggs interrupted, as if changing his mind. "Not enough. Take Tadlock—"

Benton's satisfaction broke downward.

"—and a few more of Captain Yandell's company," Skaggs pieced out. "That will do it."

Something warned Benton not to protest. "What are we to look for, sir?"

"A wagon train from Fort Smith with Confederate escort. You should be able to approach and make inquiries without suspicion. You will send me word without delay. Under no circumstances must they reach Fort McCulloch."

"Anything special in the wagons, sir? I mean we're to find out about?"

"Nothing for you to concern yourself about."

Nothing, Benton said silently. *Nothing but a hundred thousand in silver you aim to beat Pike to.*

"Dismissed," Skaggs said and stared a little longer, harder, underscoring, his nail-hard expression unaltered. Then he mounted and touched spurs, Yandell at his side like a part of him.

Alone, Benton's first impulse bade him hurry to camp so they could slip away and go up trail until they found the escort.

He held still, hearing, over by the wagons, behind him, an outburst of coarse, jesting voices to the accompaniment of Mears' teasing harmonica, and realized he'd have to abandon Mears if he pulled out immediately with Doyle and Hart, and an instant protest told him he could not.

He could feel the pressure of diminishing time as he started toward the wagons and the men standing around the flow of fire, thinking to himself what excuse he might use this early to call Mears out. In turning, he noticed the dim square of the flag over Pike's headquarters, high up, in the soft, fading, reddish haze of the darkening sky. The sight worked on him oddly, nagging, and he paused. All at once, he understood why he had lingered in his watching that afternoon. He thought, it's been this close and I'm just now getting it.

In a moment, he was taking rapid steps.

Mears was showing off the captured buckskin skirt and beads when Benton walked up. He stopped and an awareness came. Mears, he grasped now, Mears with his lively stories and music, was suddenly the key. Mears must entertain a while longer if all of them were to get away without Tadlock and the other Yandell company men. There was a crowding and elbowing forward, with much ribald laughter, and Benton drifted around, unnoticed, until he had the ambulance in view. Lettie Jo sat on a box, somberly watching, hands folded on her lap. He did not see the driver and guessed him somewhere in the crowd.

Benton angled across, at an even walk. He saw the upfling of her head as she recognized him, and her startled unguardedness when he continued ahead.

He waited for some mark of gladness from her, but it did not come. To his surprise she got up and turned for the rear of the ambulance. As she walked away without looking at him, he realized she was going to avoid him. He lengthened stride and came up from behind as she was starting up the rear step.

"Where's your driver?" he asked, and laid his glance around.

"Over there." She nodded toward the crowd. "I was just going in."

It was clear she was trying to send him on. But he said "They'll be busy a while. Listen. I'm going to tie a horse in the timber behind your wagon, so you can ride out of here to General Pike's headquarters."

"Ride out?" Her dark head was thrown back.

"Go through the woods until you come to the road that leads to the bridge. Just follow it to the tent where the flag flies. General Pike's an honorable man. Tell him everything. He'll give you protection. I know he will."

Her voice was flat, wrung dry of the agreement he expected. "Benton, you're going away. I know it."

"Tonight. Pretty quick. Why we have to hurry."

"Where?"

"Colonel's sending scouts back up the road."

"Will you come back?"

"What makes you ask?"

"It's the way you talk. Like it's the last time."

"Well, I don't know." He was uncomfortable, at a loss how to answer and yet not discourage her. "I don't know."

He was hurt by her fleeting expression of pain that seemed weary and curiously knowing, touched with disappointment; a young-old look about the fine eyes that ought not to have been there. He saw her in that moment not merely as a pretty girl, very young, but as a young woman, matured, sweet-lipped, possessing an acceptance much older than her years, someone who had known gentleness and afterward the realism of crushing heartbreak and was now wise enough to realize life's brutalities could hurt again.

He sensed the clouded force of something here, between them, in himself, in her, alive and yet uncertain, and he was leaving it unfinished, incomplete.

"In a few minutes," he said, keeping his voice impersonal, level, "when you see me leave the timber and walk out to the men at the fire—you go get the horse."

She withdrew a step, not meeting his gaze; she looked off with an odd unconcern. "Never mind the horse," she said. "I can walk out whenever I got a mind to."

"You're going pretty quick," he said absolutely. "While the guard's gone. This chance won't come again!"

"Benton, you don't understand. I don't want you to steal a horse for me."

He was baffled by her incredible indifference, her strangeness, her air of detachment. "You want to stay here—with him?" He shook his head. She didn't speak and he eyed her a lengthy moment, with a new perception; then he said, "If you're afraid I'll get in trouble—if that's what's holding you back—put it out of your mind. This is nothing to what's going to be."

Still she didn't answer.

To encourage her, he said, "Now get your things ready and watch for me."

Not until he had reached the timber did he look back to catch a glimpse of her climbing into the wagon.

Relieved, he turned to his right and swung on, aiming for his camp. It looked as if most of the men had gone to watch Mears, an attraction on which Benton counted heavily now; but not all had and others were still drifting in that direction.

Shortly, however, when full darkness fell, a few stragglers wouldn't matter.

Some distance on he found Doyle and Hart and told them his news briefly, omitting only Lettie Jo.

"Just head out—that it?" Doyle said and slapped his thigh with excitement.

Hart was slower reacting. "Sounds risky. I don't like it."

"This morning," Benton said, "you were the one howling to take chances. It's this way or have Yandell's men on our necks when we have to act."

Hart stood stiffly, in silence.

"You can stay," Benton said. "We're going."

In slow motion, Hart shrugged his resignation; his moon face lost its rigidity. "We're all in this together, bound by a single duty." Amiability smoothed his voice. "I stand over-ruled."

Benton said, "We pull out soon as I can jerk Mears away from his road show."

"Leave him," Hart said. "He's no good to us. A play-actor."

Benton was going when Hart spoke. He wheeled in anger but controlled himself. "Just be ready when I get back," he said flatly.

It took longer than he had figured to locate a picketed horse he could take. Saddling quickly, he led the animal to the woods behind the ambulance and tied it up. Mears mouth organ carried to him quite clearly, untiringly, its floating shrillness reassuring on the windless, early night The ambulance was dark; he saw no one, but he could visualize Lettie Jo in the darkness, waiting, ready to come out he hoped.

He passed the ambulance and stopped on the fringe of the crowd, trying to estimate the time needed for Lettie Jo to find the horse and start. As he paused before calling to Mears, he noticed several of Yandell's scouts leaving, a departure he didn't understand, in view of the early hour and the scarcity of entertainment.

After several minutes, he edged through the press of gamey-smelling listeners. Mears played on, apparently enjoying himself. He finished a number with his customary flourish, and Benton called him out. As Mears rose, there was a chorus of grumbling.

A Jew's-harp was twanging half-heartedly behind them when Benton stopped Mears and explained.

"It's just as well," Mears said, his laugh careless. "I was getting bored with my masculine audience."

They walked rapidly. Doyle and Hart had the horses saddled and packed.

Benton had the reins in his hand when a horse trotted up and halted. He couldn't distinguish the rider; there was no need to wonder as Tadlock called:

"Kinda sudden, ain't yuh, boys?"

How, Benton thought, in amazement, had Tadlock happened up? Had he been watching all the time? Doyle made a movement toward Tadlock, then seemed to catch himself and wait.

Benton said, "Just forming a scout detail."

"Jest four?"

Decision hardened in Benton, toughening as he took a stride, determined to drag Tadlock down and knock him senseless before he could cry out. Doyle stood nearby, a helper Benton counted on mechanically. In the next step

Benton paused, catching the shine of more horseflesh forming behind Tadlock and encircling the four Union men.

"Seen the commotion over hyar," Tadlock said in a voice as dry as time. "Figgered yuh was goin' out. So I got some hands ready."

"Mighty obliging of you, Tadlock."

"Jest the way I am, Soldier Boy. O' course I could ast the colonel about this. Why jest four is goin'."

That, Benton knew, chewing his lips, would bring mean and sudden trouble; it would stop them. "Suit yourself—come along," he said and dropped his hands and stepped back to his horse, pretending to tighten the cinch, lashed by an intolerable reproach. By taking time to steal a horse for Lettie Jo he had needlessly robbed his men of a chance to break away. But there had been time, he knew positively, ample time, if Tadlock hadn't turned up with such strange opportuneness.

He thought about that, grimly, angrily, as they rode south, the river on their left, Tadlock and his men following.

They forded the Blue and bore northeast, feeling their way, swinging wide, later picking up the rutted indentations of the Texas Road under pallid light. Miles on, Benton pushed into timber and ordered camp. As they unsaddled and groped for places to picket horses and spread blankets, he went to Doyle with the question that had been hammering in his head.

"Did Hart leave camp after I went back for Mears?"

"Didn't budge," said Doyle, his wondering tone telling Benton that he shared a like puzzlement.

Benton left him, glad that Hart was in the clear, yet unable to account for Tadlock's timely appearance. He sat on his blanket and eased off his boots. Before sleep drugged him, Lettie Jo filled his mind. He could feel, with certainty, that she had reached Pike's headquarters; it was a comfort to sleep on.

CHAPTER 12

Northeast, winding away, a creek's timber cut the trail and dodged raggedly across the up-and-down grade of hill and prairie. They were camped on a wooded rise, in position to observe any passage on the road below. A pretty landscape, but a wearying one by now, Benton thought, on this third morning.

The four Union men watched together. Tadlock and the other Yandell company troopers were farther down the rise, now and then glancing at the road while they marked time, smoking pipes, chewing, talking.

Doyle muttered, low, "Not a hair's passed in two days," and whittled faster, deeper, expressively, on the wood in his left hand. "When they come, what do we aim to do with Tadlock's bunch on our backs?"

Benton let the question ride a while. What he feared most was that Pike, his Seminoles growing restless, would send patrols to meet the annuity guard.

Mears, dozing, hat pulled over his face, murmured laxly, "Yeah, Sarge. What's order of the day? Rust on our butts?"

"I've thought of a way," Benton said, glancing again at the empty, mocking road. "Yet I don't say it's the best."

"So . . ." Hart hoisted himself around, interested.

"If the train don't show up in another day or so," Benton said, "Pike will be shoving patrols this way to see why. If so, we're cooked good. We can wait too long. I think we should move up the road by this afternoon. If the wagon train hasn't crossed Clear Boggy, we go on until we find it."

Doyle stopped his knife. "With Tadlock?"

"With Tadlock," Benton emphasized, and watched surprise touch their faces. "He has ten men. We'll need them." Mears sat up abruptly.

"Afraid I don't get you," Hart said, shaking his head. "How?"

"They help us take the train. Then we take over from there."

Mears snapped down his hat brim, his whole face gathering in a roguishness, a reckless carelessness. "Now that's more like it, Sarge."

But Hart wasn't sold. "I'll have to think about it."

"Had two days to think," Doyle growled, closing his knife with a distinct click. "Me, I like it. Goddamn this roostin'!"

"What do you say, Captain?" Benton directed it squarely at Hart.

Hart wiped his jaw, dropped a hand to his belly and scratched. He looked up, his glance sweeping. "Need time, I'd say, to work it out."

"I just thought of it, Captain. Hadn't counted on Tadlock dogging us, you know. You got a better idea?" Truth was, it had come to him the first day. For a reason not completely clear to himself, unless it was born of caution, after Tadlock's inexplicable appearance the night they had left Fort McCulloch, he had delayed bringing it out until now.

"I do not, at the moment, though to me this idea is foolhardy," the captain said. And yet, to Benton's surprise, Hart followed up with a two-handed gesture of resignation. "But I can't say I have a better plan. We must take the initiative. Too, the vote is three to one against me," he concluded.

Something had drawn Doyle away, intently observing the road. "Don't fret about th' election, Brother Hart!" he said, excited, in elation. "Theah's a wagon train comin' right now!" Benton sprang up, gazing at gray horsemen filing up from the creek, visible on the outskirts of the timber, alongside two mule-drawn wagons, whose drivers were reining in to blow their triple teams after making the crossing.

Tadlock and his bunch came scrambling over, and Benton turned to them, giving orders—orders, he thought wryly, such as Skaggs himself might give to surprise a Union wagon train. He said nothing of the silver. There was talk for a minute or so as each man's part was detailed.

Before long, as Benton led in, the wagon's escort was forming again, an irregular line on each side. Twenty-five or thirty men. Militia. Arkansas militia. Road weary and not caring a damn, Benton saw, grown lax after riding for days in Confederate country. As yet, no one near the wagon seemed to notice the approaching horsemen. Benton halted to provide that opportunity, his men trailing in column of twos. When an officer, busy lining up the sluggish escort troopers, wheeled finally and rode out, Benton raised his hand in recognition and took his detail in slowly, properly.

At a still proper interval, he halted his men and rode forward alone to salute a first lieutenant on a horse wet-slick to the lower shoulders from fording the creek, at the moment a harried, overtaxed officer, who couldn't have been two years the senior of Ernie Fletcher. Judging from the tracks of worry marking the young, tight jaws, and the hollows under the tired eyes and the milling still going on at the wagons, Benton knew there was a great deal of careless confusion here, of poorly disciplined, half-insolent volunteers in no hurry to carry out their youthful commander's orders.

Benton said, "Sir, General Pike sends his respects from Fort McCulloch. We're escort for a wagon train from Fort Smith. Reckon you're it."

"Mighty fine . . . but ah been told the gen'ral just had Indians in his command," the lieutenant drawled, red-filmed eyes dubiously on the well-armed column halted rods beyond.

"Until recently," Benton agreed, presenting a solemn face. "When we had Yankee trouble."

"Yankees—heah?"

"Yankee guerrillas, Lieutenant. Jawhawkers. Cut the Texas Road a time or two through here. Reckon they're still in the vicinity. Why we're here." The lieutenant's glance jumped left and right, in worry, and Benton went on. "General Pike's pulled in all the cavalry he can fetch. Some Texans, like me." He paused and said quietly, "he sure aims to protect your train. Needs that silver to pay off his Indians, start 'em fighting again."

The Confederate went perfectly stiff; then he said, "Wrong wagon train, Sergeant. Ah'm totin' supplies."

"Now that beats all," Benton said, in a puzzled way. "Don't see how we missed it, on patrol, back and forth, between here and Muddy Boggy." He gazed at the wagons. "Reminds me. We're plumb out of sidemeat. Could you spare us a side? Need it if we wait for that silver train."

Benton was aware that two wagons hardly constituted a

supply train bound for a fort. Twenty would be more like it. Neither was it usual practice to triple-team light, fast wagons, such as these. Of a sudden the lieutenant seemed eager to render a favor. "You boys go on up the road, an' reckon we can fix you up with a little sidemeat to take along." He reined back and Benton followed, waving the detachment to string along. Coming to the first wagon, the lieutenant directed the teamster, "Fetch a side of bacon fo' these boys."

Benton halted at the head of the six-mule team, big mules, stout, and saw his short column close up, Doyle and Tadlock in front. Watching the teamster scrambling inside the wagon, he experienced a renewed doubt. There wasn't much to go on except timing, the lieutenant's unconcealed eagerness to travel on, and his distrust of non-Indian troopers.

Then, staring down, Benton noticed the ground under the wagons; the extra deep tracks left by wide wheel rims crushing the soft creek-bottom soil. He settled back, motionless. When the lieutenant handed him the meat in a cotton sack, Benton draped it over his saddle, said his thanks and added distinctly, "We'll pass on now," and motioned his men ahead.

With Doyle and Tadlock each heading a single file, the detachment of twos, splitting smoothly, fanned by, outside the careless escort militiamen flanking the wagons.

"You can make Fort McCulloch by dark," Benton said, with an eye to the road. "Good trail on in." He saw Doyle, near the end of the escort line, slow down, and he said clearly, "Now, Lieutenant, if you'd oblige me with some plug tobacco—"

At the signal, the outside horsemen swung quietly in, practiced, together, Navy revolvers pointing at the nearest trooper. At the same time, Benton covered the open-jawed lieutenant.

"Tell your men to drop their weapons, Lieutenant."

The young man's widening stare was hung, perplexed on Benton's uniform. "What th' hell—?"

"No time for explanations, Lieutenant. Either give the order or get yourself and your men shot."

Looking on both flanks of the wagons, the lieutenant could see his men covered. He said in a dull, dry-throated voice, "Put yore rifles down."

A scattered clattering of rifle butts followed, slow to start, but, once begun, obeyed in concert. All but one man. The teamster of the first wagon hadn't thrown his rifle down. Neither did he act as if he'd use it. He was just slower than the others.

Benton saw Tadlock move, his hand jerking. The teamster was slumping with the explosion. He spilled out of the seat across the front wheel to the ground.

"Tadlock—damn you!" Benton roared. "There was no call for that!"

"I'll cut my own pie," was the sullen answer.

Benton drove another damning look at him, realizing once again that killing a man meant no more to Tadlock than shooting at a post, and ordered the militiamen to dismount. When they had, he called, "Tadlock, take ten men and move these prisoners across the creek. Start 'em up the road. On the double."

Tadlock didn't move. "How come?"

"Want to herd that many prisoners by yourself?"

"Hell, no. But hit don't take ten men."

A guardedness flecked Benton. Why should Tadlock even question the order? "Don't give a damn how many men it takes, just get 'em over there!"

Tadlock worked his jaws a moment, then singled out five men, who began shooing the glum Confederates toward the crossing, with the lieutenant, his face a sickly white, the last to go. Tadlock stayed, however, and Benton scowled, thinking: makes it six with him, six against four. A near balance that would endure only a few minutes, he knew, until the bushwhackers recrossed the creek.

Benton raised his voice. "Mears! See what's in the first wagon."

"Whut yuh after?" Tadlock inquired, riding over, his tone exaggerated and innocent. "More sidemeat?"

"Maybe to see whether it was worth killing one teamster," Benton said.

Mears left his horse and nimbly climbed the tailgate. Riding closer to watch, Benton could see Mears pawing and shifting things. This went on for a space, until Mears relayed back in disgust, "Just a little flour and bacon. Big stack of quilts."

"Dig under 'em," Benton said, and for a moment thought of sending Doyle to check the other wagon, only to douse the idea. He wanted the big man near, for he was going to call on Doyle in a minute if these wagons contained what he suspected.

Tadlock edged his horse up to the tailgate, peering in beside Benton. Hart crowded in also, looking past them. Doyle was behind Hart, between the wagons. Inside, Mears was backhanding quilts, flinging them like a hound after a rabbit. He stopped suddenly and kneeled, grunted and slid something heavy across the flooring, pitching quilts out of the way as he rolled the object toward the tailgate.

It was, Benton saw, a stout little wooden keg, newly-staved, bearing large black CSA markings.

"Must be twenty back there," Mears panted, straight-faced.

"Mought be powder," Tadlock ventured. "Why'n't we see?"

Mears waited for Benton's go-ahead. Benton, watching sideways at Tadlock all craving to see, and feeling Hart at his hind quarters, said, "All right—open it." Mears turned the keg upright and opened his pocketknife.

To Benton it seemed unusually still after the violence of moments ago, no one talking, no sounds except the horses stamping and the prying and gouging of Mears' stubby knife blade. The wood was thick and tough. Mears attacked a split, widened it, slipped the blade under one end and pried up. He got a finger under, another, his whole hand, and as he ripped upward with a protesting creak of new oak, silver dollars—big Mexican 'dobe dollars—suddenly lay exposed in a glittering vein.

Benton made ready, in hand the revolver he had drawn on the lieutenant, the assurance of Hart behind him and Doyle spaced behind Hart.

Sound erupted—boots beating hard, mixing with Doyle's yelled warning. But as Benton dropped a shoulder to cover Tadlock, something rammed into his ribs from the rear.

He found himself staring into Hart's moon face, then down at the pistol poking him.

"Don't be foolish now," Hart said. He bared his teeth in

the facsimile of a grin. "Mears, take the gentleman's pistol and carbine."

Beyond, two bushwhackers, apparently having slipped around the rear wagon while Doyle's interest strayed front, held carbines on the Texan.

As Mears took his weapons, Benton's disgust broke. "You, too—"

"Sorta looks that way, doesn't it, Sargie?" Mears gave a scoffing grin as he hefted the Navy Colt.

Doyle spat.

Benton was still stunned, beginning to shake with rage, remembering Hart's sleazy co-operation, his dodging of responsibility all the way. Too late, he knew he should never have trusted Hart. But Mears had been different. He had failed miserably when better was expected of him as a man.

"Face up, Sergeant," Hart said. "Why, hell, you didn't have a chance from the moment Tadlock came in."

"When?" Benton choked. "When'd he come in?"

"Oh, long time ago, in Missouri. Early. Tadlock lined up the others, too. We watched you all the time. Like the other night at McCulloch, when you tried to pull out. Tadlock was watching. I didn't have to lift a hand. He got the boys ready. Knew something was up when Yandell called you out." The red mouth inside the whisker thicket curled. "I always plan well. Perhaps you realize that now, Sergeant."

"And I took you for a Union officer," Benton said.

"Naturally. The man whose papers I took was a Union officer. *Was.* Even General Curtis was impressed with my credentials. But, then, Union generals are easily fooled, or they wouldn't be Unionists. Though you never trusted me completely, did you?"

"Not quite. The mistake I made was trusting you at all."

"But enough."

Hart had been gloating; suddenly he barked an order to dismount. Benton stepped down numbly. Beside Doyle, he marched into the woods, and the forbidding black shade and the edgy stillness suggested Cabin Creek again, with the light greasy-dull on the fixed faces of the Union Indians.

"Halt!"

Benton did and pivoted on "Left face!" as he turned seeing the engraved cut of Doyle's taut-jawed helplessness.

Tadlock jumped his horse over and waved his revolver. He stared venomously at Benton. "Soldier Boy, I'm gonna kill yuh right here!"

Hart broke in, "You're not the only one's taken guff off Wall. I want a hand in this. We will have a firing squad. You men tie those teams, then line up."

Tadlock started to protest, then nodded, chewing on a cheekful of tobacco. Making the lead mules fast, the bushwhackers returned and formed a line. Hart, appearing to relish his own suggestion even further, stood at one end of the line, Tadlock next to him.

Only Mears didn't line up.

"What's wrong?" Hart questioned with a scowl. "Getting chicken-hearted?"

Mears shrugged and looked bored. "No bark off me what you do with 'em. Your direct method is just a little out of my line, is all. I'll watch."

"Wasn't sure about you for a while," Hart said; his expression firmed. "But you came through. Keep it that way."

"As long as I get my share."

Mears sauntered out, oblique from Hart and Tadlock, and turned, carelessly shoving Benton's revolver inside his belt and letting the muzzle of his carbine droop.

Benton swiped a hand across his mouth and measured the distance to Mears and knew he could never get that far. It was coming and he felt sorry for Doyle, caught up in a mission that had been impossible from the start.

"Tell me something"—Benton said in an unnatural voice he could hardly recognize as he split his bitterness between Hart and Mears—"who told on Ernie that night?"

Hart threw back his head. "You were fooled there, too. You thought maybe Mears did it. He could've, but he didn't. I got up and tipped Tadlock when you went to stand watch with Doyle. My idea to show Tadlock he could trust me."

"You Jayhawk sonofabitch!" Doyle snarled.

Hart's face roughed up so swiftly Benton thought Doyle would draw a bullet then. He said bleakly, in hurry, "You have all the time in the world, Hart. One more question. Tadlock, who killed Lettie Jo's folks in Missouri?"

Tadlock spoke contemptuously. "We'uns did, Soldier Boy. Too bad you'll never live to tell her. Be a pleasure to gun yuh down after all I've took."

Benton scarcely noticed as Mears started a stroll to one side. "You murdering son-of-a—" he began, anger boiling up in him.

"Shut up," Hart ordered. "That's enough. Let's finish this."

Mears was still in the careless stroll. Benton forgot him, for there was no more time left. He was dry-mouthed, stiff, wooden, no breath in the shallow pools of his lungs. Now he just waited.

Mears stopped with an indolent scuffing of his boots. He made a half turn to his left, and Benton saw him swinging the carbine in the same smooth motion.

"Drop them!" Mears said, grinning. "Sarge, ease over for your pistol. Doyle, theah's a shotgun on the ground to your left."

Hart and Tadlock stared, their mouths dropping open. The other men were too startled to use their weapons. One by one the carbines fell.

It broke as Benton rushed toward Mears, seeing that neither Hart nor Tadlock had released their carbines.

"Drop 'em!" Mears cried.

Hart's hands blurred, a short, savage movement. Mears was just as quick. There was a double blast, with Mears' shot deafening this close. Benton heard him grunt as he grabbed the revolver and wheeled, catching sight of Hart doubling up and Tadlock shooting at Mears.

Benton fired once, saw Tadlock buckle. Not pausing, Benton wheeled in time to see the bushwhackers scrambling for dropped weapons. He cocked and pulled, and a man jerked. He kept it up, the pressure of numbers hurrying him, realizing he couldn't stop them all. Mears still had his carbine, but he couldn't seem to use it.

A shotgun coughed hoarsely, throwing its ear-splitting boom, and again, almost at Benton's shoulder. Through the grayish smoke, three figures seemed to falter, slip downward, dissolve.

It was Doyle—Doyle charging up with a scooped-up shotgun. Benton glimpsed Mears on one knee, and started over, stopping when Mears shook him off, an odd look bunched in his face. "Go on—they'll be coming back."

Swinging up, Benton saw Doyle, already anticipating trouble across the creek, drop the shotgun for a carbine and take position behind a tree. Benton ran over.

Their wait was brief. On the hard-traveled road bending in to the crossing, five riders came flogging horses. They pulled up indecisively, staring hard.

Benton and Doyle fired almost together.

One man pitched down. Another grabbed leather, trying to hold on as he followed the panicked backward rush of the others. He rode only a little way before he fell, his horse galloping on.

Benton went quietly back with Doyle, feeling the drag and letdown of reaction. Hart was dead as a post, having taken Mears' slug in the throat.

"Tadlock's still alive," Doyle said suddenly. Benton saw the yellow eyes close and open. "Let him rot," he said and took a deliberate step away.

Mears was groaning, all humped over, knotted up, both hands holding his stomach.

Swearing in sympathy, moving to him, Benton unbuttoned the bloody blouse and went taut at the still bloodier mess underneath. Mouth drawn, he slid an arm under Mears' shoulder, muttering, "We'll fix you up," and heard Doyle searching the second wagon.

Mears' slim face was wan, but behind the blue eyes Benton could see a hint of mockery. "Whiskey's man's best medicine, Sarge. Some in the first wagon. . . . Prop me up against a tree—on the shady side."

Doyle ran up with a flannel shirt. Benton tore it into strips and went to binding and wrapping. Finished, he moved back and dropped his hands, staring at the futility of his crude, ineffective work. Remembering the whiskey, he got it from the wagon, and then they carried Mears to a better place in the shade and leaned him back and gave him a drink.

"Ah . . ." Mears smacked his lips and asked for another. A new brightness enlivened his eyes, a false brightness, Benton knew all too well.

Benton said earnestly, "You saved our necks."

"You bet," Doyle said, with an overheartiness. "Yo're a real hard-assed horse soldier, boy!"

Mears made a grimace. "Afraid not, Doyle. See, I went in with Hart before Tadlock did. Stayed 'til he snitched on Ernie." Reddish foam beaded his mouth now. Awkwardly, Benton wiped it clean. Mears mumbled for another drink and got it. "Couldn' do anything but play along with him after that."

"You don't have to explain anything," Benton told him.

Mears' face wore a clamped doggedness. "Aimed to desert—go to Old Mexico." An immense weariness, growing by the moment, seemed to press upon him, to bear him down.

Benton said, "Rest a bit," and stood, motioning to Doyle.

They walked beyond Mears' hearing. Doyle smashed his fist into his palm. "Goddamnit, what can we do, Sarge?"

"Nothing."

Benton stared off at the muddy creek, high in its banks, hearing the wind rousting through the trees, feeling the vastness of lonely, open country, so still now.

He said, "We're not far from Boggy Depot. They've heard the firing, they'll send a patrol. Can't stay here much longer and we can't tote this silver."

"More kegs in the second wagon."

Benton observed the creek again, up and down it, and was preoccupied. He turned to find an expression on Doyle's face. "Maybe we're thinking the same thing."

"Dump it in the creek?"

"Where else? No time to bury it."

"But not heah, by the crossing."

"We can take the wagons down a way. Come back for Mears."

They were in motion with the words. Benton told Mears and forced added cheerfulness into his voice. "We can fix a quilt bed for you in one of the wagons. You'll ride easy."

Mears nodded, but the pallor of his skin sent an ache through Benton. "Just leave that bottle handy," Mears said, brief, drawn.

Doyle uncorked it and settled Mears' right hand around the neck. Mears leaned his head back, a remnant of his roguishness playing on the big man, half taunting. "That shotgun was real finessey, Doyle. Real finessey."

Benton drove the first wagon and when the creek made a bend and the eroded bank sheered steeply down, he pulled through the trees to stop the mules within feet of the water. Doyle halted farther down.

With the tailgate down, Benton began sliding the short, fat-bellied kegs out and heaving them; they sank like stones, and to make discovery more difficult, he would change position, up or down from the wagon, and toss from there.

When done, he leaned against the tailgate, winded, and estimated the creek to be eight or ten feet deep at this point. A sharp-eyed man knowing about the silver, he realized with misgivings, could follow the rim tracks and divine the story. Even so, recovery would have to wait a while, for the creek was running high. Time and mud would hinder the finding further.

Driving back to the road, they headed the wagons as they had found them, bound for Fort McCulloch. The loose saddle horses had wandered out to graze on the prairie.

Other than to turn his face to the creek, Mears hadn't moved, it seemed. He still gripped the bottle. Benton jumped down, hurrying. He stopped in full stride, speaking softly, "He's gone, Doyle. He's gone," and felt, all at once, the pain of Mears' loneliness, his searching and never finding. Little Mears, he thought, who'd scoffed at honor and duty; now he had died for them.

Doyle dropped his head and swore.

It was a while before Benton spoke again. "Can't leave him like this. But first we'd better try to brush out those wagon tracks going down creek."

Doyle agreed glumly. "Remember the time he stopped at the farm house, came back with the chicken? When he showed the girl garter an' we drank his whiskey? Y'know, Sarge, he really won that garter fair; didn't buy it just to show off. I know that now."

They chose a shaded place off in the timber, a place safe from the creek's overflow, and went to digging with spades found in the wagons' toolboxes. It was slow work in the hot timber. They dug steadily, pausing only to scan the other side of the creek.

An awkwardness came at the last when, hatless, they stood by the fresh mound, marked by the crude cross of sticks Doyle had fashioned by tying the horizontal piece with his bandanna.

Doyle stood there, head down, dejected, unable to stir. Benton thought he understood. Doyle was a man of few attachments, and those he had he guarded and sealed off within himself. But it was time to think of the saddle horses they would have to catch now; and so it was then, as he thought of Red River and nothing to hold them here, as movement sawed across his senses, that he knew they were no longer alone.

He made a sudden turn and flinched still.

Butternut men, afoot, spaced like skirmishers, carbines at the ready, were advancing through the woods, so close now that he recognized Captain Yandell's stocky figure.

CHAPTER 13

Yandell's thorough gaze was a question mark on the grave.

"Private Mears," Benton said. "We were going back for the others."

"Going back? Why'n't you dig a trench?" Yandell jogged his pistol at them to move on.

Benton said, "Aren't you a little mixed up, Captain?"

"We saw the wagons. Looks fishy. Tadlock's dead."

"I can explain."

Yandell's answer was an order that sent his carbine-wielding detachment behind the pair.

Benton supposed a patrol had taken them. However, as he walked alongside Doyle, the rest of Yandell's scout company appeared, posted about the wagons. And looking down the road to Fort McCulloch, he was surprised to see Skaggs' entire command moving, closed up, column of fours, complete with transport.

A swift apprehension seized him when his eyes fell on the ambulance. A second later he realized it had a place there whether Lettie Jo rode inside or not.

Yandell, leaving his prisoners under guard, mounted and dashed out to meet the column.

Foreboding filled Benton as he watched Yandell return with Skaggs, conversing as they rode. Halting, the colonel jabbed the angry probe of his gaze at the prisoners, shifted it to the dead men, and back again.

"Well, where is it?" Skaggs demanded of Benton.

"Where's what, sir? This is all the wagon train we found."

"I mean the silver, you stupid fool! You were supposed to intercept a wagon train from Fort Smith carrying silver to Pike's Indians. Now these empty wagons"—he cut an enveloping hand about—"everything picked clean."

"You didn't say anything about silver, Colonel, and there wasn't any in the wagons. We surprised the escort. Made sure they came from Fort Smith, first. You said they weren't to get through. One of the teamsters—that dead one over yonder—opened up with a shotgun. Hurt us, as you can see." A cold sweat coursed out on the skin underneath his shirt. He was piecing together a story as he went, striving for conviction where there was little conviction, he feared, because there were no dead militiamen and a heap of dead bushwhackers. "The escort bolted across the creek. Just Arkansas militia. We'd just buried the first of our boys when Captain Yandell came up."

"Buryin' in a single grave instead of a trench," said Yandell, his dogged suspicion on Benton never slacking. "Funny to me, Colonel, there's no dead militia. Ain't like

182

our boys to let folks off easy."

"Anyway," Benton said firmly, "that's what happened."

He saw emotion shuttle over the colonel's face, frustration tangled with rage.

"Your orders were to notify me immediately."

"No chance to yet, Colonel. This just happened."

"In addition, you were to make inquiries without getting involved in a fight. Furthermore, I can't see your small detail disarming an entire escort. How many men were in the train?"

"About twenty-five, sir."

Skaggs arched up in his saddle, even more amazed. "Twenty-five men escorting a hundred-thousand-dollar wagon train? Too extraordinary, Sergeant!"

"But we found no silver."

"You tell me, then, why this train was headed for McCulloch? Captain Yandell informs me it carries no supplies."

Benton said, "The lieutenant in charge said most of his men quit him when he lost the bulk of his train crossing the South Canadian."

Once again, Skaggs' studied the bushwhacker dead. "You had other men in your detail. Where are they?"

"Checking on the militia, Colonel."

Skaggs was pinching at his beard. Before he could resume the questioning, the trotting of horses intruded from the off side of the creek. Skaggs' attention lifted from Benton.

Three riders approached the fort at an uncertain trot. One waved and a man by the wagons beckoned them across.

Benton turned swiftly cold, recognizing the three Yandell scouts. He watched them ride into the stream and run their dripping horses up the bank, watched them slow down as they passed the bodies and then spur faster to the wagons.

Pointing at Benton and Doyle, the front rider cried, "You got 'em, Colonel. They drove us off. Wouldn't let us cross back."

Skaggs' gesture silenced the man. "The silver—where is it?"

"In the wagons. In kegs."

"He's lying," Benton said. "There wasn't any."

"We seen them kegs!"

Skaggs' eyes glittered. He nodded fast, biting his lip. "Kegs! They've got to be close! There are ways to make a man talk." Behind him a rider left the column, the running of his mount falling across the colonel's remarks. Yandell wheeled back and flagged the man down and rode out to intercept. The trooper shouted something, and almost without stopping Yandell was whirling his horse, spurring, something vital and serious in his headlong rush.

Benton heard him clearly. "Pike's Indians comin' up!"

Skaggs didn't seem surprised. He answered calmly, while Yandell fought his horse still, "We beat them here, anyway. Crossing below the bridge gave us that much jump, though I didn't expect them to make contact this soon."

"Colonel," Yandell exploded, "this ain't no patrol! Looks like Pike's whole command! Ever' damned Indian he's got!"

Skaggs gave a start. "Place these two men under guard," he directed, and started back.

Dust thickened down the road, and through the rolling amber haze, Benton marked a column of fours in violent motion, a huge man leading. Pike, he thought, come for his money.

Pike tossed his arm and his command slackened, and immediately Benton saw a company cutting away, aiming for a flank. As yet not a shot had been fired. The first volley rattled as Skaggs sent his wagons flying into the timber, while he deployed his companies in front. Mules went wild-eyed and crazy in the singing fire; those hitched to the two Confederate wagons lunged and started off. Men ran out in time to catch bridle bits of the lead animals.

Benton said to the two men guarding them, "Want us to help?" and received a severe muzzle-jabbing in the ribs for his trouble. Both guards resumed their worried watching of the skirmishing going on behind the pall of dust.

Other wagons rolled in, the ambulance last, in a swaying turn, its driver cursing above the rapid rumbling. Closing up behind came a single rider.

Benton went oddly still—seeing a dim face, a girl's face, Lettie Jo's, behind the driver, screened off as the ambulance hurtled by, to come to a half-circle stop, its rear pointed toward the creek. Benton saw her again when the driver climbed down and haltered his skittery mules to a tree.

Heavier firing caused Benton to look down the road again. A foglike diffusion of dust and smoke covered the prairie, drifting slowly on the wind, obscuring the road, making phantoms of the charging horsemen. And the guns sounded nearer.

Was Skaggs, unaccustomed to meeting a stubborn, head-on foe, giving ground?

"They're pushing you back," Benton jeered his fidgety guard.

"Like hell," the man replied, without conviction. He shifted his boots, watching nervously.

Beyond, in the smoky confusion, in the hoarse crying and racketing rolls of sound, the force of an unseen pressure seemed to strike. Lead bit the earth, throwing up little geysers of dirt. Benton crouched down. He saw a teamster drop. One rear mule screamed and the five harnessed to him suddenly boogered. A teamster rose to stop them; he pulled on a bit, was dragged off his feet. His cry cut back.

Both guards half rose, watching the mules tearing off.

It was as if he and Doyle had the same thought. Benton read Doyle's sidelong look, saw him jackknife up with a clubbing swing that struck his guard broadside on the temple. Benton, farther away from his man, dived low and felt his shoulder smash knees. Grappling for the swinging carbine barrel, he took a glancing blow across his head. Half-blinded, he caught the barrel and pushed it away from his face. He was straining to twist it free when he heard a tremendous blow, like wood on bone. The struggling body over him went limp, the carbine came free.

Shaking his head, getting up, he saw Doyle standing clear, in his hands the carbine he'd swung like a club. Together, snatching revolvers and waistbelts weighted down with cap and cartridge boxes, they legged to the guards' tied horses, freed reins and swung up, the boxes flapping. Benton ran his horse southward for the white smudge of the parked ambulance, Doyle pounding after him.

A bullet whined and a pistol popped. Benton discovered the driver crouched by the front wheel. Benton drove straight at him. Fright bulged the teamster's eyes. He reared up to run, made a panicky pivot, his pistol pointing, and Benton thrust out his own handgun and thumbed off the shot. He saw the man flinch, twist, break and roll under the wagon.

Swerving front, Benton came upon Doyle, already alongside, extending an arm to Lettie Jo. Her face had a whitened look as she put a foot on the wheel rim and stepped out, taking Doyle's arm, and swung in behind him, astraddle, and caught Doyle's waist with both arms.

Benton flung up an arm, pointing south. They dug away, going around the wagon's rear.

Several miles south they paused to rest hard-used horse-flesh. Lettie Jo was too tired to dismount at first. She tugged at her tight skirt around her knees, gave up and rested her head against Doyle's wide back. After a moment, Benton gave her his hand. She slid down to him and stumbled, and he steadied her before she could fall. Strain lay in taut, dark tracings across her face.

He said gently, "What stopped you from going to Pike's headquarters?"

"I didn't try. Guess I hoped you'd come back."

Doyle left them abruptly and walked out a way, head cocked north to the continuing, unslackened din. He listened a minute or more and came back. "Movin' this way. If it keeps up, Pike will drive Skaggs down to the Red."

Benton nodded. "Sounds like it. At any rate, Pike's Seminoles won't be in any shape to march on Kansas."

When they mounted again, Doyle turned curiously. "Where to, Sarge?"

"Why . . . the way we're headed. Texas."

"Uh-huh," Doyle murmured.

"Thought we'd get Lettie Jo started for Sherman. Has kin there."

"Still the gentleman, eh?" Yet Doyle spoke without malice. "Wal, to be honest, I was hopin' you'd keep on."

"As if it made any difference to you," Benton said, smiling. "As if I could stop you."

With the pressure off and the way clear, there was, he could feel, a kind of released cheerfulness upon them. He paused, expecting Doyle to add something—and saw that Doyle had no reply for that, intended none. And so the fine moment had evaded them again, as it had other times. Benton was disappointed, but he wondered if he did not see in this powerful, enigmatic man a likeness of his own close-mouthed self, all else locked out but a singled, guarded purpose.

As they rode south over the dipping prairie, the air turned sultry. By late afternoon the clear sky had changed, darkening, oppressive, threatening, and wind gusts whipped at the travelers. The horses tired, lagged. Benton had Lettie Jo switch more often.

Filing down out of the last moulding of gentle, rounded hills, through high, weaving grass that tickled a horse's belly, down to the flat, rich bottomlands pressing against the copper-colored river—it was almost like coming home to Benton. Except, he thought bitterly, for Crockett, who had shared these sights and smells with him.

A light, wind-hurried rain was falling when they entered the dense growth of cottonwood and willow lining the north bank of the Red.

Safely over, Benton overcame the temptation to camp in the first sheltered spot, and led inland, on familiar ground, away from any main wagon road or stock trail, to an isolated cabin sitting lonely and dark off the edge of a field.

Here, as late evening fell, they got down at last, chilled through, used up, enormously hungry.

Lettie Jo was shaking badly. Benton gave her pallid face a quick search and stepped through the narrow doorway, into semi-darkness and the musty odors of a place long empty, made cheerless by the cold breath of the wind seeping through breaches in the chinked walls. He waited for his eyes to adjust and found the stone fireplace, and, feeling down, dry hay and a bed of brittle boughs in one corner on the dirt floor.

Using flint and steel, Doyle sparked up a fire on the hearth, kneeling, blowing on hay and twigs, while Benton packed in fallen limbs. As the blaze grew and light lengthened over the bare room and heat began to penetrate sodden clothing, they huddled in close to dry out.

Lettie Jo unbuttoned her shoes, removed them and alternately arched a small foot at the flames. Her dress was plastered to her, outlining slim legs and thighs, and high, firm breasts. Her long dark hair was matted, her face gray with cold.

Benton admired her for a moment, recalling she hadn't complained.

Doyle went out and returned, bearing a lumpish knapsack and two ponchos. "Water-soaked bacon an' hardtack," he announced. "Wal, it beats hay." He was, Benton recognized, in rare good humor. There seemed no limit to his energy. In rapid order they were cooking bacon strips on ramrods and munching hardtack, and, afterward, hovering before the fire.

Lettie Jo was shivering again. Benton started to drape his damp jacket around her shoulders, but she moved back and shook her hand, thanking him with her eyes. "You have tc stay warm, too." She took up a poncho and went barefoot to a dark corner. "Look the other way. I'm going to take off my things and dry them."

"You'll have different clothes tomorrow," Benton said, thinking of Hannah Richmond, and turned his back.

When she came into the yellowish light, the black poncho enveloped her to her ankles. As she began drying her under-garments and dress, Doyle and Benton walked into the cold rain where the horses stood sheltered under an oak.

"Know where you are?" Benton said, unsaddling.

"Bonham's due south. First place is old Major Barr's. Next the Egans and Richmonds."

"You know it, all right. I plan to take Lettie Jo to the Rich-mond's for clothing. Maybe she'll rest up there a day or two."

Doyle uncinched, peeled off the saddle with one hand and stripped the blanket. "Meanwhile—?"

"Well—" Benton checked himself in time, and knew, with conviction, that he didn't wish to involve Doyle fur-ther in his own personal problems. "Let's talk about it in the morning," he said, instead, being vague.

"Shore," Doyle said amiably, but just as evasive, and took his gear to the cabin.

Coming inside, Benton flanked his saddle down, spread the horse blanket to dry on the saddle, and went to the fire, crouching, watching vitality color Lettie Jo's cheeks. She had contrived to shake out her hair, which fell to her waist. At intervals, she would turn her head to catch the heat, just as she had, he thought, that late afternoon on the sunning rock. From somewhere she produced a bit of blue ribbon; looping it, she caught her hair at the base of her neck and tied it.

"I never knew fire could feel so good," she said, hugging hands to shoulders.

A growing comfort replaced the chill in the drafty room and mingling with the steamy damp of clothing was the rankness of drying horse blankets. Contentment spread through Benton, a feeling dispelled as Tadlock's bloody boasting came to mind. He had to clear up the fate of Lettie Jo's parents; he had to do it now. And, presently, he told her and added for conviction, "Doyle heard it with me."

"That's right, ma'am," Doyle said.

Lettie Jo's eyes, hurt, slid to Benton. "It wasn't that I didn't believe you."

"Well, it is hard to believe. Until you remember Skaggs played both sides. I wanted you to get it straight from someone besides me."

She sat a while longer, then took her dry clothes to the darkest corner. Benton heard the crush of hay as she went to bed. She called a drowsy "Good night." Later, when he rose, she was sleeping soundly, in exhaustion, an arm thrown over her head.

He stretched out upon the hay and boughs, swept under by a wave of physical depletion, his mind empty. One moment he was listening to the wind flailing rain against the shake roof, and the occasional spitting of the fire—the next he awakened to a gust that struck the cabin with a violent shaking. The endless rain whipped harder, drumming in Benton's ears like metal. He heard Lettie Jo cry out and stir. He turned over and found her hand reaching for him, groping, needing. He clasped it and could feel her shaken by a trembling she could not control.

"Benton," she said in a blurred voice. "I'm afraid."

He slipped an arm under her shoulders and pulled her in, hearing her unsteady breathing, feeling the chill of her body. She stayed contentedly within the circle of his arm, her face turned to him. Carefully, so as not to disturb her, he pulled more hay over them and lay back. After that, a greater warmth came. Her breathing became regular. He felt her body relax beneath her undergarments and the thin slightness of her dress. He was dropping off into a heavy sleep when she stirred again, a slight shifting of her face as she pressed her mouth to his cheek for an instant and kissed him. More like a drowsy child's kiss than a young woman's, instinctive, secure. Then she lay back and they both slept.

Pale daylight filled the cabin when Benton opened his eyes. The rain had stopped; there was no wind. He turned his gaze, not seeing Doyle. Lettie Jo was still sleeping. He eased his arm free without rousing her and sat up, supposing that Doyle had gone to look about the horses and gather wood. Dully, not glancing where the saddle gear lay, he stood and went stiffly to the door and pushed it open, rubbing his eyes.

One glance knocked him instantly awake, struck him rigid. Just a single horse stood tied under the tree. His own.

Doyle had gone.

CHAPTER 14

Nothing had changed at Windwood, it seemed to Benton, riding in ten o'clock sun up the lane, Lettie Jo astride behind him. The two-story clapboard house under the shading oaks, the general air of well-being, the neat Negro groom trotting out on the graveled drive at the sound of hoofs—everything was in place. Benton took in the cool veranda, staring. There was something missing, after all. Colonel Richmond in his high-backed rocker; it was gone also. Another close glance showed tall French windows; which hadn't been there previously, and through them he could see the iridescent flashings from prisms on crystal chandeliers.

As he gave up the reins and stepped upon the veranda with Lettie Jo, a Negress he did not recall appeared in the doorway. He inquired for Miss Hannah instead of her father. "Tell her Benton Wall is here."

"Come in, Mistuh Wall."

Inside, as the Negress turned to climb the circling staircase, Benton ran his eyes around and found a vast change: an impression of richer tones, more luxurious than ever, in this high-ceilinged room where he and Crockett had visited that last day. New blue velvet draperies and new dove-gray carpets; the glistening chandeliers; an oil portrait of Hannah, full-length, in a blue evening gown.

"She's very beautiful," Lettie Jo said. "Perfect."

"Yes—she is beautiful," he said. Seeing Lettie Jo glancing in dismay at the ruin of her own dress, he gave her a reassuring look. "Hannah will take care of that."

Some minutes passed. Still longer. An uncommonly long time. Getting up, letting his eyes trail again over the new furnishings, he wondered at their acquisition in war time, at the increased atmosphere of soft living here. A sound on the stairway attracted him.

"Benton!"

He saw Hannah Richmond pause on the top landing. For a second he had the effect of a deliberate entrance, forgotten as the lively excitement of her face drew his eyes. She seemed to float down the carpeted stairs while she held up the hem of her hoop skirts. Benton went to the foot of the stairs, a strong sensation sweeping him. In a flurry of tiny rustlings, she was down and coming to him, bringing a delightful scent of soap and perfume. She lifted her face for him to kiss, and then he was returning the pressure of her lips. A long moment and she stood off in astonishment, eying him up and down.

"You—in Confederate uniform!"

"What did you expect, Hannah—Yankee blue?" He smiled back, in that moment recalling his manners. "Hannah," he said, "there's a young lady with me who needs your help," and saw her turn, as if aware of Lettie Jo for the first time, an awareness that, somehow, erased a particle of prettiness from the full and perfect mouth.

Lettie Jo made a curtsy, her eyes impressed with the elegance she saw. Hannah, after a moment, smiled her greeting.

"Lettie Jo's had a rough experience," Benton felt called upon to explain. "She has people in Sherman. She needs clothing. I thought—"

Hannah's eyes, estimating, lifted from Lettie Jo to Benton. "I'm happy you did. Whatever she needs."

Benton, reassured, wondered why he might have doubted his reception here. This was the Richmond hospitality he'd counted on for Lettie Jo. "Thank you, Hannah."

"The house is yours," she said, waving a gracious hand. "You know that, or should. But why the mystery?"

"There is none. I'll explain later."

Whereupon, Hannah murmured to Lettie Jo, "My dear, why don't you run upstairs? Rachel will show you your room, bring water for your bath. I know you need a bath."

A small stitch of feeling quivered in Lettie Jo's face, a defensiveness which Benton sensed himself sharing. She said, "That's kindly of you, Miss Hannah. I'll go up now. Know you-all want to visit."

Benton put out a hand. "I'll say goodbye for a little while, Lettie Jo. I'm leaving."

"Leaving?" She looked truly taken back. Her face fell.

"In a day or two I'll take you to Sherman."

Her chin seemed to stiffen. "A bother—a big bother."

"I promised to and I will."

"No need, if Miss Hannah could loan me a horse."

"Of course," Hannah said, showing amusement. "But it's hardly ladylike."

"You can't ride alone," Benton said.

"I'm not afraid." There was something unfinished. Words seemed to rush to the dam of her lips, words she wouldn't let out.

Hannah murmured easily, "My dear, perhaps theah's a personal matter you'd like to discuss with Benton before he leaves. I'll be back in a moment."

"Now what is it?" Benton said when Hannah had entered the library.

She studied him for a beat of time, searchingly. "Benton, you aim to kill somebody, don't you? That's why you're leaving."

He hadn't expected that; he had no answer.

"It's so—I feel it. There's something. Like when you stole

the horse for me."

"There are some people, Lettie Jo—a man I have to see. Can't say what will happen. But nobody—nobody can stop me from coming back as long as I'm alive. Will you wait?"

She nodded. Her mouth was trembling, but her voice reached him firmly. "Just watch yourself. Benton. Watch harder than you ever have!"

Hannah appeared in the library doorway. Lettie Jo noticed, then went quietly toward the stairs.

He was watching her climb the stairs when he felt Hannah's fingers on his arm. She drew him to a paneled sideboard, poured sherry and handed him a glass. "To your homecoming, Benton," she said, raising her glass.

He sipped and his interest wandered over the room. "Your father, Hannah? I keep—"

"He passed away. Last summer."

"I'm sorry. I respected him."

Her voice shaded off to a matter-of-factness. "He was a poor business man, but I suppose you knew that. I've had to change many things."

He viewed his glass and turned it in his fingers.

"I've learned to look out for myself, Benton. Had to. Heavens knows I've had to . . . I'm hauling cotton, wool and hides overland to Matamors. I'm making money. I intend to make a great deal more."

Thoughtfully he put his glass on a cherrywood table, and his mind, going back, retreated to Pea Ridge and thinly clad Confederate dead scattered on rocky slopes, lying in the raw March wind, some without shoes.

"Look, Benton—" Hannah was gesturing with her glass, indicating her portrait. "Monsieur LaVelle journeyed all the way from New Orleans to paint me. Don't you think it's a good likeness?"

"Excellent," he said, "—and very expensive."

"Oh, come now, Benton. Surely you don't begrudge me a little profit." She showed him an appealing expression.

His tone halted her. "A fair profit, perhaps."

"And *perhaps* you don't understand. In exchange for what we haul to Old Mexico, the South gets needed military supplies and medicines. Isn't that helping? Isn't it? Unless we make a profit we can't help the South, can we?"

"We," he said. "Who's we?"

"I'm not the only one. Others are in it," she said indifferently.

An ugly thought flared. "Larkin Knowles, maybe? Sounds like him?"

Her set-down glass made an emphatic click. "I see now. You're after him because you think he killed Crockett?"

"Think? I know he did. I was there *when he did it*. What surprises me is that you know. Did he tell you?"

If he had flustered her, there was no betrayal in her manner. "Benton, how forgetful you are! But I can understand with the war. When you came heah with Crockett, that last time, you said you'd just had trouble with Larkin. Remember? Naturally, I assumed he was responsible for Crockett's death. Father and I both did." She moved all the way to him this time without pausing, confidently, looked up and fingered the front of his soiled jacket. "Do you realize you've told me nothing about yourself—absolutely nothing? You simply disappeared. Some folks thought you'd joined the Yankee army. Some thought you'd drowned. Now you come home in a Confederate uniform, a strange girl with you."

"The uniform should speak for itself," he said. "There's little to tell." Yet, in defense of Lettie Jo, he felt he was compelled to give an explanation of sorts. Sketchily, he related a story along the lines he had told Skaggs, except that he had joined the Confederacy in Arkansas, before being captured at Pea Ridge. He added his fall-in with Skaggs' bushwhacker command, an account which Lettie Jo could confirm.

She placed her cheek against his chest. "I will send that girl on to Sherman for you, today. You look tired, Benton. Very tired. You've ridden hard. You can stay heah a while with me. Just the two of us." She tilted her flawless face back, gazing up at him. "I think you've always wanted that, haven't you? Even before we had any war? When we couldn't do anything about it?"

He was still surprised at the calculation he saw. She could have been talking again of cotton, wool and hides, something to be bought and hauled at her whim. He said, "No man could be unaware of you, Hannah."

"We've waited a long time, Benton."

"Yes," he said, "a long time. Maybe the mistake was in waiting."

She freed her arms abruptly. "Mistake?"

"Yes. Maybe we'd understand each other better now if we hadn't. Maybe I'd know what you really want. I regret that I don't. I honestly do."

Her eyes were blazing, the little muscles pulling at the corners of her mouth. "It's that trashy girl, isn't it?" she flung at him.

"No," he said quietly, "she has nothing to do with it. The

war's changed you and me both, Hannah." He was silent a moment. "I've come a long way," he said finally, "and I won't be put off. I'd be obliged if you'll fix me a pack of food. I don't want to waste any more time in finding Larkin Knowles."

He watched the change strike across her face, thinking again that he knew neither himself nor her.

"If you wish, Benton." She still had the same look of waiting intimacy, the same willingness, yet a matter-of-fact willingness, but her voice carried to him in a different way, sharper somehow.

Passing down the lane and out on the open road to Bonham, Benton restrained his impulse to pound straight into town. Well known in the district and remembered as a Union man, he would be recognized and regarded with suspicion by his Southern friends, even in Confederate uniform, just as Hannah had first expressed doubt. An over-hasty daylight dash into Bonham could spoil his one great chance at Knowles, and doubtless there would be just the one chance.

He dismounted and rested in the shade, his mind shifting, aching for the sight of Cherry Point only a few miles away. Hence, his first move crystallized. He would scout around the old place, find some of his darkies, question them, then strike out for Bonham. Failing to locate Knowles in town, he would look up Henry Jackman or Todd Vaughan or Jim Trask, in the hope that one of them had not gone off to war. The mere thought of these men, once his friends, riding with Knowles was galling to remember. True, they hadn't joined in pursuit of Martin Abel, but Benton had often wondered if, under cover of darkness, they had taken part in the

Cherry Point ambush. He could trust no one, he realized.

He started up as a rider cantered down the lane. When the man took the Bonham road in hard gallop, Benton saw a darky in the saddle. Hannah's groom.

Avoiding the road, he picked his way across the burgeoning countryside. And as his eyes hungered again upon familiar fields, idle today for cotton planting because of last night's downpour, he saw the face of Crockett as he had looked; he felt Crockett riding beside him. He went on. He saw the gables of his home, like sad eyes in the swaying green mask of towering pecan trees. Just glimpsing the house hurled everything back. A kind of clear-headed purpose guided him now. He circled north, wide of the house, cut back and followed along the bottom of a shallow, wooded draw, within a hundred yards of the house. When the little grove of cedars he was seeking came into view, he tied his horse and went slowly up the slope.

He took off his hat and became still, his throat swelling at the sight of the picket fence of split cedar enclosing the cleared plot and three graves. Two bore weathered headstones, his mother's and his father's, side by side. At the third stood a board. He read and wondered over the carefully whittled inscription:

CROCKETT LANE WALL
BORN AUGUST 2, 1840
DIED APRIL 17, 1861

Lemon sunlight and the pungency of gnarled cedar favored this silent, protected place. A soft breeze imparted a sense of movement, of life still going on. But after all the warmth of living before the war, it was hard to think of his people lying here. Crockett the hardest of all, for he had been young.

He pushed the gate in, drawn by the bunches of roses withering on the graves, and he wondered again and turned his eyes. The plot had been weeded, the grass kept down. Over there a pink azalea glowed softly. A yellow rose bush showed its muted, delicate face.

"A coon's age ah been a-waitin' fo' you to come home, Mistuh Benton."

Benton whirled toward the voice, caught off guard.

Ned, so stooped that Benton did not recognize him for a breath, stood in the path.

Benton ran out the gate. He threw his arms around the old man and was shocked by the thinness of his shoulders. Shifting the flowers he held, awkward, Ned clapped Benton's back, embraced him violently, and stood away, staring at Benton's face. At last he mumbled, "Ah knowed you'd come! Ah just knowed it! You—lean as a houn'!"

"It's all right, Ned. I'm home."

"Ever' Sunday ah comes heah . . . tends de graves. Dis is Sunday, de Lawd's day."

"Bless you, Ned. Should have known it was you. I was afraid they'd killed you that night."

"Shoot an old nigger lak me?"

An icy rage swept Benton as he watched Ned. This wonderful, loyal person had become a shuffling old man, broken, defeated, confused, with a kicked-in fear and hurt in the depths of the brown eyes. "What have they done to you?" he said gently.

"Dey—" Ned shook his white head. "Ever'thing's

changed, Mistuh Benton." He looked up and Benton saw the damp glint in his stare. "Dat white trash Larkin Knowles he libs in de big house. Done took it."

Something exploded through Benton. He did not realize he was moving toward the house until Ned's hand caught him. "Dey'll shoot yo' head off."

"I'm going to kill him, Ned." Benton was loosening Ned's grip with firm gentleness.

"He ain't dere, Mistuh Benton."

"Just because you helped bring us boys up, don't sly around. Not now, Ned. This has to be done." He started off.

Ned's hand shot out again, surprisingly strong. "Sho' it does. De good Lawd's gonna see 'bout dis, too. Now lissen." Ned's pleading had gone to a patient firmness, instructive, correcting, yet always encouraging, a tone that sent a pang through Benton. This was Ned as he had been in another time. Crockett and himself. Just boys, listening to Ned while they followed coon dogs in the silver pallor of a crisp autumn night, signaling each other with whip-poor-will whistles, or fishing the deep pools along the copper river, or stalking bushy-tails in the tall bottomland timber. Ned toting of Squirrel-Eye, his double-barreled shotgun. "You know ah don' sly aroun', Mistuh Benton. Just when ah has to."

"All right"—Benton wished he could call back his hot words—"I'll listen."

"Wal, dey's white trash aroun' dey house. Dey come an' go. Larkin Knowles, he got a big sto'house in town. But he comes heah most ever' night or two, lak he owns Cherry Point. Got him an uppity New O'leans nigger at de house. Ah'm a field hand now, Mistuh Benton. But ah still watches de house. Knows what goes on."

"You're too old for field work," Benton said, angered again.

"My place. Ah won' be Larkin Knowles' house nigger." Excitement hurried Ned's voice. "You hide out down in de draw, Mistuh Benton. Come late tonight, we kin meet heah. If dat white trash comes in, ah'll know."

Benton agreed. He had ridden here without much thinking, surrendering to sentiment, to the powerful pull of the familiar. Ned's plan was sound, as if he had thought it out long ago in the intuitive knowledge that Benton would return.

Later, in the cover of the wooded draw, Benton loosened the saddle cinch, ate from his pack and began the long wait until night. He reflected bitterly that Hannah might at least have told him Knowles had Cherry Point.

The setting sun dipped and the countryside fell muted and lonely, its stillness nagging. Other years rolled back to him like a tide, when evening meant reawakening and contentment, work done, when heat had left the brown land. Before neighbor killed neighbor. He put it all from him. He was a stranger hiding out on his heritage. He wrapped the reins around his left wrist for readiness, for flight, turned on his side and slept.

When night took over, he made his way up the hill to the cedars and posted himself to watch the path. Time seemed to stop. He judged the hour to be ten o'clock when a whip-poor-will call sounded down the path. Moments later Ned shuffled up.

"Dat Knowles he ain't come in," said Ned, sounding puzzled.

"Probably in town. Guess I'll have to smoke him out."

Ned's voice was sharp. "Stay 'way from town. Folks done think you joined th' Yankee army. Dis is de best place. No white trash gonna snoop aroun' dead folks."

"A safe place," Benton agreed, "but I can't hole up and find him." He started moving off. "Meet you here tomorrow night, whether I've got him or not."

"Ah wish you wouldn't, Mistuh Benton. Wish you wouldn't."

Benton paused by the split-cedar fence. "I'm curious about something, Ned. The headboard you made for Crockett. It's very nice. I'm mighty grateful."

"Mistuh Jackman, Mistuh Henry Jackman, he put de words down on paper fo' me." Ned was proud. "Den ah whittled 'em out big. 'Co'se ah knowed de times when you boys was born in de big house."

Henry, Benton thought, in surprise. Henry.

CHAPTER 15

Several times on the way to town the following morning Benton turned off into the woods as rumbling wagons approached. It was on his second return to the road that he noticed spires of angry smoke behind him, rising far to the north, black, menacing, in the neighborhood of the river. The smoke stuck briefly in his mind, backtracking to last March, when the Army of the Southwest invaded Arkansas, and burning farms marked the flanks of advancing Union cavalry.

Bonham presented scarcely a livelier face than the drowsy country through which he had just passed. He saw a lone buggy drawn up in front of the courthouse and a few riding horses on the quiet street. A scattering of oldsters rested on benches under the wooden awnings of the stores. He drew mere nods as he rode by the first knot of loungers; it gave him satisfaction to know that, in his shaggy appearance, unshaven since leaving Fort McCulloch, his hat pulled low, he could pass inspection at a distance, for several of the faces were familiar.

His objective was Knowles' stock barn, at the drag end of the street. As he approached, however, his impression of a town nodding in the steamy morning sun suddenly faded. Where a slovenly building had been now stood a broad one of recent construction. In giant lettering, like a black banner painted across the yellowness of new lumber, he read:

MR. LARKIN KNOWLES
Cotton, Wool & Hides
Salt for Sale

Benton rode closer, noting the signs of a big operation. Saddle horses—blooded horses, more than he'd seen along the entire long street—crowded the hitching rail. A man walked out hurriedly, mounted and tore down the east road. Jammed with parked vehicles, many new, a huge wagon yard spread between the building and town, enclosing boat-shaped Conestogas, the shorter prairie schooners, light wagons and even high-wheeled Mexican carts—indeed a contrast, Benton reflected, to the South's usual miserable battlefield transport. High, stout corrals and feed sheds massed to the rear. He got the feel of coming and going, of intense preparation, as he saw darkies loading at the rear of the main building, which, he understood now, was a two-storey warehouse.

A tatter of thought pegged in Benton's mind, something Old DeWitt Richmond had said about men getting rich off the war while others ate poverty pie.

He rode to the hitch rail and dismounted.

The instant he entered he regretted his intolerance of delay. He was in a barn-like room, partitioned off from the warehouse section, the floor littered with cigar butts, splattered with tobacco juice, in a room reeking of the rancid hides stored just beyond. A punished counter ran halfway across; behind it, perched on a high stool like an owl on a limb, a stoop-shouldered clerk posted entries. Between counter and doorway five men idled, long-booted men in black suits, gaudy silk waistcoats, string ties and gray beavers, their flat, curious stares fixing him.

Two faces touched off an elusive recognition, but as he nodded and walked to the counter, a deeper inkling clawed. Both, it came to him now, had ridden with Knowles after Martin Abel. The cussers and spitters and ranters; he'd bulled right into them.

He felt a cool tracing up his spine as he turned his back to them and spoke to the clerk.

"I'm buying remounts. Colonel Ewing's cavalry."

The clerk continued to write, concentrating on the point of his pen. "Must be a mistake," he mumbled, not looking up.

"I was directed here. A farmer on the river."

"Then he ain't been to town in a year," came a hoarse-laughing voice behind him. Benton turned. A small, cat-like man, who would have been meek looking except for the light greenish-gray quality of his eyes, was giving him a ridiculing grin. "He shore ain't."

"You no longer deal in horses?" Benton asked.

"Shore don't, soldier." He winked ironically at his companions. "Just might be able to hustle you up a few, though. Depends, o' course, what the pay's in."

"Drafts on the Confederate treasury," Benton replied to discourage him.

The man made a backing-off gesture, highly amused. "At sixty-five cents on the dollar? Afraid you won't git any horses."

One of the two Benton had recognized, a moody, taciturn man of big bones and a curly beard covering most of his face, was observing him with an increasing interest. Benton resisted the wish to tip his head downward and said to the first man, "A name was given me. Larkin Knowles. Understand he can help me locate stock."

There was a vague head shake. "He ain't here."

Benton waited, hoping for a clue. None came. He said, "I need to talk business. Any idea where he is?"

"Out of town."

"Well, I can come back. When do you expect him?"

"Hard to say, soldier."

That was the extent of it here, Benton knew. For some reason Knowles was being careful, almost as if he'd been warned and was in hiding. Benton noted the big man again. He took a sideward step, staring harder. Benton kept him in the corner of his vision, at the same time wondering if he'd have to knock aside the men by the door to make free to his horse.

He said, with a blunt look for all, "I'm looking for volunteers, too. Colonel Ewing lost a passel of men at Pea Ridge. Anybody interested?"

He had spoken short of manner, taking them off guard. He saw them grow quiet, saw their glance-trading. The runty man, the spokesman, replied after a moment, "Happens we're on special details. Takin' wagon trains to Matamoros so you Yankee-killers can have supplies."

"Been mighty lean where I'm from," Benton said.

"Too bad. When we ain't he'pin' out with the trains, we serve with the Home Guard or the Vigilance Committee. Look out for nigger trouble. Fires, poison wells, such."

Benton knew what bothered them: a battlefield veteran's contempt for well-fed home-fronters. Somehow these men had avoided army service, probably through Knowles' influence. He said mildly, "I see. Well, we can't fight without supplies. I'll ride by in the morning. Be obliged, in case Larkin Knowles shows up, you tell him I'm in the market for horses."

He moved easily toward the door, holding himself to a stroll.

Then he was on the porch and down to his horse, pulling the slipknot and mounting. As he reined around, he glanced inside. The bearded man was talking earnestly to the smaller one, jerking his head in Benton's direction.

Benton set his horse in a trot up the street. He traveled by the stores, by the friendly idlers, taking their nods again, and came to the street opening on the river road. Turning into it, he looked back.

Three horsemen were leaving the warehouse, loping in his wake. They struck up a gallop as he watched.

Once out of sight, hidden by the buildings on his right, he

sent the gelding galloping north out of town. Houses fell behind. He had a two-hundred yard start by the time they took the corner, but after another run he saw that their blooded stock was gaining. Ahead the narrow road made a curve. He ran through it and saw, not far, a second bend. There, he hauled in briefly and swung right, into the woods. He rode fifty yards beyond sight of the road, came down and held his horse under a close bridle, ready to stifle a whicker. Soon he heard horses clattering past on the road. It was time to ride now. He swung up, going north.

Walking the gelding now, he scouted out to the road; it was empty in both directions. He crossed and took stock of his surroundings, remembering the direction of Henry Jackman's plantation to the northwest. Heading that way, he couldn't miss the pall of black smoke hanging high in the sky toward the river. He eyed it at length, unable to think of a logical explanation. Since his ride into town, its dimensions had increased.

An hour's riding placed him in the vicinity of the Jackman place. Coming up to the clapboard house, he had no idea what to expect, whether Henry was home, even alive. His gesture in writing out the headboard inscription had been a year ago.

When Benton's boots sounded on the porch, a familiar voice called from the house, "Come in!"

Benton, not answering, entered and stopped just inside the door, wary, uncertain of his greeting, watching the man intently cleaning a brass-mounted Enfield.

Not until then did Henry Jackman glance up. He withdrew the ramrod and turned his eyes, both hands stilled, his face wrinkling, flashing a pleased recognition. In one rapid motion, Jackman set the ramrod and rifle aside and pushed out of the chair, limping across, one hand extended—an angular man, prematurely gray, amiable blue eyes set deep under thick brows, his nose prominent, his mouth large, expressive.

"Benton Wall! Thought it was one of the neighbors."

Benton stared at the hand; he did not take it.

Jackman didn't seem offended, his amazement was yet so great. He drew back, resting weight on his right leg, which gave him an off-keel look, and peered keenly at Benton. "Guess I've seen everything now—you in Confederate gray. Sit down. We'll have a drink on this."

"No thanks, Henry." He could not, Benton felt, drink with a man he was about to accuse. Jackman looked tired; he returned to his chair, limping badly, favoring his stiff left leg.

"Where'd you get that?" Benton asked.

"In Tennessee. On a damned six-horse patrol. Got sent home when I could ride as well as any man they had. Trouble is, you have to do some walking, even in the cavalry." Jackman's eyes were reading him. "God knows where all you've been."

It wasn't a question in one sense, in another it was, Benton knew, a damned pointed one. "Colonel Ewing's Third Texas Cavalry," he said. "I'm on furlough."

"Ewing's command." Jackman nodded. "But damned if it isn't hard to believe, Benton. You know . . . we all thought—"

"—I'd joined up with the Yankee's," Benton said for him.

"Well, yes, now you've said it. What you'd naturally expect when a man went as far as you did for his convictions. I wouldn't believe it now if I weren't lookin' at you." His upraised hand routed all argument. "Anyway, you're just in time."

"For what?"

"The war's come home to us, Benton, heah, in a way I never expected. Our people robbed and killed. Homes plundered, stock taken. Started yesterday. Outlaws—conscription dodgers—I don't know what they are. Deserters seems to fit, since they're uniformed like Confederates."

Benton sat up stiffly. The smoke—the smoke he'd observed over the bottomlands: suddenly it had meaning. Skaggs had crossed the river. Rather, Pike had driven him. Now, Skaggs was taking out his defeat and thwarted command and loss of the silver on the unsuspecting countryside south of the river. In short, he'd gone to bushwhacking again.

"Whatever goddamned breed they are," Jackman resumed, outraged. "Murdered Major Barr this morning. Burned the house, took his horses, ran off his beef cattle. We know that much, God pity folks along the river we don't know about."

Hearing Jackman, Benton discovered a surprising insight which he thought had no longer existed: for an instant he shared a portion of Jackman's feeling, even though the valley people had persecuted Union men to the death and allowed so-called Vigilantes to rule by the rope, masking private grudges and ambitions behind treasonable accusations. He crushed the emotion before it could rise higher and sway him. "Sounds like bushwhackers to me," he said noncommittally.

"How can you explain the uniforms?"

"Oh, they probably have blues, too. That way they can assume any role they wish. What size force you figure?"

"Hundred and fifty or so. Maybe more."

Pike, Benton was aware, had indeed done some sharp whittling. About half of Skaggs' command. He asked, "What's the Home Guard doing about it?"

"You sound like something should've been done already," Jackman said, and grimaced. "In the first place theah's damned little to do with it. That's the trouble. I'm in command of this district. My darkies are out now, takin' word around. We'll form here. Be night 'fore we can count noses."

"You sound discouraged."

"Wouldn't you be, with only fifty-odd? Half of 'em invalided out of the army. Rest boys, old men. Just about ever'body's in the army or on the frontier with the Rangers."

"Not everybody," Benton corrected acidly. "Knowles and his crew are still around."

"That speculator!" Jackman exploded.

"How does he stay out? He's under thirty-five. There's a conscription law."

"Mr. Knowles," said Jackman, exhibiting a mocking airiness, "is engaged in pursuits vital to the Confederacy—and himself, I should add. If that didn't exempt him and his crowd of dude cutthroats, he has plenty of slaves to get him by. Under the law you can exempt one white man for ever' twenty darkies you own."

"Doing all right for himself, isn't he?"

"Not bad," Jackman conceded bitterly. "With cotton a dollar a pound on the world market. Salt so high a man can't buy enough to cure his winter meat. Knowles charges twenty dollars a sack in Bonham. That's two hundred pounds, and he holds nigh ever' grain around heah." He seemed to have a sudden comprehension. "So you've been to town?"

"Just left."

"You didn't see Knowles?"

"I think he's hiding. Three of his men took after me outside of town."

"What happened?"

"I gave 'em the slip. I want Knowles."

"Furlough, hell! You came home to gun Knowles!"

"Guess I've got reason. And I think you can help me flush him out."

"How would I know where he is?"

"You might, Henry. Last time I saw you you were riding with him." Benton knew it was a cruel charge, more so because Henry was plainly glad to see him, had welcomed him. But once and for all, he realized, he had to know where Henry stood in Crockett's murder.

Pain entered Jackman's angular face, lodged there. "Once—that day. A man can grow up in a year's time, thank God." He moved his head from side to side, in regret. "I can't help you because I don't know. Haven't seen him in months."

"I know you didn't go after Martin Abel," Benton said, unyielding. "Was it because Crockett and I were there? Did you join Knowles at Cherry Point after it got dark? You Jim Trask, Todd Vaughan? Where are they?"

One side of Jackman's mouth pulled up in disgust. "Jim's in a Yankee prison. May be dead by now, starved. Captured at Fort Henry in February."

"Todd?"

"Dead. Killed at Shiloh last month."

Benton considered him, believing when he wished not to believe, sensing that Henry Jackman spoke solid, rock-bottom truth. He had a distinct twinge of shame. "Sorry about Jim and Todd. I mean that."

Jackman shrugged. "It's funny you haven't found Knowles," he said.

"What are you trying to say, Henry?" Benton asked.

"Just this. Why don't you ask Hannah Richmond?"

"Because she's in the same business?"

Jackman was surprised "Don't tell me she admitted it?"

"Same as did. Indicated there were others in it."

"Well, the war's changed a great many things heah from the way you knew them, Benton." Jackman was speaking with reluctance. He made a gesture of dismissal. "I'll say no more about Hannah."

"I've talked to her, and I've been to Cherry Point," Benton said, shaking his head.

"She didn't tell you Knowles had taken over?"

Benton shook his head again. "Ned told me. Who gave Knowles the authority?"

"He claimed your place was being impressed to raise cotton for the government. Said he had the necessary papers."

"Anybody ask to look at 'em?" Benton said.

"Not that I know about." Jackman went on with a sheepish, half-regretful expression, as if remembering something. "I think maybe I could've beaten him to Cherry Point for you. Held it."

"Then why'n hell didn't you?"

Jackman's jaw muscles twitched. He looked squarely at Benton. "And be in Knowles' boots right now? Have you thinkin' I murdered Crockett—tried to murder you—to get possession of Cherry Point?"

"Except you had no hand in Crockett's death," Benton said apologetically. "I'm glad to eat crow."

"Would you if I had Cherry Point?"

Benton couldn't reply at once.

"See theah," said Jackman, though somewhat mollified. "I'd feel the same way in your place. Now, by God, we're going to have that drink if I have to hold your nose." He limped to the other room and returned, bearing bottle and glasses.

In a while, after Jackman had his whiskey, his eyes fell penetratingly on Benton. "Benton, you got to help us run these bushwhackers out."

"Why me?"

"Why!" Jackman almost shouted through his astonishment. "Merciful God, man, these people are your neighbors!"

"Once—" Benton said. "Once. They were never in any hurry to control Knowles' Vigilantes. They let good men be persecuted and murdered. Furthermore, what've they done about Knowles in a year? Not a solitary goddamned thing! He's bigger than ever. Tell you what I think, Henry, I think it's coming back to 'em."

Jackman's voice trailed him to the door. "You still don't understand. They're helpless—I'm helpless. Knowles is within the law."

"You mean he *is* the law."

"Look," said Jackman, straining for reason. "You've got rights now. You're in the Confederate army. You can have Knowles moved off Cherry Point."

"Who'll do it—me with my bare fists?"

"Damnit, you can take care of him later. I'll help."

"He's long past due," Benton said over his shoulder. "I can't wait."

"Neither can your neighbors."

Benton was on the porch, not stopping.

"Where you going?"

"Windwood!"

He did not glance back as he stepped to the saddle and spurred off, the gelding breaking into a startled run.

CHAPTER 16

Benton used the gelding unmercifully for a distance, until the striking sun registered between his shoulder blades and he realized that he faced a long ride to Hannah's home. He slackened and went over the whole string of events, including his conversation with Hannah.

He rode up to Windwood warily but the cool dark oaks so cloaked the long face of the house that he was unaware of trouble until he came into the open, on the back side of the graveled drive. He stopped uncertainly, a chill like sudden nakedness running over him.

Riders rested on the shaded veranda while a groom held their sleek horses. Long-booted men. Civilians in gray beavers.

Benton retracked with a sweep of the reins, instinct warning him to go quietly, on the chance that he was still unobserved. Before he had covered two rods he heard running boots crunch gravel. He heard a rousing yell. At the first noise of discovery, he was sinking spurs and throwing himself low in the saddle. Then came the snarling of bullets and flat cracks that seemed to linger and echo in the hot air. Something tore his hat off, whisked it sailing away.

. . . The afternoon was spent when he found the wooded draw north of Cherry Point. He got down and led in, the dead-beat horse making a stumbling racket behind him. When he came to where he had made camp before, he stood for a time, legs braced, swaying with fatigue, just listening. Assured, he unsaddled and picketed the gelding close, finished the food in his saddlebag and sank down, drained of energy, of thought. His mind fuzzed at details of his wearying, round-about, circuitous ride, and the men he'd managed to lose in the woods between Windwood and the river.

But the circling and indirect riding had run the bottom out of his horse, and he'd come to the only refuge he knew: this shunned place, the unforeseen and unlooked for, near his own dead.

It was late when a whip-poor-will's whistle came beyond the cedars, brief, muted.

Benton answered back, hesitantly at first; then he heard the almost forgotten notes shrilling between his lips. He moved nearer the cedar fence and waited.

Ned materialized like an unhurried ghost, shuffling out of the shadows into the clearing's uncertain light, mumbling, "Reckon you ain't hongry, Mistuh Benton?"

"Lord, yes!"

"Mebbe ah kin hustle you a bite or two." Ned had his

hands behind him, as if hiding something. Slyly, his slowness tantalizing, he thrust a sack at Benton, who caught the aroma of cornbread and bacon.

"Ned, you haven't changed a bit!"

As Benton dug inside the sack, Ned said worriedly, "Dat ole Knowles he come in while ago, but he's gonna be hard to git. Lak a coon in a tall holler tree."

Feeling soared in Benton, his weariness forgotten. "How many men with him?"

"Nigh 'bout ten. Dey got guards posted aroun' de house. Ah couldn't git close. Seen 'em ride up 'bout dark."

"Think he'll stay the night?"

"Looks lak it. De house is quiet."

"What room's he using?"

"Downstairs—in yo' bedroom," Ned said, incensed. He was objecting almost as he said it. "Now you ain't gonna bust in dere, is you?"

"I don't know, Ned. Just trying to think of something." Approximately all he had succeeded in during the hard day, he chided himself, was to make Knowles increase his bodyguard and post lookouts around the house; whereas, if Benton had stayed here as Ned had suggested in the first place, the general atmosphere might be more relaxed, even a little careless. Benton said, "The horses—where they got 'em?"

"In de barn. Under guard." Ned's voice trailed off, puzzled. "Sho' some funny things goin' on t'night. Dey sho' is."

"Hows that?"

"Seen a man circlin' de house same time ah was."

"Wasn't it one of the guards?"

"Didn't get no closer'n ah had to." Ned seemed to be thinking to himself. "It was de way he moved, Mistuh Benton. Watchin' de house 'stead o' lookin' out from de house."

"Knowles' men are posted all around, you say. Had to be a guard, Ned."

Benton dismissed the matter and began taking his fill of the sack's contents while he considered Ned's report. He put down a mouthful of cornbread and said thoughtfully, "Is the old carriage house still standing east of the barn?"

"Yeah."

"Could you set it on fire?"

"Mistuh Benton"—Ned was genuinely shocked—"you ain't gonna burn ever'thing down?"

"Not a stick if we don't have to. We won't decide now. First, I want you to show me where the guards are posted."

"Dat's better." Ned was relieved.

Benton deposited the sack by the fence and picked up his carbine. He paused as he started up the path, thinking of Ned. "If there's shooting, you run—get away from me. I want you to understand that plainly."

"But—"

"You'll do as I say, Ned. No slyin' around."

"Sho', Mistuh Benton. Sho'."

A short way along the path, Ned stopped Benton with a tug on his arm and vanished. He reappeared within moments. "Brung Ol' Squirrel-Eye fo' company," he said in a chuckling whisper. "Keep 'im cached in a holler tree."

They went on in strict silence, in the milky dimness of a first quarter moon. Thereafter, Ned communicated with a single hushed word or a touch of his hand. It was formless going until the cedars played out and open ground lay between them and the pecan grove hiding the house. Ned led straight into the taller trees, never hesitating. Once under cover again he bore away to the north. As they changed direction, Benton glimpsed faint light on the lower floor of the house.

Cigar smoke, strong, near, made Benton sniff; simultaneously, he felt Ned's staying hand, heard Ned's almost inaudible and whispered, "Dere one is."

Benton wouldn't have located the man had they been still among the low-growing cedars. But the lofty pecans were long-shanked, and, dimly, beside one, Benton marked a standing figure. The guard was restless; he strolled off and back and off again.

They skirted him and spotted the next man about thirty yards to the northwest. Across the double lane of trees leading to the Bonham road, they discovered a third watcher. In all, half an hour later, after completing the circle, Benton had accounted for five guards, including one stationed at the barn door.

"Leaves five with Knowles," he said.

"Dey's a man at de front an' back po'ches," Ned supplied softly.

"Puts three inside, then."

Three or four or five, Benton thought bleakly, it was a totally one-sided undertaking.

On their return they did not go directly down the path, the end of the circling scout having left them south of the cedars. Ned led in from that side and started down.

The darky's abrupt, stopping hand stilled Benton.

Someone, walking light and fast, was coming up the path.

Dodging right, Benton got behind a cedar and sensed Ned's presence vaguely in front of him. For the moment he had no thought except to escape detection. But, as the boots advanced and he made out, faintly skylighted, the shape of a man and his swinging rifle or carbine, he remembered suddenly his horse tied in the draw. This man could be taking news of that discovery to the house.

There wasn't time to signal Ned his intention. When the boots came even, Benton, rising, took quick, light steps to the path and closed in, prodding the muzzle of the carbine into the walker's back.

"Drop that gun and turn about!"

He heard an astonished grunt; a moment and the weapon clattered down.

Benton pulled a revolver from the right-side holster, slipped around and gave his prisoner another muzzle jab that headed him back the way he had approached.

"Get along—move!"

Benton was preparing to lay the edge of the barrel across the man's head if he didn't obey when the shoulders in front of him swiveled around, and a drawling Texas voice exclaimed, "Sarge, keep that up yo're gonna bust my backbone."

Benton let the muzzle sag. His mind raced. "—Doyle," he got out. "Just ready to crack that skull, you damned runaway. Where you been?"

Doyle didn't answer.

"Mule-head," Benton said warmly. "Don't you know you'll get shot prowling around here?"

"So'll you."

"Where's your horse?"

"In the draw, where yore mount is."

"Let's go down a way and talk."

Doyle was the first to speak when they reached the clearing. "Got any rations, Sarge?"

"Cornbread and bacon in that sack over yonder. Thanks to Ned, here. Help yourself."

Doyle sat down and Benton let him satisfy himself for a minute before he interrupted. "Wondered what'd happened to you."

"You had Lettie Jo to worry about."

"I left her at Hannah Richmond's."

"Now," Doyle said, "both of us prowlin' th' dark." He ate wolfishly for an interval. "You after him, too?"

"Knowles? Sure." Benton explained why—and added, "This is my place—or was. Crockett's and mine. Knowles has impressed it in the name of the Confederacy, if you know what I mean?"

"I know." Doyle's grunt was explosive. His loaded hand paused halfway to his mouth. "Might a-figgered somethin' like that made you so beaverish to cross the Red. Theah was nothin' else—no other reason?" he mocked softly.

"Lettie Jo was the other. Noticed you didn't object, however."

"Naw, I wanted to git across soon as we could." Doyle wiped a hand across his mouth, and when he spoke again his tone was back on the familiar track Benton remembered, bitter, belligerent, defiant. "Can't say I gained much by myself. Took yesterday, today, to locate him." He reflected a moment and resumed, grim and wondering. "Funny, you an' me, Sarge. All time after th' same sonofabitch—this Knowles. It was him—him an'

222

his bunch that killed my pappy."

Benton's head snapped up. "When was this?"

"Early last summer."

"Your father wasn't an abolitionist. He didn't preach slave uprisings and fire."

"Didn't preach secession either. That was enough, an excuse. Made Knowles look like a real Johnny Reb."

Benton felt an immediate and powerful sympathy. As it formed, the enigma of Doyle suddenly vanished, became clear. Doyle's dark moods, his defiance, his violence, his clumsy, unexpected gentleness when Mears had died, his obscure but unvarying hatred of something never named until now—they weren't strange actions at all, just those of a person deeply hurt, deeply wronged.

"Tried to stop 'em," Doyle said, living it again in his harsh voice. "They held me, made me watch while they slapped th' horse out from under 'im. While they hung 'im, him an old man, helpless—th' sonsabitches! But I saw a thing—it came to me, Sarge." Benton stayed still. All Doyle's guarded turmoil was rushing out, released, at last. "Sarge, it's this—a true Christian's never afraid to die. Never. My pappy didn't want to die. He wasn't ready to go, but he wasn't afraid. He gave me somethin' right theah, right when I'd give up. I fought 'em—I was next—I broke away. Hid out two days an' nights, 'til I could cross the river. Guess I've never been afraid since. That's about it, Sarge," Doyle said quietly.

Nothing more was said until Doyle finished eating and stood. "Knowles has got to be heah. Too many men on guard duty."

"He is. Ned saw him ride in, about ten strong."

Doyle seemed to figure hard on the arithmetic of that. Both were silent, and then Benton said, "We can't handle more than a guard or two without raising a squawk, and just busting into the house won't solve everything. We figure Knowles has three men inside with him. I'd like to cut down those odds."

"How?"

"Draw 'em out somewhere beyond the house. Some, at least. Both the outside and inside men."

"Wal," Doyle said, his tone suggesting, "you know what's on yore place better'n me. Go ahead."

Just the sound of Doyle's rough voice gave Benton courage, that, together, they could make possible an impossible scheme. He said, "Ned could fire the carriage shed east of the barn. It's close enough to make them worry about their horses. If the barn catches, all the better. We'd set the barn afire, but there's a guard with the horses and Ned's taking too many chances as it is. When the shed's going good, you and I jump the house from the west. That means taking care of at least two men on the way in—the one along the road under the pecans and the man on the front porch. Inside, we'll go for the bedroom down the hall to our right. Knowles sleeps there." Translated into words, the plan sounded like a very thin chance. There was no assurance that the fire would attract enough men to make much difference, or any at all. Benton said, "I hope you can think of a better way."

Doyle held his reply for a time. "Ain't no easy way; its all chancy. Only thing I say is wait as late we can. Little 'fore daylight, when they're half asleep an' ass-tired o' guard duty."

Benton said, "All right we'll do it that way."

A profound quiet was everywhere except for the plaintive, early morning bird cries, a quiet so unbroken that Benton could hear Doyle, flattened out beside him on the edge of the ploughed field, drawing on the stem of an unlighted pipe. Beyond, toward the house made invisible by the pecan grove, there was darkness and silence. Not many yards away, in the trees to their left, a rifleman guarded the road running between the double file of trees.

Benton thought of the approaching moments with a mixture of cold exultation and dread. He noted a faint change in the sky, and remembered suddenly the urgency in Lettie Jo's voice warning him to be careful.

A small measure of time passed, another, and then, shrilly, a ripped-out yell erupted across the stillness.

Benton and Doyle seemed to rise as one and go forward in unison, staying near the trees. Other than the yell there had been no further outcry yet.

They checked suddenly, sighting a shape. From here it was impossible to tell whether the guard's attention was on the fire or not, but it was a chance they had to take. Benton stepped faster.

Some sound or sense seemed to warn the man at the last moment. He jerked, whirling with his rifle as Benton crashed his pistol barrel downward. It was a chopping blow upon the crown of the gray beaver, all his strength laid in behind it. He heard the crunch of breaking bone. Doyle tossed the loose rifle into the field, stopped again, and came up jamming a spare revolver inside his belt.

They went faster, long striding. Benton heard the strike of boots bearing in from the north, and voices rising on the east side of the house. And there was increased light, a crimson brightness that smeared the eastern sky, but left the west porch in deep shadow.

His pulse leaped when he saw two men instead of one at the southwest corner of the house, watching the inflamed sky.

He held up, hoping the pair would be drawn toward the fire. After a moment's pause, he realized they weren't going. The shouting and running in the direction of the fire said others were taking care of the horses. Neither, it flashed upon Benton, could the two be left at the corner to cut Doyle and himself off when they ran from the house.

He swung toward them, walking lightly, Doyle in step. Benton winced as their boots scuffed gravel. It was that brittle sound, though faint, that gave them away. Before they could come any closer, the nearest man turned.

"You boys git back to yore posts." The second man faced about.

Benton and Doyle, abreast, continued their approach.

"Our horses—" Benton said.

"They're bein' looked after. You boys git back . . ."

Benton knew then they'd never get in close—knew it as the speaker seemed to stiffen all at once, high-shouldered, big-hatted, outlined against the tawny light.

Benton shot him and heard Doyle's pistol an instant after.

Without pausing, they ran to the porch. Benton tried the door, found it locked or jammed. He kicked—nothing gave. He kicked again. The door crashed back, and he went in at a crouch ahead of Doyle, feeling carpet under his boots, aiming for the bedroom at the hall's end.

He moved on memory of the room's arrangement; for

several steps he moved in a false hush; nothing happened. What little he could see made an unreal, obscure scene, dimly lit along the east windows by the blazing shed.

He was still advancing when the nose of his revolver bumped back in his hand, lodged on a man's soft belly. Benton hammered the gun barrel twice across the blob of face, brutally, just then realizing that he did so instead of firing because he'd sensed hesitation. A chair broke as the man folded.

Upon that, the back door jerked open and a figure, outlined there, started spraying lead into the room. The man Benton had knocked down screamed. Window glass crashed. The outburst of shooting ceased on the deafening roar of Doyle's pistol ahead of Benton's. Afterward, Benton heard the plop of a body on the rear porch.

Somewhere on the east side of the room another gun spoke up, the hissing shots searching, beginning a broom sweep of lead. Benton tasted gunpowder, acrid, warm, felt Doyle scrabbling out of the line of fire. Benton crawled after him and reared up behind the couch, trying to fix the gunman. The firing quit. He could hear somebody stumbling into furniture.

Benton tried a shot; it stirred the man over there to action again. He started shooting, wildly, too high, too fast, blue muzzle flashes marking his position.

Benton's reply and Doyle's clapped close together.

The gun flashed once more, then went out altogether and the sliding thump of a body filtered across the room.

Benton wasn't alerted for the speedy passage of boots breaking down the hall and behind him, the sound already past him, out the door and beating off the porch, even as he whirled up, late.

He was just a step ahead of Doyle springing through the doorway and across the porch, pausing only long enough to mark the runner's direction. West—a crunching flight on telltale gravel toward the double-filed trees. The strengthening light verified what Benton had sensed. It was Knowles.

Benton shot twice, quickly, as Knowles passed inside the tree row. Knowles didn't let up.

They were tearing after him when men ran around the southwest corner of the house. Before either could turn, Benton heard a roar and saw Doyle falter. Benton spun, the pistol snapping empty. He emptied the carbine and ran on. Doyle was still on his feet. It seemed they were out of it, shielded briefly by the trees curving with the drive.

Benton had dropped behind when he answered the shots, and he'd seen the men hold up. Now he saw Doyle lose stride, stumbling, badly hurt, which told Benton why Doyle hadn't returned the fire.

The big man was starting down when Benton caught him.

Doyle raged at him. "Go on—git th' sonofabitch!"

Benton looked back, hearing the running pick up. He eased Doyle down, he waited.

"He's takin' off across th' field!" Doyle's urging voice was weaker.

Pursuit grew louder, men in a stomping run.

Benton fumbled for Doyle's Navy gun, found it. He was ready for them when a single boom crashed, and another, the brassy, deep-throated tones of a shotgun. He heard cries, a floundering on the gravel. He waited for the boot-steps to advance, for the first man to show himself around the curve of the trees.

But nothing appeared. The silence back there persisted.

"Sarge—he's gittin' away!"

Benton put out a quieting hand, thinking of the curious, opportune shotgun blasts. He heard slow steps approaching, but he was careful to hold his fire. The steps became more distinct, quickening. Not boots—but a softer, hurried shuffling. There emerged a bent over shape toting a shotgun, a shape with a black face and a cottony head.

Benton waved Ned on, indicating Doyle, and struck out, soon stretching his stride to take the furrows. For a minute or more he ran, so long he began to doubt his direction, long enough to cause him to stop and scan all about. Was Knowles circling for the horses? But, as the light fell stronger, he discovered a gray motion to the west, off toward the Bonham road. He started running again. But now the scattering light, to his advantage a moment ago, went against him.

He saw Knowles halt and turn. A ball hummed. Benton hit the fresh dirt and shot at the blurred target, saw Knowles flattening out just as he was. He thumbed and pulled again and the hammer fell on an empty cylinder. Ducked down between two furrows, Benton began reloading, sweat dripping on his hands as he poured and dropped, rammed and removed the used caps for fresh ones. Another ball whirred, followed by the popping report of a revolver.

Benton tried a shot, drew a ball in return. He could see nothing except an exposed hand or arm because of the sloping land. At a range of thirty or forty yards each was wasting loads. He started counting back. That last shot was Knowles' third.

Knowles kept peppering away, nervously, erratically. Benton replied once. After Knowles' sixth shot, he waited out a pause. He inched up and nothing happened. Knowles was still down, flat.

Benton sprang up, watching for Knowles' arm to come up. Knowles didn't move. No gunfire greeted Benton as he ran and he expected none now, not if he could close in before Knowles reloaded. Knowles remained down, making no effort.

Benton slowed his rush, seeing Knowles stand up, arms to the sky.

Benton covered the intervening distance in a deliberate walk, his pistol grimly ready, hammer back.

Streaks of dirt and sweat traced Knowles' face; field earth browned his fine clothes. Benton's eyes clawed at the cinnamon-colored coat and its double row of white plated buttons, at the green silk waistcoat and the dun trousers. But to Benton he was still the same overdressed opportunist holding a hangman's rope as he sat his blooded gelding on the dusty Bonham road.

His finger coiled tighter around the trigger, tightened and eased. His breathing became ragged. He couldn't do it this way, even to Knowles.

Knowles waited, his empty hands hanging.

Benton lowered the revolver and made a half-turn, apparently to start his prisoner toward the house—and whipped back, pivoting, as Knowles dug for the derringer inside his waistcoat.

Benton wasn't conscious of pulling the trigger. He heard a shot and felt the pistol kick backward. Across the space, an utter and terrifying surprise was framed in Knowles' eyes. As it was, he managed one shot, a bullet spurting dirt between them, just when Benton let go a second time.

Afterward, wearily, Knowles dropped the little hook-handled gun and sat down. He put a hand to his chest and coughed, a gagging cough, strained to rise, and fell over on his side.

Benton stared at him, long and hard, without remorse, until he was certain it was finished, and started back, dreading what he would find. As he ran, the line of trees seemed far off under the changed and open sky. In the pasty, fooling light, he had pursued farther than he had realized.

Doyle lay as if sleeping, on the soft ground under the pecan trees. Benton, short of breath, looked once and glanced hurriedly to Ned and saw, confirmed, what he had already sensed, with a sinking heart, that Doyle was gone.

Ned said, "He tried to hold on, Mistuh Benton, 'til you come back."

Benton hacked for wind. "Did he . . . say anything?"

"Jest a little." Ned worked his mouth. "He say, 'You tell Sarge he done fine fo' a gent'man.' "

It was almost as if Doyle stood across from him again, sneering in black-eyed anger, fists ready, the greasy Missouri mud sliding under his churning boots. Benton said, "But he didn't know I'd be back."

"He was mighty sho'. Mighty sho'. Somehows he knowed when he heard dem las' shots."

Benton turned away, shaking his head, and pressed a hand to his eyes, half-closing them. Something of himself lay over there, just as part of him lay with young Ernie and Mears and Crockett.

CHAPTER 17

Benton rode late and without haste for Windwood, behind him a dismal duty completed. Doyle rested in the family plot at Cherry Point, not nameless like Mears up in the Choctaw country. When the opportunity came, if the damned war ever ended, if he survived, and if he could come back here to live—that would be taken care of properly. He hadn't concerned himself with the other chores until, considerably later, he had returned from the cedars.

Ned spoke. "Don't you worry, Mistuh Benton. Ever'thing's done been took care of. Ain't gonna be no fuss. Naw, suh, 'pears lak dem mean white trash jest up an' plumb disappeared."

"Disappeared?" Benton repeated wearily; then he began to understand.

"Yes, suh." Ned's manner was unusually solemn. "An' dey say dat ole river quicksand is mighty close-moufed, too."

Benton didn't know what to say. Then, in reflection, he knew that Ned had the best solution. Questions would be asked, certainly. Chances were, there would be an official inquiry because of Knowles' higher-up connections in the cotton ring. But the local people wouldn't push too far. They detested Knowles and his privileged kind, living high, profiting, while friends and kin fought and died or wasted away in Yankee prisons. Henry Jackman's fiery sentiments had echoed their feelings. If only, he thought, bitter again, they'd tried to do something about Knowles. Another thought grew. Bushwhackers were operating in the district, killing, pillaging. Knowles could have encountered them.

Benton, half-smiling, had to marvel at Ned; then he remembered the last thing he must do. While going through the big, empty house, while waiting for the darky grave-diggers to finish, he had written down a matter long on his mind. Without speaking, he gave Ned the papers.

"What's dis, Mistuh Benton?"

"Free papers. Yours and every family at Cherry Point."

"You mean"—Ned didn't quite seem to understand—"we'se free?"

"That's right. You can leave Cherry Point."

"Mebbe, when de wah's over, ever'thing'll be de same agin."

"I'm afraid the war's going to last a long time, Ned. Things won't be the same because they've already changed."

Ned had a stricken look. "What's us gonna do now? Go hongry? Leave Cherry Point—home?"

"You don't have to leave. You can stay. But you have a choice."

"Dat's mo' lak it! All us needs is somebody to run de plantation while you is gone. Somebody lak dat Mistuh Jackman."

Coming to the Bonham road, Benton turned from habit to examine the sky over the river. Smoke was still visible, a dirty smear that had moved southwest since yesterday. He had dismissed the bushwhackers the moment he left Henry Jackman, excluding them from the circle of his concern. But, now, the sight commanded his attention longer than usual. He wondered who might be in trouble today and judged the location to be that of the Prather family. Nearby were the Masons. Small farmers. All people he'd known—like the others scattered through here, some, a minority, holding Unionist opinions; many differing.

He kept looking for Lettie Jo as the groom took the reins and he crossed the veranda to the door.

Hannah appeared immediately, in contrast to her habitual delay. He had the impression that she was expecting company, important company. But his surprise hardly equaled hers. Her eyes dilated enormously, her face whitened, she froze without speech.

"You're not looking at a dead man," he said, entering, even though she hadn't invited him inside. "But it's no fault of yours. I could have had my head blown off."

"Benton," she exclaimed, "what in the world?"

"I believe," he said, "you were expecting someone else. Certainly not me. You're dressed for a guest."

"I was hoping it would be you," she said, her smile easy. "You said you'd be back. Yes, I was expecting you. Sometime today."

"Even after yesterday—when they jumped me outside your door?"

"Oh, those men . . . they stopped for water. I heard the shots. They rode off. How could I've known it was you?"

"They did. Can you think of anyone else they'd be after?"

"Benton, you don't understand. I'm relieved—I'm happy you got away."

Hearing her, watching her, it was hard not to believe her. Two days ago he would have. He said, "Too bad it isn't that way. Hannah, I know you warned Knowles."

He awaited some betrayal, some small revealing sign. He saw nothing, except she became more rigid.

"How could you imagine such a thing? It isn't true!"

"You're lying," he said, disgust in his voice. "You sent your groom to Bonham with the news soon after I left. Only you got in too big a hurry. I saw him on the road. Next day, when I rode to town, Knowles was hiding out. His committee suspicious, primed for trouble." He broke off impatiently. "Why tell you what you already know—where's Lettie Jo? I'm taking her out of this house of friendliness."

He saw a different look begin in her eyes; it grew until her cheeks and mouth were a part of it. "*That* girl!" she said, giving the words a special twist. "Benton, you continue to surprise me, yes, even amaze me. I do believe you're in love with her. I was watching from the window the day you rode up. Oh, it was most tender. You, the gallant soldier. Her"—Hannah's lips curled—"her with her bare ankles and legs showin'. Her astride, like a man. Both arms around you. 'Most naked, in rags, when she came into my home. Like common white trash you'd picked up on the road."

His face was hot. "Where is she?"

"I don't know. She left."

Benton gripped her shoulders, shaking her. "Where is she?" Hannah gave no reply and he shook her again, more forcibly. "You're going to tell me."

Resignation laid a slack dullness across her face. Her head sagged. "She rode off this morning."

"To Sherman?"

She wouldn't speak, and he shook her again and got no response.

"Why'd she leave?"

"I'll tell you nothing more," she said. Her voice was flat and final.

He thrust her away and went back to his horse, his mind already miles from any pleas she might make.

Benton learned from the groom that Lettie Jo had left some hours before. Following the shod prints chopping the soft soil of the narrow, seldom-used wagon road, his mind leaping ahead with the motion of his horse, Benton ran through the groom's story again. Instead of going south on the Bonham road, Lettie Jo had inquired how to cut across and pick up the Bonham-Sherman road southwest of Windwood. There was a way, but it was chancy if you didn't know the country, twisting, dim in many places, following the edges of fields, winding through the hills and woods.

. . . The tracks wound west. He worried his gaze at the troubled sky. A multiplying uneasiness assailed him as he realized she was heading into the smoke, which was much nearer than when he had left Windwood. Not that she had lost the road, faint as it was at times. Here the cluttered pattern said she had stopped to weigh and consider before venturing ahead; here she had correctly divined a tangle where two other roads, no more than dim trails, entwined, ran as one for some distance, then went vaguely off, one by one.

He traveled upon Mason land now. Wind-carried smoke scattered its pungency of waste. Turning as the road twisted, he came in sight of a cottonwood grove cooling the Mason house. Rather—he discovered—where the Mason house used to be.

He pulled up, a pause he broke by sinking spurs. But he was hours late; there was no life. A silence as complete as the bottom of a well dominated where a comfortable two-storey house had stood. He passed the smoke-bubbling rubble of the house and its skeleton chimney spire, the burned-out smells clinging inside his nostrils. He wished he could feel detached. But his feeling of indifference was turning to a quick anger, mounting the longer he looked.

Lettie Jo's trail lost identity in the milling hoofprints. He picked them up on the road about a hundred yards from the house. Here, it looked, her mount had shied violently at something. As he started on, his gelding spooked sideways and then he found the two bodies in the weeds. A darky and an old white man, face up. He forced the horse across.

The white man was August Mason, too old for the war, but the war had come to him. Both bore the trademark, shot between the eyes. Feeling his stomach crawl, his helplessness, he could imagine the scene. Confederate-looking horsemen approaching. A soft-accented voice calling to the two standing on the road, calling, drawing them closer, merely a convenience of pistol range for the men bent on murder.

Well, he could do nothing here, and he rode faster after the tracks, a new alertness in his hunting, a thought clarifying. He minded that these people suffered, he minded powerfully. The only thing that puzzled him was why he cared. Was it because he was also to blame for the rise of men such as Larkin Knowles, back in those early, wavering days of the war, when Knowles was just growing strong, when there was still time to check him? Had he, it suggested itself, been like many, unwilling to act, hesitating, waiting hopefully for another to do what he had neglected? Were his neighbors more to blame than he? As his mind sought, the gap between them and himself lessened.

Of one truth he was positive now: he could never separate himself entirely from the people here. Inwardly he hadn't, he understood now, even when in his blackest accusing moments.

. . . He wasn't immediately aware when the tracks lengthened, the iron shoes digging deeper. It was just there, a knowledge gripping him: Lettie Jo was running from somebody. At once, the marks leaped the road into a field, her horse's stride shortened by the soft footing. Benton followed the deep hoofpocks at a fast lope, thinking there was only one reason for her to leave the road, a reason he dreaded to face.

Her tracks, going south, paused before an oak clump and cut east, stretching out again. Benton swung with them.

Not fifty yards away the puzzle ended. Horsemen from the north, the ones she'd originally fled from, and those breaking out of the oak clump, the ones she'd come upon in surprise—they had run her down here.

The wretched picture filled out further. Yandell's scouts, he thought, a patrol. Or a detail out foraging.

That knocked the drive out of him, left him halted, head bent over the snarled signs even after he had the story. He started off after a while, going doggedly, northwest, toward the river. . . .

He was rounding the face of a rise, intent on the gouged imprints, and didn't see the butternut riders, until he was almost abreast of them, filing north by twos, leaving the dense woods to his left. There was time to run for it, and he reined back. But as more riders came into view, he held up, watching a ragged cavalcade take form. Some were adequately mounted. For the most part, however, they straddled mules and heavy-footed workhorses. They seemed to have little order and less concern for silence. He could catch voices rising above the clumping advance, even laughter, as he trotted toward them, waving. The front horsemen halted and the irregular line closed up like loose-jointed parts, bumping, jostling, noisy.

Henry Jackman, in the lead, cut Benton an amazed recognition and swung out, his face lighting up.

"You didn't catch up any too soon. They're just three miles north, camped in the woods. What changed that mule head of yours?"

Benton rode in alongside him. "Passed the Mason place couple hours ago. He's dead, shot—him and a darky. Everything looks like one big campfire." Was it August Mason or Lettie Jo, alone? Was it both? It wasn't important now that he was throwing in with them.

"I was afraid of that when August didn't show up this morning."

Jackman was a pretty grim sight. He carried the brass-mounted Enfield across his saddle, an enormous horse pistol at his belt. His dusty hat was crammed low upon his head. An etched frown puckered what was normally a cheerful face, and a vexed and thwarted expression worried the blue eyes. His mouth was a trap, the lips squinched together. Benton understood; it was a familiar look. He'd seen such bedeviled harassment on regular army officers handed the painful duty of forging discipline into larking volunteers fresh off Missouri farms.

Benton turned his gaze to the brief, drawn-up column, nodding to the faces he knew, and experienced a like dismay. Up close, the picture was even more discouraging. The scattering of weather-stained butternut tunics he'd noticed at a distance seemed to belong to men possessing only parts of themselves. Then he realized they had been invalided out of the Confederate army, missing a leg or an arm, or, like Jackman, too crippled to walk and hardly able to ride, not a whole man among them. The others were mere boys in their early teens and bearded elders, too old to go off and fight Yankees, living on the embroidered exploits of memoried clashes with Mexicans and Comanches. And they toted the damnedest assortment of muzzle-loaders, carbines, revolvers and shotguns Benton had ever seen. In fact, in all, they resembled a disorganized posse more than anything else.

He said gravely to Jackman, "You intend to close right in?"

"Aim to do something, by God. Got to! We're just a poop in the wind, as you can see, but we're all theah is between those house-burning murderers an' the folks in Bonham an' Sherman. Reckon the enemy hasn't heard us coming. We're not just going in blind, though. Got scouts out. Boys that know every foot on to the river." He waved his fifty-odd company into motion. "They're really not as bad as you'd think, Benton. These kids can drill a squirrel's eye at fifty paces. An' those old cusses back yonder, they didn't settle heah when it was a picnic ground."

Jackman's little command followed quietly, in a rhythmic squeal of saddle leather, jingling curb chains, rattles and the muffled roll of trotting animals.

"Want me to fall in somewhere?" Benton asked.

"Stay right where you are. Gonna need you, I think." Benton settled down to watching the shifting face of the land. As the column wound around, he lost the tracks he had been following, but he had no doubt as to their destination;

they trailed north on approximately the same line of march being taken by Jackman, in fact held to a more direct going.

Jackman displayed a progressive vigilance as the country fell behind, turning to make use of cover, constantly inspecting his flanks, carefully keeping his double file closed up.

Within the next mile, a boy straddling a light-legged mule shaped up in considerable hurry. "Them scoun'ls are headed this way!" he reported, excitement thinning his voice.

"How many?" Jackman asked.

"Thirty-forty, I reckon."

"Go back an' watch," Jackman instructed. "Were comin' up!"

The scout cut away and Jackman took his company forward in a swinging trot. Not long afterward a shot stroked the stillness ahead, followed by a flurry of banging. It ceased all at once. During the next minutes Jackman's men rode into a hushed quiet of scattered timber and low hills and rolling prairie.

Three riders falling rapidly back made Jackman halt and bark, "Column o' fours! Foo-ard!"

Crowding, bumping, the Home Guard riders executed the order and eventually ended up in formation.

Jackman winced visibly, swallowing his distress.

They were, Benton gathered, doing the best they knew how. But—and the prospects were sufficient for consternation—they were no match for trained guerrillas. They had little conception of this particular enemy. Neither did Jackman.

And now, pressing after Jackman's retreating scouts,

Benton observed a wedge of gray horsemen; the distance between the two forces narrowing. At about four-hundred yards the attacking riders loosed shots, wheeled and drifted back. It was a tantalizing maneuver, not too fast, just slow enough to suggest successful pursuit.

Benton scowled, sensing something vague but familiar. The exact meaning evaded him.

"By God, they're running!" Jackman cried elatedly and spurred faster. The enemy, retreating north, also quickened. Jackman, impatient, stuck a gallop.

Benton roweled ahead, even with Jackman, yelling at him to pull up.

Jackman, surprised, barely slowed.

"Pull up!" Benton roared above the hammering hoof roll. When Jackman kept on, Benton cut in front of him, forcing him to slow down. "Henry—this is a decoy!"

"Decoy?" Jackman, reluctantly, tossed his arm for the company to see and hauled on the reins. "Damned if you don't seem well informed," he muttered sourly. "I don't understand you."

"Told you I saw 'em operate in Missouri. Damnit, they're trying to draw us in."

"Never catch up now," Jackman said, disgruntled, shaking his head. "Sun's low."

"Henry, we're no farther off than we were. See, they're pulling up, too. Reason is we're not following. I think they want to hem us in between the woods," Benton said, pointing right and left.

Jackman, Benton saw, was more concerned over what he considered a lost opportunity for victory, a feeling shared by his grumbling men.

"What's holdin' us up, Henry? We had 'em on the run."

"We come to hang up some scoun'ls' hides. Not squat an' jaw."

Benton raised his voice for Jackman and those nearest him. "They want to suck us in. It's plain as daylight."

"Hell, they're on the run," a voice argued. "Henry, let's go git 'em!" Others took up the clamoring demand for action.

It was all too much for Jackman, himself as eager. He turned on Benton, his eyes stony with suspicion. "Maybe you don't want us to catch up?"

Benton made a gesture of despair. "You're in command, but for God's sake don't suck in," he replied curtly, and realized that all the reason in the world couldn't sway them now.

Jackman ripped out a long Rebel yell and they charged. Somebody let go a futile shotgun blast. Immediately the column of fours lost alignment, the lumbering workhorses even slower than the mules and the mules unable to keep up with the faster saddle horses. They rushed on like an unruly mob, whooping, spurring, whipping, already beginning to string out. Up ahead, the clot of gray horsemen had retreated a little and stopped, apparently prepared at last to make a stand.

Jackman rammed straight at them, Benton wondering if he intended to bring his command into line on a wider front. Then Jackman stood high in his stirrups and flung up an arm and set his horse back on its haunches, Jackman's abruptness causing the farthest riders behind him to collide with those just ahead.

Benton saw it at the same time—gray cavalry streaming out of the woods on both flanks, precisely, like exact figures on a drill field. In concert, the bait bunch that Jackman had blundered after jumped forward in a springing charge.

Jackman's face blanched. But for all his overeagerness, he didn't hesitate now. There was one way out of this and he took it quickly, rearing in his stirrups, crying and motioning back. His voice failed to carry far, but the signal of his arm was enough to start them turning.

It was better than a hundred-yard run to the woods they had skirted coming out on the prairie. A mule went addled in the sudden singing fire, buck-jumping violently. Its young rider spilled and sprang up running. Another boy raced up, paused and the runner swung on behind. The one-armed Confederate riding next to Benton dropped his rifle and slipped sideways, dead before he hit the grass. Jackman was shouting above the hammering din, the animal-grunting and the rattle and slap of gear:

"Go back—go back!"

Benton, like Jackman, on the outer rim of the about-wheeling column, found other shapes at irregular intervals left and right of him. As if drawn by old training instincts, a scattering of men in pieces of worn linsey-woolsey had fallen back to cover the retreat. They fired and shifted carbines and rifles to rein hands, they drew revolvers, or lacking two hands, shoved the long weapons into saddle boots.

Benton saw gaps appear in the onrushing line, riderless horses cavorting wildly, stirrups flying. Together, Jackman's rear guard fell back, released another uneven volley, and fell back some more. Their sudden resistance had caused more surprised hesitation than damage, Benton saw, but it had delayed an expected dash through these seemingly demoralized country people. The woods were at his back when he squeezed off another bullet and dodged his horse in under the oak branches, swung down and commenced reloading. Before he could finish, he heard them coming hard. Bullets whined through the timber. He felt a dribble of branches. He pressed on the last cap and ran forward to a tree, glimpsing the old men and boys kneeling, spread thinly, others hustling horses and mules to the rear, some of the invalided veterans still mounted.

Benton shot at a beard-darkened face; it fell away. Someone within arm's length fired a muzzle-loader, its roar ear-splitting. Shotguns boomed, brassy, bellowing. Powdersmoke formed and drifted, caught in the thick timber. And through the grayish fog Benton saw the charge slow and waver as horses and men crashed down. Another volley and it curled away, horses wheeling off.

Scattered carbine shots rattled back. Swiftly they were gone, hurt, drawing across the prairie.

A ragged cheer rose, spread the little company's length. Benton cheered with them.

Benton continued to kneel a moment, his ears still ringing, like the others claimed by reaction, staring dully. Here and there lay a shape, but out on the grassy plain lay more. Someone moaned, crying for water. A boy staggered up, suddenly retching.

It was Henry Jackman who shattered their lethargy, who drove them up and stirring, to tending the wounded and seeing about the horses, collecting bushwhacker carbines, revolvers, cartridge and cap boxes.

Jackman came over to Benton. "I was wrong. Everybody was but you."

"We got out. That's the thing. We'll know what to do next time."

Soon supper fires were blazing and the sun had slipped behind the western wall of the long-shadowed hills when Jackman called his people together. First, he appeared to size them up and ascertain their general mood.

"We know what to expect now," he said gravely. "We're outnumbered, outhorsed. No match in a stand-up fight. Guess some of you figure we should send across the river, fetch help from Fort McCulloch. Well, General Pike's not responsible in this district—we are. If he could give us a hand, be day after tomorrow gettin' heah. An' we can't wait—we can't wait past daylight." He viewed the tip of one boot with extra attention. "I've said my piece. It's up to you-all. Do we go home or pitch into 'em again?"

A period of silence held until a crippled Confederate said, "Better fight together heah than home, alone. Cain't we Injun in on 'em some way?"

After that, it seemed that everyone was talking at once, having his say.

Jackman let the babble spend itself before he spoke again, nodding. "I'd rather go forward knowing what I aim to do than have them come at us an' not know. We're keeping the fires low and steady. Not too high." His grunt was short, humorless. "Just enough so they can see how scared we are of the dark." He became thoughtful. "Figure it will take two, maybe three hours, way we'll have to circle around. Just so we're in position, ready, before daylight."

"Sounds good," Benton said. But one detail was yet left. He hadn't informed Jackson of Lettie Jo, not thinking it necessary. Now, he realized, it was. He waited until after supper and when Jackman passed by him on his rounds, he said without any preliminary, "Be obliged if you'll pass word to watch out for a girl. Be hard to tell her in the dark."

"A girl—God Almighty!" Jackman, drifting on, executed a sharp turn.

"One of their patrols took her this morning. I was on their tracks when I met you. No need to go into details."

A shred of disappointment squeezed out through Jackman's voice. "So that's why you joined us . . . over a female?"

"How many reasons does a man need to fight on? Maybe August Mason and Major Barr make another. Maybe not. Take your choice. I just want to pass word along so she'll have a chance to stay alive."

"I can do that," Jackman said slowly.

"I'm obliged," Benton said, stiff-voiced, the heat of his feeling still burning.

He didn't know when the next thought had been born in his mind. It was there even before Ned had uttered it this morning, like a reminder; possibly it was forming yesterday, unheeded, unknown, at Henry's house. As Jackman started off, Benton called him back.

"If we come out of this," Benton said, "I intend to make you a proposition. Short and sweet."

Jackman came in a slow step.

"Lease you Cherry Point for the duration," Benton said.

"Isn't Knowles there?"

"Was."

"Was? You trying to tell me . . . ?" Jackman's question straggled off.

"Let's just say he's not there any more. Won't be."

"Oh—" said Jackman on a drawn-out, understanding gasp.

"Somebody will have to run Cherry Point. When tonight's business is finished, I'm leaving. Henry, I want you to take it. Will you?"

"Why," said Jackman, uncertainly, "why—I don't know what to say. But—I guess so. Sure. If you're certain you want it that way?"

"I wouldn't be offering if I didn't," Benton said, sharp of tone. "Your land is poor. Cherry Point will get you through. This damned war's going on and on, 'til everyone's down to his last pinch of corn meal. Having Cherry Point will make up for a few things, I hope. Like when I doubted you—Todd and Jim."

"I never thought," Jackman said frankly, marveling, "you'd change your beliefs."

"Beliefs, politics—they don't have a damn thing to do with it, Henry. I'm concerned with people. They mean more to me than any mealy-mouthed spellbinder's claptrap, North or South."

"I'll not argue that," Jackman said in a quiet voice, letting the matter pass. Then, curiously, he asked, "I take it you're going back to Arkansas? Colonel Ewing's regiment?"

"Where else would I go?"

"A foolish question, I admit. But I've got to be frank, Benton. Knowing you, I can't see you changing your convictions. I can't."

Benton heard his own bitter voice saying, "I'm sure there are a great many men in the Southern army who still believe in the Union. Men in the Yankee army who love the South, hate to see it cut up and served on a politician's greasy platter. You tell me, Henry. What happens to them after the war?"

Jackman seemed to search the far corners of his mind. "Benton," he said after a bit, solemnly, "I don't know. I just don't know." He turned away before Benton could speak again, and then Benton realized there was nothing to be said.

CHAPTER 18

Sometime after midnight Benton heard the scuffling cadence of hoofs advancing from the south, and, in a while, lowered voices, among them Jackman's, questioning, directing. Ten or fifteen men, Benton judged by the sounds, counting the detail sent back with the dead and wounded. So they had gained a few, but not many.

Jackman, limping badly, returned to the timber, his approach a signal rousing sleep-dulled men to their feet. "Chunk up those fires a little more. Move to the rear. Form fours. I don't want a strung-out command stumbling over hell's half pasture in the dark."

There seemed no end to the saddling and milling. Finally, the groups slowly dissolved by twos, threes and fours, men walking their mounts to the vague line forming under Jackman's curt instructions. There confusion ended and order came. Falling in, they filed out to the west, beginning, as Jackman had explained that evening, a lengthy semi-circle intended to place them in position behind the bush-whacker camp. Leather squeaks, rattles, clanks, curses, the hoof-snapping and horse-snuffing—it all sounded excessively loud to Benton. But as the company swung into motion, the noises settled into a muffled rhythm which became a part of the inscrutable night. Behind, the spaced fires glowed brightly.

Jackman seemed to march forever west, winding, twisting. When he did turn north, it was to go but a short distance and rest briefly. In motion again, he pulled his men in tighter with temperish words. An order was passed:

"Close up! Close up!"

Jackman's progress over the blurred land was plodding but unhesitating, much like that of a person feeling his way across a darkened but familiar room, knowing by intimate sense the location of each indistinct object. They halted once more while Jackman rode back to check for stragglers, after which he led eastward. Hereon, Benton felt the muggy breathing of the unseen river on his left, murmuring behind the screen of black bottom-land woods.

The column paused while Jackman sent two mule-mounted scouts ahead. They returned within half an hour, looming up abruptly in the curdled murk.

"Camp's quiet," a young voice said. "Few low fires goin'."

"Not so quiet they've pulled out on us?" Jackman questioned.

"Naw, sir. We could see plenty horses."

"What about their sentries on this side?"

"Couple on the horse picket line."

Jackman scanned the sky a judging moment and took them forward somewhat faster. When he halted, a pale tone had invaded the eastern blackness for the first time.

Jackman reined back midway of the halted fours. He said, "I'm reminding you again about the young lady. Watch sharp. She should be around the wagons somewhere. Now—you will deploy in a single-file front, forming on me in the center. Idea is to walk our horses in as close as we can. I want eyeball range for our shotguns. Don't fire until I yell. That understood?" He waited. Nobody spoke and he said, "Uncle John, can you blow the *Charge?*"

"Blowed 'er down to San Jacinto, Henry."

"That's what we need. You ride with me. When I yell, cut loose. Keep buglin' long as you got a puff of wind." Still speaking softly, Jackman named four men. "At intervals you boys yell, 'Company—charge!' Rest of you holler big. Make a racket. We've got to sound like the whole damned Confederate cavalry's just arrived." He sat a moment, silently. "And stick together."

As the riders fanned out to line up, Jackman turned in beside Benton and held up, speaking in an undertone. "I should have told you sooner. But I had to straighten out some matters in my own mind. Just as you did, I reckon. I've been doing a powerful lot of thinking tonight. Couldn't get those Southerners out of my mind, the ones you spoke of in the Yankee army. Made me wonder if one—just one, mind you, blast his mule head—wouldn't like to come home after the war?"

All movement had ceased along the line; it was formed, waiting. Jackman went forward and Benton, with him, heard the rustling whisper of horses walking through tall grass. Nothing was visible beyond him. He had the feeling of riding into a void, vast, endless. Farther on, he felt his horse rise with a low swell. It was then, in the distance, that he saw the glow of several fires hugging the land. It seemed only a passage of moments until he distinguished bulks which he knew were picketed horses and behind them, traced by the banked fires, the hooded wagons.

Jackman led on, holding to a walk. They were advancing quietly, not near enough to charge in, when over on the right wing a shotgun coughed nervously.

Jackman cursed and hesitated no longer, a yell tearing from his throat:

"Yip-yip-yaw—aw-awwwww!"

Uncle John Acker, gabbling in excitement, was hissing frantically into his bugle, frozen, unable to sound the call. But as Benton drove spurs, the first brassy sputters came through and the headlong, staccato notes of *Charge* began beating across the fading night.

"Company—charge!"

Already the line was crashing forward, yelling full voice, mouthing a fearful and tremendous racket, mingling with the din of running horses and mules and the scrambling bugle blasts.

A sentry's shot cracked down.

There was no let up. And short ahead the terrified animals on the picket lines, neighing and whistling and lunging against stake ropes, suddenly burst free and like a dark swirling eddy poured backward into the bivouac area, striking with an audible shock, trampling the rising, screaming men, scattering coals, slamming into wagons and tree trunks.

"Company—charge!"

In the bewildering dark, figures cried out and dodged. Spurts of flame marked a rallying point. The ping of carbines began to swell from the woods, whipping at the onrushing line.

Jackman's Rebel-yelling bunch charged straight ahead, pell-mell, in close, guns booming. A mule screamed and plunged down, rolling over its rider. One of the wagons had caught fire from the showering coals; by this thrown-out yellowness Benton saw a knot of crouching men disintegrate, shotgunned, fleeing, others knocked sprawling as more crazed horses, picket pins flying, bowled through them.

He cut for the wagons and found the ambulance overturned, and hauled up, calling her name, swinging back and forth, searching, seeing only uniformed figures lying still or crawling and the strewn fragments of a wrecked camp.

A man ran into the circle of dancing light, carbine swinging up. Benton fired at the same moment. The man dropped. Benton felt nothing and rode on, hearing a stiffening exchange of gunfire kick up on his right. He could hear Jackman bellowing over there, crying through the tumult. Benton leaped his horse out to come upon a savage, close-quarter tangle in the muddy gray waves of breaking light. Jackman's men were stopped, on the edge of faltering, when a ploughhorse, wounded, uncontrollable, bolted into the crackling carbine fire.

Jackman seemed to sense a turning point. He lifted a great shout and everybody surged in yelling.

. . . The prisoners stood sullenly in the trampled woods, bearded, unkempt men, dejected now, haggard, showing the strain since Fort McCulloch and General Pike's Indians. Questioning them after another futile search of the wagons, Benton had learned little. They'd seen the Missouri girl come in with some of Yandell's scouts. Been in the ambulance, they reckoned, when the command bedded down. That was all.

Jackman was listening. His anger ripped loose. He had scattered them all over hell and back, he and his neighbors, set them afoot, whipped them to a frazzle with a third their number, hurt them terribly at buckshot range. But the cost, though not high, was still appalling to him. He said grimly, "Let's stretch a few necks. Cure some memories quick!"

"No use, Henry," Benton said, with a shake of his head. "They're telling the truth. They just don't know what happened to her after the shooting started."

"Maybe they've murdered her?"

"I don't think so."

"Bet their commander could tell us—"

"Where?" Benton interrupted. There hadn't been time to think of Skaggs.

"—If he was alive," Jackman finished. "Had on a right pretty lieutenant-colonel's uniform. Least it was before his picket animals stampeded through his tent."

Benton mounted and started a dogged circle, too weary to think clearly other than constantly widening his hunt. He looked for footprints, knowing ahead of time he would find none on this hoof-slashed ground. A single conclusion fastened as he searched along: Lettie Jo had to be afoot. That seemed logical, knowing as he did the strict watch Skaggs had always set over his picket lines. A wide-awake sentry had fired on Jackman's men. Too, with the suddenness of the attack, she'd had no chance to fetch a horse. He tried to piece together what must have happened—crazed horses knocking the light ambulance over, Lettie Jo running blindly away from the gunfire and terrified animals.

All meaning of time passed. Vaguely, he was aware of Jackman's men in the same search.

He was scouting the shaded bottoms northeast of the bushwhacker bivouac, farther even than he thought a frightened and bewildered girl might possibly wander, scouting through here because he had discovered not the faintest sign of her anywhere—when his eyes seized on a patch of white just ahead.

He spurred over fast, and there he found her. She lay on her side with an arm flung forward, as if she had fallen in that position, spent, unable to go on.

Turning her over, he found thicket scratches and dirt smutches, the stain of dark and complete exhaustion on her face. She wore the same thin, pathetic dress she had on the day he had taken her to Hannah's, and the dress was a story in itself. For she had accepted nothing from Hannah, then— nothing, when she needed everything.

She felt cold to his touch; for a few breaths panic had him. He wrapped his tunic around her and rubbed her hands, and spoke to her. After a while, she moaned and opened her eyes.

"You're all right now, Lettie Jo."

Her gaze wandered—it was open, vacant. It threw a fear into him, that yesterday and this morning, maybe, that everything had been too much for her mind.

Then she seemed to find him for the first time, but in utter disbelief. Her face quivered, crumbled. Tears formed in her eyes. He felt the sudden, rigid pressure of her arms and hands.

"You didn't wait for me at Hannah's," he chided gently, humoring her. "You ran off."

Her mouth parted in protest. "She said you'd been killed." Her voice caught. "Killed—and I thought you'd never know how much I loved you. I wanted to die."

She turned her face upward for him and closed her eyes. Afterward, he could feel the slow, wonderful warmth returning, spreading through her. He continued to hold her that way for a long time, afraid he might lose her again. He was holding her still when he heard Jackman's men enter the timber.

Center Point Publishing
600 Brooks Road • PO Box 1
Thorndike ME 04986-0001 USA

(207) 568-3717

**US & Canada:
1 800 929-9108**